LATENT FLAW

XENOPHOBIA SERIES – BOOK 2

ANDREAS KARPF

ISBN: 9798842349180

Cover Art: Sean Vecchione and Andreas Karpf

Books in the Xenophobia Series

Prelude to Extinction

Latent Flaw

PART 1: SUBTERFUGE

Chapter 1

Jack activated the radio and said, "Lunar Control, this is UN Shuttle four-three-B; current position is sixty degrees past L4-line at a lunar altitude of twenty-five thousand kilometers. Request direct flight path to L2 station."

There was a brief pause before a female voice replied, "Shuttle four-three-B, new security protocols are in place for L2. State your names and positions with comm cameras on."

"Jack Harrison, Director of Alien Technology," Jack said tersely. He glanced to the co-pilot's seat as his companion stated, "Sarah Freeman, Associate Director for Tech."

Sarah leaned over and asked, "When did you authorize the security upgrade?"

Before Jack could answer, the voice said, "Shuttle four-three-B, voice print, and biometrics confirmed; permission granted. Proceed on direct approach. Dock at port gamma."

"Confirmed…UN Shuttle four-three-B on direct approach to L2 Station; docking at port gamma." He released the transmit button and looked at Sarah as he continued, "It wasn't me." Jack instantly regretted his statement. The near-constant flow of new directives and oversight from central command was becoming suffocating. It wasn't the new procedures that bothered him so much as having to constantly explain and justify them to his teams – justifications that didn't always feel genuine. Sarah's unbroken stare prompted him to continue, "The report I read said it was in response to more threats against the alien tech. program."

"Who from?"

Jack didn't answer immediately as he banked right. A crescent moon set against a jeweled field of stars gracefully slid into view. The thin arc of its crater-filled landscape easily drew his mind away from the conversation he wanted to avoid. Long, inky shadows cast by jagged crater walls cut sharply into the pockmarked ashen terrain. Deeper into the jet-black lunar night-side were the lonely peaks of a smattering of mountain tops, catching a few last rays of sunlight. His eye continued probing the pitch darkness below until he spotted a ring-shaped cluster of faint lights – Copernicus base.

"It's not because of that manifesto the Times printed, is it?" Sarah pressed. "You know…that nutcase who claimed he was going to prevent humanity from killing itself off by activating some hidden alien weapon?"

"No…no, that's total bullshit. Believe it or not, we get two or three of those every week in the security briefings…the Times just got lucky and caught wind of that one. This alert's different…" Jack's voice drifted off as he glanced down at his primary display. The mostly black screen showed a gently curving green line that wound its way through the thin orange arcs of the system's gravitational field lines before eventually ending at a red circle marked 'L2.' To the left of the line was a blue icon representing the shuttle. Beneath it was a simple message: 'L2 course injection – Confirm Y/N.' Jack gently tapped the 'Y' and felt the pressure of the engines firing as the blue shuttle icon merged onto the green line of their new course.

Sarah allowed a few moments of silence to pass before finally asking, "What's different about this one?"

"An intelligence analyst found an anomaly in one of the data sets from an alien tech test."

"Go on," she said with a hint of impatience.

"You know how noise in a data set should be random, like static in an old-style analog radio transmission?"

"Of course."

"Well, the analyst was running pattern matching algorithms across the entire storage system – looking for hacks or other breaches. Of all things, her program flagged the background noise in some data from one of the experimental engine tests. It caught what could be two distinct shifts in the baseline noise level. It's probably nothing since the size of these changes is about the same magnitude as the larger random noise fluctuations. But, the analyst listed data manipulation as a possible explanation."

"So, you're not convinced," Sarah said, not expecting an answer. She took a breath before adding, "At least it's not in the engine data itself."

"True...but while intel finishes their analysis, central decided to treat it as an attempted system hack and activate the security protocols."

Sarah didn't answer. Figuring there really wasn't anything else to say on the subject, Jack turned his attention to the now-receding crescent moon out the cockpit window. It had shrunk noticeably, washing away the details he had admired earlier. Gone were the jagged ridges lining the larger crater walls. All that remained were the shrinking elliptical forms of distant craters on the thinning crescent. As the shuttle's trajectory carried them deeper into the lunar night-side, the moon evolved into a jet-black disk – a hole in the blanket of stars. Jack's eyes strained, hoping to pick out the lights of Tycho base – the largest inhabited colony on the moon. A lunar village of five hundred, it was sizeable and covered nearly a square kilometer. However, they were much too far now to see it.

Jack's eyes continued probing the darkness; the emptiness was almost peaceful. The black lunar disk slowly sliding out of view was his only hint that time was passing. All that lay before him now was the glowing, grainy band of the Milky Way. His eye, though, was drawn to a small cluster of bright silver dots that stood out against the myriad of surrounding stars. He stared at them for a moment before finally saying, "The L2 station doesn't look like much from five-hundred kilometers out, does it?"

"It is pretty isolated," Sarah answered softly. "But, that's why they chose this location, isn't it? Sixty thousand kilometers behind the far side of the Moon – literally, the middle of nowhere. Far enough away that the damage would be limited to just this station if there was a problem with the engine test."

"I know," Jack replied barely audibly. "Still, I sometimes think too many people are working way too hard to find worst-case scenarios with this." He avoided her gaze as they accelerated toward the station in silence. The growing structure showed itself to be a cluster of six cylindrical modules, all connected at right angles to a central node. Their smooth metallic surfaces were interrupted only by the raised ridges of support struts and the occasional window. Though Jack knew these were Spartan accommodations, they glistened in the sunlight, giving them an almost elegant appearance. His eye, however, was drawn to a thick, dull metal disk connected to the end of the starboard module – a radiation shield designed to isolate the station from the prototype ship docked on its far side. At better than twice the module's diameter and at least half as thick, the shield dwarfed the experimental craft: a ship that was little more than a silver dot at this distance.

Positioned a few hundred meters above and below the station were two moderate-sized observation ships. Designed to work purely within the Earth-Moon system, they looked more like mobile orbital platforms than traditional spacecraft. Each was comprised of a central, pressurized cylinder set within a metallic framework that held a wide array of instrumentation. The modules' front faces were lined with a patchwork of brightly lit windows and stood in stark contrast to the small dark engine units positioned to the rear of each ship. The space around them twinkled from dozens of tiny, remotely piloted craft – each monitoring some critical aspect of the upcoming test.

Jack brought them in gracefully, and the L2 station quickly showed its size, dwarfing their shuttle. He swung around and ran parallel to the nearest cylindrical module. Its silver skin rushed by beneath them until Jack abruptly pulled back on the control stick. Barely a second later, they were drifting a few meters away from a large set of crimson letters that spelled out, "Port Gamma – Keep Clear."

"Station command," Jack called into his radio, "UN Shuttle four-three-B ready to dock at port Gamma."

"Proceed," was the unemotional reply.

Jack pointed at the crimson letters and a bright, holographic orange circle appeared, highlighting the docking port in front of him. "Computer, proceed with docking," he said softly. The ship automatically swung around as a telescoping adapter extended from the port. A few seconds later, he heard a series of metallic latches take hold of the shuttle. The mechanism slowly pulled them closer until there was the solid metal thud of the docking port, making a solid seal.

"Docking complete," an automated voice announced. A moment later, it added, "Adapter pressurized."

Jack waited barely a second before unbuckling his harness and saying, "Shall we?"

Sarah smiled as she answered, "So how long has it been since you last saw them?

"Kurt and Nadya?"

"Who else do you think? I'm looking forward to meeting them."

"Not since the last time they were back on Earth…about three months." Jack pivoted as he drifted above his cockpit seat and gave himself a gentle push. He glided toward the rear of the small shuttle and continued, "It's really been too long, but our schedules never seem to overlap. In fact, I really haven't seen much of the old crew."

"That's too bad," Sarah said as she followed him to the rear door. "After more than a decade together on the Magellan, I would've thought that somehow you'd all keep close."

Jack activated the rear hatch and said, "Unfortunately, it's sort of natural – we all have very different specialties. I don't think many of us would ever have met under normal circumstances. Still, I wish…"

The door slid open, and the bright white station interior caught him by surprise. His eyes adapted just fast enough to see Kurt's and Nadya's smiling faces as Kurt nearly shouted, "Jack!" His friend quickly moved in to embrace him and then slid aside so that Nadya could give him a long hug and a quick kiss on the cheek. "It's been much too long!" she said.

"Too long," Jack answered, not even trying to suppress his own ear-to-ear grin.

"Captain?"

The words caught Jack off-guard, and he looked past his friends, searching for their source. Janet Kinkade pushed her way forward to hug him as she said, "It's great to see you!"

Jack took a deep breath and said, "You know, I haven't gone by that title in nearly three years."

"Old habits die hard, don't they," Janet answered.

"I'd heard you got yourself first seat on this test flight. Ten years piloting the Magellan, and now this? That'll put you at the front of the line for the next interstellar mission, won't it?"

She just grinned in response, at which point Jack added, "You really must hate Earth."

"Hardly, but you know…there's no way I could pass up a chance at this…especially testing out this new tech."

After a quick laugh, Jack glanced behind him and said, "I'd like to introduce you to our new associate director for alien tech applications, Sarah Freeman."

Sarah made her way forward with her hand extended and said, "It's a pleasure to meet all of you."

Kurt shook her hand first and answered, "Nice to meet you."

Nadya followed as she said, "I didn't know they assigned a new associate director yet. It is good to meet you.".

"It happened very quickly after Giovanni's death," Sarah replied. "The secretary-general didn't want to waste time. It seems being the liaison officer between Don Martinez's science group and planetary defenses made me a logical choice. But it's meant playing some serious catch-up.

I've had to spend a ton of time working with Jack to get up to speed. There's just so much...hell, I haven't even started wrapping my head around the work you and Kurt have been doing up here. It sounds amazing; I just need time to get a better handle on it."

Nadya smiled and said, "I think we could give you a quick overview now before we start the flight readiness review." Nadya turned to Jack before continuing, "It shouldn't take too long."

"I don't see a problem. I already signed off on the official tech review before we left. The in-person thing's more of a formality." Jack smiled before adding, "A formality that gave me a good excuse to come up and be here in person for the actual test."

Nadya laughed as she said, "Follow me." She turned left and gave herself a good push down a stark white corridor. At only a meter and a half wide, they had to follow single-file. The white plastic paneled walls were interrupted every few meters by identical, dull, metallic gray doors. The hallway's smooth, off-white floor and ceiling did little to break the monotony. The only way to differentiate between floor and ceiling were the small room numbers on the doors and rows of lights running along the edge of the ceiling. It took barely a minute to reach the end of the corridor. Stopping in front of a steel bulkhead labeled in bold red letters, 'No Unauthorized Personnel Beyond This Point,' Nadya said, "Sorry, but security's been a little strict here with the upcoming launch."

Pointing to a camera above the door, Kurt added, "You don't need to stop as we enter…just look at the lens when you go through. It uses standard biometric identification."

"I figured as much," Jack answered.

Nadya deliberately looked up at the camera, and barely a second later, the door slid aside. One-by-one, they made their way through a small, equipment-laden compartment labeled 'Communications Suite' before entering a large, circular room lined with computer consoles. The bulkhead automatically closed behind them, and Nadya said, "This is our control center. We'll track and control the whole mission from here." Looking over to Sarah, Nadya asked, "So how far have you gotten reviewing this tech?"

"Honestly, not very. I know the engine is based on the Magellan's – it uses matter-antimatter annihilation. But from what I gather, the breakthrough is how you harvest the antimatter itself. If I understand correctly, you've actually succeeded in pulling it directly from the vacuum. But, that's something I'm still in the dark on."

"Exactly! It's harvesting the antimatter that's the key," Nadya said with some excitement. "As I'm sure you know, the vacuum – empty space –

isn't really empty at all. It's literally a sea of quantum fluctuations…all extremely short-lived. We take advantage of the fact that these fluctuations actually have the characteristics of real particles of matter and antimatter. It's as if pairs of particles – one each of matter and antimatter – spontaneously appear and disappear uncountable numbers of times per second. The time that they spend existing, however, is infinitesimal…so small that without very special equipment, you'd never even know they were there. That's why we still refer to space as empty or a vacuum.

"That much, I understand," Sarah said.

"Good," Nadya replied with a smile. "So, then you're also aware that even before getting access to the alien knowledge, people conducted a large number of experiments confirming these particles' existence. All these did, though, was tell us that there was something there, beneath the vacuum. We didn't learn much more than the virtual particles' basic behaviors. As far as we knew, actually separating and drawing them into interacting with the rest of our world required huge amounts of energy. So much so that even if you harvested some of this antimatter, you'd have expended way more energy getting it than you would gain from using it. So, it was a losing situation – it had no benefit.

"The breakthrough lay in the information Alpha gave Jack. One of the first things they taught us was that the vacuum – empty space – is actually structured. It has sets of well-defined energy levels sitting below what we call the zero point. They showed us how to skim some of these particles off the top without the huge energy cost."

Sarah leaned in intently and asked, "How?"

Nadya paused and glanced at Jack, who said, "Sarah's a physicist and probably the only one here beside you who can really understand this stuff."

"Hey, you know, I'm here too," Kurt chimed in.

Nadya ignored Kurt and laughed lightly as she looked back to Sarah and said, "Sorry."

"No problem. But, I am curious about how you got around the energy barrier," Sarah replied.

"We can go into the real details later, but we basically target just the highest-level virtual particles – those least strongly bound to the vacuum. Alpha's information showed us that all we had to do was create an extremely strong, standing-wave electric field that's resonant with a targeted vacuum energy level. This pulls the antimatter portion of the virtual pairs away before they can recombine and disappear. We then use a strong, pulsed magnetic field to funnel it directly into the engine unit. So basically, we have an unlimited fuel source without having to carry any of it with us."

"Damn, that's clever…it's like stimulated emission…" Sarah said without hiding her excitement. "What's the final yield in terms of engine power?"

"Since we don't have to carry large amounts of fuel anymore, it's huge. Right now, we're limited only by the tech necessary to protect the humans on board the ship itself."

"What do you mean?"

"I honestly think we could get up to ten g's of acceleration out of this – we're talking thirty times faster than the Magellan. But, no one could survive that for a prolonged period of time. The prototype Janet'll be piloting will test it up to three g's. Even then, we're going to protect her by suspending her in a special fluid-filled compartment. We can schedule some time after the test to go over this in-depth with you."

Sarah smiled as Jack said, "Take all the time you need later."

"Which means," Kurt said with a smirk, "we can move forward with the real reason you're here – the engine test."

Jack answered his friend's attempt at humor with a simple, "Yes."

Kurt just smiled back and said, "Ok, let's get started." He entered a command on his hand-held terminal, at which point the room darkened, and a golf-ball-sized, holographic image of the Earth appeared near Jack. A gray orb the size of a marble hovered about a half-meter away. Its miniature craters and dark basaltic plains made it obvious it represented the moon; a short distance beyond it was a brightly glowing red dot. "The L2 station is located here," Kurt said as he pointed to the dot. "We conducted one last inspection and feel confident with our original plan…give the engines a good run out to Mars, which is over there." Jack looked to Kurt, who was pointing at a small reddish globe floating near the opposite end of the room. "This way, she won't be too far out if something goes wrong."

Nadya turned to Sarah and said, "Actually, we're a little lucky right now with planetary alignments. Earth and Mars are near opposition, so we're only a couple million kilometers beyond closest approach."

"How far are we talking?" Sarah quickly asked.

"Closest approach is fifty-four point six million kilometers. Right now, we're fifty-eight million kilometers apart. So, the idea is to take it out to Mars, and if all is going well, swing around and bring it straight back here. Janet will accelerate out for half the trip, turn the ship around and decelerate the rest of the way in to Mars." Kurt paused to type in a command, at which point a bright blue line appeared, leaving the L2 station and heading directly for the Mars hologram across the room. At the halfway mark, were floating blue letters spelling out the word, 'Midpoint.' Kurt continued, "It should take just short of thirty-six hours to get to Mars. Then assuming everything's in good shape, she'll head back here."

"Damn, that's fast," Sarah muttered.

"They say I'll get up to nearly half a percent of the speed of light by midpoint," Janet added. "And, that's in a little over seventeen hours of acceleration."

"That'd change a lot of things," Jack said thoughtfully. "I was out to Olympus Mons base on Mars only a few months ago, and it took me the better part of three weeks to get there. You're talking about a day and a half."

Janet smiled back in agreement.

"Have you done any shorter test trips yet?" Sarah asked.

This time Nadya answered, "No, just some test runs of the antimatter harvesting system. Even those were at a very reduced load compared to this. Kurt oversaw those tests, so I'll let him give you the details."

They turned to Kurt, who seemed completely distracted by something on his handheld computer. Jack allowed a few seconds to pass before he said, "Kurt…Nadya said that you could tell us more about the harvesting test."

Ignoring the question, Kurt suddenly looked up and turned to Jack. "There's a priority message that's just come in for you. Do you want to take it on this?"

Jack took the device without hesitation and quickly entered his passcode. The cryptic message read, "Inbound KBO 14 and 15 identified. Earth impact probability 70%. ETA 78 and 83 years. Contact SG Office ASAP." He stared at it in disbelief. A single thought echoed in his mind – this can't be right.

He had no idea how much time had passed before Nadya spoke, her elevated voice telling him she was repeating something she had just said. "Jack, what is it?" she repeated.

He looked at each of them before saying, "They've identified two more Kuiper Belt Objects on inbound trajectories. There's a good chance these are on a collision course with Earth."

"Two more?" Kurt said with obvious exasperation.

"Yes," Jack answered solemnly.

"That's a total of what…fifteen? How long until these are here?" Nadya asked.

"Seventy-eight years for one and eighty-three years for the other."

"So, it's about the same as the others," Sarah said.

"Roughly," Jack answered. "The other impact dates range from sixty to about a hundred twenty years from now."

"Then, it's nothing we can't handle, right?" Nadya asked. "Deflection missions aren't that complicated. With those dates, there's plenty of time to map out and launch one for each of these KBOs."

"Normally, yes…we have the tech in place for this. The problem is so many…each mission takes several years to plan and decades to execute. Dealing with fifteen KBOs is pushing us to our limit."

"I think you're missing the point," Kurt protested. "This is getting ridiculous! I mean, it's crossed the line to being a statistical impossibility. You can't say that fifteen KBOs were disturbed by the unstable AGC we used, and they're all on a collision course with Earth?"

"That's not what I'm saying," Jack answered calmly. "We've identified about a hundred whose orbits were perturbed one way or another. Of those, about fifteen have been identified as having the potential to collide with the Earth, Moon, or Mars. Hitting the Moon or Mars would be bad…we've got a lot going on, on them. We're talking large-scale evacuations. The Earth, however, is a different story. These inbound KBOs are bigger than the object that took out the dinosaurs."

"Fifteen percent intercepting something with human populations..." Nadya said softly. "That's still too large a fraction."

"Yes," Jack answered with concern. "It's pretty clear something's not right…" He took a breath before continuing, "It's the progression of data that gets me too. I mean, they're spotting one or two every week now, and that's starting to make people a little panicky back home." Jack turned to Sarah and said, "The secretary-general wants me to contact her. It's a safe bet that we'll have to head back to Earth immediately."

"Immediately?" Kurt asked softly.

Jack looked at him and answered calmly, "They're going to have to convene an emergency meeting of the planetary defense council. I have to be there for that."

"So, what do we do now?" Kurt asked.

"Continue with the engine test – that's important. I'm just sorry I won't be here to watch it. In the meantime, I'm going to need a secure room to contact the SG."

"Of course," Kurt said.

"Thanks," Jack answered. He turned to Janet and said, "You be careful out there. Don't take any unnecessary risks in that thing. And I expect you to tell me all about it afterward."

She smiled back, "I'll contact you as soon as I return."

Jack looked back and said, "Sarah, I'll meet you at the shuttle in an hour."

"Ok."

He turned to Kurt, who immediately said, "Ok, follow me."

Chapter 2

Jack stared longingly out the shuttle's side window. A thousand kilometers below lay the airless, lunar landscape. With the sun directly overhead, the surface looked almost smooth; the myriad of craters showed themselves as little more than ring-shaped highlights on a mottled gray expanse. Only the largest of the impacts gave texture to the bland expanse – their jagged walls casting short, sharp shadows against the surrounding soil. Off to the right, the terrain turned distinctly darker and smoother – the edge of a lunar sea. If he was right, it was Mare Tranquillitatis, the landing site of Apollo eleven. He thought for a moment about how it had been over a hundred and sixty years since Armstrong and Aldrin first walked there. The fact that they pulled those landings off – with barely any technology – always amazed him. Jack's eye, though, pulled his mind back to the endless details in the terrain below. His gaze followed a depressed channel from an ancient lava tube as it randomly wound its way through the flat lunar plane. It meandered like a river seen from a jet back on Earth, though this had nothing to do with water.

All Jack felt was a desire to be down there, exploring – perhaps uncovering some new detail in the history of Earth's nearest neighbor – anything to be away from what waited for him back home. He glanced to his right. Sarah was carefully examining something on her terminal; he didn't care to find out what. As he turned back to the window, the computer's voice called out, "Incoming transmission from the Secretary-General."

Jack ignored it and continued staring at the cratered field beneath them. Their close fly-by of the Moon would soon be over, though it would still take another four hours to reach Earth.

"Incoming transmission from the Secretary-General," the computer repeated.

"Connect us," Jack replied. After pausing for a second, he continued, "Madame Secretary?"

"Jack, sorry for the delay in getting back to you, but things are evolving pretty quickly back here. Bottom line is, we're not going to have time to meet when you land…the KBO situation's got everyone on edge. Instead, I want you to head immediately over to Don Martinez's group. The security council is demanding a thorough reanalysis of how the unstable AGC could have caused this. I want you to work directly with them on their review."

"Understood," Jack replied. He took a quick breath and continued, "You do realize we've been through the data at least a dozen times – so it'll be a waste of time."

"Maybe…maybe not," she replied. "We both know something's not right here. Think of it; fifteen percent of the KBOs disturbed by your AGC are on a collision course with Earth or a populated outpost. Simple orbital dynamics tells us it should be way less than one percent. And on top of that, all of the inbound objects are large…capable of eradicating civilization."

"You don't need to tell me what I already know," Jack shot back, though he quickly regretted the abrasiveness of his tone.

"What you don't know," she said flatly, "is that Don's team has been running more and more complex models of the belt, and they still can't seem to predict any of this. That's what's unnerved the security council. Think of it from their point of view: each deflection mission has to start within the next few years. With this large a number and the fact that we don't understand why there are so many, they're starting to worry that we're not capable of neutralizing all of them."

"You know we can handle that number. It's a matter of…"

"Jack," she said firmly, "this isn't the time to argue numbers. We both know there'll be real problems if we find even a few more inbound KBOs. Don's report says that if the numbers climb over twenty or thirty, then some of them will start being close enough to gravitationally interact with each other…that'll scramble all of our orbital calculations. The bottom line is that we have to get a better handle on what's happening ahead of time. Simply put, we need to understand the dynamics of what's going on out there right now. That's the only way we'll have a chance to solve this."

"So why have me sit and watch them re-run their simulations?" Jack pressed.

"Because I want you to look at it from another angle. If the engine test works today, then maybe we can speed things up and use that tech and send a mission directly out to the belt. Think of it…we'd have the ability to go from KBO to KBO and accurately map out what's really going on. That's something we can't do using our current ships. Look in detail at what Don's team is doing and report back to me if you think it's feasible."

Jack instantly knew it was a good idea. "I can do that. Where's Don now?"

"He'll meet you when you land. Tell me what your first thoughts are, asap. Also, let's keep this between us for now."

The transmission ended with a quick burst of static before he could reply. He looked back down to the lunar surface and wanted to escape back into his dreams of exploration, but Sarah broke the silence. "The secretary-general's idea makes some sense, right?"

"It does," Jack answered noncommittally.

She only allowed a few seconds of additional silence to pass before finally asking what she really wanted to know, "Why keep word of this quiet?"

"There's still a lot of political crap going on. It can't look good for her to put me in charge of another high-profile project…"

"What the hell are you talking about?" When Jack didn't answer, she continued, "What? Do you seriously think they're still holding the AGC thing against you? Everyone knows there was no way for you to see what would happen. And besides, those inbound ships would have ripped Earth to shreds. You destroyed them."

"People have short memories. Destroying those ships happened three years ago. Those inbound KBOs are happening now. That's all they care about. Simply put, if it wasn't for me, we wouldn't be facing this threat."

Sarah just stared back and said, "Bullshit. That's just what some assholes in the media are pushing. The SG, the heads of state, they know better. They're not buying into that crap."

"No, but it's a convenient pressure point for some of them. A lot of those at the top hate me for holding firm with distributing Alpha's tech equally to everyone. Let's just say a few of them have made it very clear that they want me to do the honorable thing and retire. You know, get out of their way. That'd let them control the knowledge the way they want. The KBO threat is just a convenient way to stir up the public."

"What does the public have to do with this? You don't have to deal with them or run a campaign."

"If they hate me, then it makes it a hell of a lot harder for anyone in the government to support me. It's meant to isolate me and put more pressure on me to get out. So, to say the least, putting me in charge of a high-profile project like this could really blow up in the SG's face."

Sarah just stared back at him for a few seconds before saying softly, "At least this means she's supporting you, right?"

Jack took a deep breath; this wasn't a conversation he wanted to have. It was almost easier to simply ignore what everyone else thought and stand firm with his own decision. In that sense, he didn't care what the secretary-general thought. He glanced out the window again, but Sarah's continued silence forced him to finally answer. "I don't know whether keeping this quiet is her way of trying to protect me or if it's her own way of motivating me to do the honorable thing. I really just can't tell what politicians think…or if their own thoughts even matter at all."

Jack deliberately avoided looking at her and instead kept staring out the window. They had finished their fly-by of the Moon, and it was now gently sliding out of view. All that lay in front was a distant crescent Earth. Its bright white clouds contrasted brilliantly against its cerulean oceans – it was almost hypnotic.

Sarah broke the silence again, asking, "Is there anything you can do to help defuse it…you know, take some of the pressure off? Maybe even compromise and give in a little on something?"

Jack ignored her.

"I'm just talking about giving yourself a little breathing space, politically speaking. I know you're worried about people hoarding destructive tech, so don't give in on that. But maybe you could delegate responsibility for some of the non-critical knowledge – like crop genetics or pollution mitigation – to the secretary-general…or even to my group."

Frustration grew within Jack; he was tired of being pushed from all sides. Everyone seemed to think they knew better, but they didn't have a clue. He'd seen what was out there: existential dangers that dwarfed any of their petty concerns. He considered lecturing Sarah on what was really at stake – even if the danger was still generations away from them. But she was well aware of it. The fact that she knew and was still pressuring him, ate at him.

"Jack, I'm not talking about giving up on your principles. I'm just saying that it would give you the appearance of listening to them and trying to work with them. It would take some of the wind out of their sails."

"No," Jack answered simply.

"But why?"

"Because this stuff Alpha gave us wasn't meant to make some greedy bastards rich. You know that's all that's going to happen." He looked at her for a moment and when she didn't reply, continued, "Let's say I give them access to plant genetics…they'll just quietly funnel some important piece to a friend with a company. That company will suddenly discover this great innovation and patent it…they'll hold it over everyone else and make billions. Everyone involved along the way will get their little piece of the action.

"The real problem is that everything goes downhill from there. They'll have had a taste of what they can get. They'll use that money and new leverage to put even more pressure on me and the government. It won't take long before decisions are being made purely for personal gain. Once that happens, what do you think someone or some country that's left out of this little deal-making machine will do?" He stared at Sarah who just looked back, and continued, "There's no damned way they'll stand by while their competition gets richer and more powerful!" Jack paused to take a deep breath and realized he practically shouted his last words. He continued in a level tone, "Let's just say I'll do everything in my power to prevent that from ever happening."

"Even if it means destroying your career and reputation?" Sarah responded.

"If giving in to them is what it takes to protect a reputation, then I don't even want one!"

"Jack, that's not what I meant. Plus, you can't really believe that they would do all of that. I mean, there are a lot of decent people in the government…"

"Don't you get it? If Alpha's knowledge isn't distributed equally, then whoever controls it has an insurmountable advantage over everyone else. We're talking thousands of years of knowledge here. There's no way anyone could overcome that. If one country or alliance had it, we're talking total domination. And don't tell me they wouldn't do it. That's been the story for almost all of human history…one country or empire gains an advantage and controls the others."

"You really think it would come to that?"

"Worse…I think whoever's on the outside…whoever's being shut out will take military action before they think it's too late. The side with Alpha's tech will use it to wipe them out and suppress whoever's left. We'd be so busy fighting each other, we'd forget the real reason we even have this knowledge…the real danger out there."

"And putting everyone on equal footing is going to remove the risk?"

"It's better than the alternative…and it worked during the cold war…you know, 'mutually assured destruction.' NATO and the Soviets were on equal footing, so neither could fight a full-blown war against the other."

"That's hardly a model to build a society on. You gotta have some faith that there are some sensible people in the government that can help find a better answer. Give them a chance."

"I am. I'm not telling anyone what to do with the tech. I'm not even getting involved in treaties or how individual governments work. That's for them to work out. The only thing I'm insisting on is that everyone has equal access to the tech."

"I mean, maybe you should let them find the fairest way to distribute the knowledge."

"You're beginning to sound just like the rest of them," Jack shot back.

Sarah didn't reply. He wasn't sure if he struck a nerve or if she'd just grown frustrated with his stubbornness. In the end, it didn't matter. He knew what he had to do. He looked back out the window, but not much had changed. The brilliant blue and white crescent Earth just sat there against the stars; it had grown a bit during their conversation but not much. "Computer," he finally said, "ETA for landing?"

"Three hours and thirty minutes," was the passive reply.

Jack looked back to Sarah, but she was once again staring intently at her terminal. That was fine; he really wasn't in the mood for conversation. Instead, he activated his own terminal and looked for something to read – anything to pass the time.

Chapter 3

Jack stared out the cockpit window as they sat on the tarmac. The bright blue sky of a spring day made him squint, but he kept looking and admired the view. Strips of close-cropped green grass separated the crisscrossing, concrete taxiways. Not far beyond were the blue waters of a few small inlets that wound their way back to the Atlantic. Clusters of reeds poked out of the water, reminding him of salt marshes he used to kayak around during summer vacations as a kid. His eyes probed further and could just make out the hazy silhouettes of the city's kilometer-tall skyscrapers – impressive even at this distance. A nearby manmade hill to his right supported large, raised white letters spelling out, "Welcome to John F. Kennedy International Airport." He smiled at the fact that his point of origin was well beyond the realm of aircraft. But, the name still made sense; nearly all of the traffic that came through here was still technically air traffic, even if a large fraction flew at hypersonic speeds near the edge of space.

The radio came to life, "UN Shuttle four-three-B, you are cleared to taxi to terminal six, gate twelve."

"Thank you. UN Shuttle four-three-B proceeding to terminal six, gate twelve," Jack replied. Then after releasing the transmit button, he continued, "Computer, use automatic mode; proceed as directed." The system took over, and the shuttle quickly followed the nearest taxiway. Linked to the central air traffic control computer, their small shuttle automatically adjusted its speed as it wove through pre-planned gaps in the lines of larger aircraft waiting to depart. Despite his years of experience, Jack knew that manually piloting the shuttle would only have slowed things down. It took only a couple of minutes before they pulled up alongside their gate. A small docking tube immediately extended from the building, making quick contact with their craft.

Jack turned to Sarah and asked, "Ready?"

"As ready as I can be," she answered.

Jack smiled as he got up, led the way to the craft's rear door, and pressed the open button. It slid aside, revealing a short, narrow, white corridor. At its end was Don Martinez, patiently waiting with folded arms.

"Jack, Sarah," Don called out as they walked toward him. "It's good to see you, though I wish they hadn't dragged you all the way here just for this."

"I know," Jack replied as they shook hands. Sarah nodded in agreement as she extended her hand.

"It's really a colossal waste of time," Don continued. "I mean…you know we've been through the numbers dozens of times. I just don't see what going over them one more time – especially with someone looking over my shoulder – is going to do."

"So, you think they sent me to watch over you?" Jack asked with sarcasm and a small smile.

"No…no. That's not what I meant. It's…hell, I don't even know what I mean." Don took a breath before continuing, "None of this makes any sense: the KBOs, the sheer number of them, the fact that our simulations aren't predicting any of this. And now we have them second-guessing every recommendation I make…it's just damn frustrating."

"That, I understand," Jack answered. "Is there somewhere where we can talk privately?"

Don looked around and said, "Actually, yes." He turned and pointed to his left as he continued, "There's a small set of meeting rooms back this way off the main corridor. Airport security lets me use them from time to time when I have people come in."

Jack followed Don as they worked their way through a small crowd of travelers. They had walked barely twenty meters before Don stopped abruptly by an unmarked gray door adjacent to a souvenir shop. He looked up at a security camera and the door obediently opened. "There's a room we can use in here." He headed a few meters down a plain white corridor before opening another door on his right. Inside was a gray, plastic paneled room with a small, white, round table and four well-worn, hard-plastic chairs.

As Don started to take a seat, Jack said, "I wanted to let you know I'm not here to try and supervise or get in your way."

"I'm sorry, I didn't mean to suggest you being here was an issue…"

Jack smiled and waved him off as he said, "Not a problem."

"But then why did they drag you all the way back here?" Don asked.

"The SG wants me to look at the possibility of a mission out to the Kuiper Belt," Jack answered. He glanced to his right; Sarah was staring back at him, her mouth slightly open. He knew he caught her off guard considering the SG's request for secrecy, but it didn't matter.

Don just sat there for a moment before saying, "But how? It'd take too long. We'd need years of planning, and then it'd take one to two years just to get out there. Plus, everything's so spread out…each of the larger KBOs is separated by at least a few hundred million kilometers, so we're talking about several months of travel time between each one. The mission wouldn't finish until maybe fifteen or twenty years from now, and we have to start developing the deflection missions well before that. Its data would be too late…" Jack cut in as Don's voice drifted off, "The plan would be to use the engine tech Kurt and Nadya are testing."

Don just stared back.

Jack gave him a couple extra seconds before continuing, "I worked the numbers on our way here. Running that engine at only one-g acceleration, including turn-around and deceleration time, we're talking about a five-week trip to get there. Plus, with its capabilities, it'd only take two or three days to travel between KBOs."

Don didn't say a word and just looked past him. Jack knew the scientist was mentally working through the numbers himself. After a few more seconds, Don finally replied, "That's…that's unreal. I don't know what to say." Excitement crept into the man's eyes as he finally asked, "How long until a ship like that could be ready?"

"I don't know," Jack answered. "But if today's test works – Janet's taking a three-day trip out to Mars and back – I imagine we could start designing and building one very soon after."

"That changes everything," Don said. "Then that's why you here?"

"Sort of. I'm supposed to look over your calculations and determine whether a mission like this could help. But that's not what I want to do."

"What're you talking about?"

"First, there's no way I could get up to speed on your code and evaluate it...not without spending months working hand in hand with you.

In my view, that'd be a complete waste of time. What I want is for you to think about what additional information we could learn from actually being out there. Tell me what your models are lacking and how we could improve them. Give me an idea of what extra data you'd need to help figure out how we can intercept these threats early on. I want to design this mission around what you think we'll need."

Don looked back at him and simply said, "Damn…" He took a deep breath and continued, "Yes, we can get that together."

"But," Jack said, "there's a catch. You're going to have to keep the rest of your team in the dark about what we're doing…about the mission."

"Why?" was the quick, exasperated response.

"Because," Jack said calmly, "there's a lot of other crap going on. Best I can tell – the SG doesn't want the possibility of this becoming a distraction. Right now, we don't have anything more than a 'what if' scenario based on the possibility that some alien tech might work. She told me a lot of people are on edge with the number of inbound KBO threats. My guess is, she doesn't want to raise anyone's hopes – especially if it turns out we're not really that close to getting this engine working."

"I guess that makes sense…" Don said with his voice trailing off.

Jack gave him a couple of seconds before asking, "Don, what is it?

"Nothing," Don replied softly as he looked down at the table.

"Don," Jack said calmly, "don't hide anything from me on this."

"It's nothing important…but I guess I'm just surprised she put you in charge of this. I mean, it's not just you. It feels like they don't trust any of us that much anymore…you know, anyone who was on the Magellan. I've heard people make comments about you and Kurt. And it's been obvious to me lately that they're double-checking everything I do. It made me think they're still suspicious that we were compromised by having those implants." Don took a quick breath before continuing, "Sorry…this isn't the place to ramble on about my paranoid ideas. Sorry."

Jack thought about saying something to ease Don's worries but decided that it was better just to answer honestly, "Truth is, I think that may be part of her reason for trying to keep this mission quiet. I'm sure, all things considered, I wasn't her first choice for evaluating this. But, she knows that we can't waste any time…and that the two of us working together would be the fastest way to determine whether this is worth pursuing."

"I understand," Don answered, "it makes sense. Still, if I can't tell my group what's going on, we're going to have to come up with a cover story for you being here."

"We won't have to work that hard… just go with the SG's original assignment: that I was sent to evaluate your work here and see why your computational models aren't accurately predicting what's happening in the belt," Jack said. He then smiled before adding, "That'll even give you a reason to be mad and not have to talk to me that much. It'll be like old times."

Don rolled his eyes and simply said, "Really? No…we'll come up with something a bit tamer. The last thing you need is my bunch acting up, thinking they're protecting me. For now, why don't I get some ground transportation set up for us so you can meet the team. Sarah, will you be coming too?"

"Yes. But I'll probably stay for only an hour or so. I've got to check in with my office."

"Ok," Don said. "Wait here. I'll come get you when we're set to go."

As Don left the room, Sarah said, "I thought we were supposed to keep quiet about the mission."

"I had to tell him. If I hid it, he'd eventually figure it out himself. First, he'd get pissed at all of the questions I'd be asking. It'd look like I was second-guessing his decisions. Then he'd start pressing me on what was really going on. In the end, I'd have to come clean. So, either way, he'd find out; by waiting, though, I'd lose his trust."

Sarah nodded and asked, "Do you think he'll tell anyone else?"

"No," Jack replied tersely. "What we should really do is check in with Kurt on the test. It should be underway now."

Sarah checked her watch and said, "Damn…it's only a few minutes to launch."

Jack pulled out his terminal and activated the comm utility. As he typed in Kurt's code, he turned to Sarah and said, "We should be up there with them."

Before Sarah could answer, the link came alive with a slightly static-filled image of Kurt sitting at a control station. "Jack, good to hear from you. Your timing's perfect. Janet pulled away from the docking port about ten minutes ago using maneuvering thrusters."

"So, everything's a go?" Jack asked.

It took a couple of seconds for Kurt's reply to come through, "That's an affirmative. We just finished the full systems check. We're pretty busy up here, so I won't be able to talk much. I'll leave the comm-feed open so you can follow along."

Jack turned the terminal so Sarah could see as he answered, "Thanks, Kurt. Good luck up there."

Kurt gave him a thumbs-up before turning to face another control panel.

Jack listened as Janet's voice came in over the feed, "L2-station, X-165 here. I'm at a distance of two-hundred kilometers and accelerating to two thousand k-p-h."

An unidentified voice replied, "Affirmative. Proceed as planned."

The video link went black for a split second before the image of Kurt at his terminal returned. He was working intently at something as Janet's voice came through again, "Distance, two hundred thirty kilometers. Re-orienting ship now."

The unidentified voice replied, "Confirmed. We see your new orientation. Engine exhaust will be clear of the station."

Nadya's voice added, "Everything looks nominal from my panel. Janet, you have a go for power-up."

"Affirmative," Janet replied.

The video cut out again.

"What the hell?" Sarah said.

Before Jack could say anything, the image of Kurt returned. "E-field generators are powering up," Janet said unemotionally. "Activating in five…four…three…two…one." There was a distinct pause before Janet continued, "I am reading antimatter flow into the drive system. Feed rate is at ten percent and climbing."

"Affirmative," Nadya answered. "I'm getting a good clean data feed too. You're now at twenty percent and increasing within specs. Prepare to..." The screen went dark. Barely a second later, it came back online as Nadya continued, "…drive system in five seconds."

"Affirmative," Janet answered. "Activating drive system now."

They sat in silence; their image of Kurt showed him typing something into his terminal. He then said, "I'm tracking your ship. We have your acceleration at one-point-two g's and growing."

"That's one hell of an affirmative," Janet answered excitedly. "This thing's got a real kick to it."

"I'm showing one-point-eight g's now," Kurt said.

"My instrumentation is showing the same," Janet replied. "Continuing to increase power now."

"Affirmative," Nadya answered. "I want you to use engine curve beta for this, do you…" The screen went black again. Jack was slightly annoyed, but the brief cut-outs were expected.

As they stared silently at his terminal, Jack felt the need to break the silence. "I hope they get this back online fast. I really don't want to miss anything." The screen, however, remained blank. His patience lasted barely ten more seconds before he brought up a diagnostic screen and confirmed that they were still connected to the network.

"Let me test our comm utility," Sarah said. "I'll place a call with someone planet-side…someone in my group."

Jack gently pushed the terminal over to her. Sarah immediately opened a new program window, typed in a code, and a couple of seconds later, the terminal came to life as a male voice said, "Sarah?"

"Hey, Ahmed," Sarah said, "I'm just testing a comm connection here."

"No problem," was the reply.

"I'll check back with you later," Sarah said softly. She disconnected the link and said, "Let's try something a bit further… one of the orbital stations."

"Go for it," Jack answered impatiently.

A moment later, Sarah had the code entered, and a blonde woman's face appeared and said, "Microgravity applications group here...oh, sorry Sarah, I didn't realize it was you at first. I'm confused, did we have a meeting scheduled?"

"No…no. I'm just testing some equipment here. We don't have anything booked until next week. I'll check in with you before then. Thank you."

"This is getting us nowhere fast," Jack said as she disconnected the call. "Contact the lunar polar base – we should have tried that first. They're the ones relaying the L2 station's signal."

"Got it," she answered as she brought up a directory and selected a code for the polar base's communications center. The screen, however, simply displayed a message stating, "Communications error."

"Try it again," Jack said flatly.

"Already on it," Sarah replied. She cleared the screen and re-entered the code, but the same message re-appeared.

"Display their data stream. I want to see…," Jack started, but stopped as the door abruptly opened. Don rushed in half out of breath and said, "Jack, we've got a problem."

"What?"

"We think there was an explosion…"

"What do you mean we think?" Jack shot back.

"I mean, we don't really have a handle on what's happened. All we know is that there was a massive electromagnetic pulse. It took all of the lunar satellites off-line; all communications with the L2 station, polar base, the monitoring ships…they're all down."

"What…how?" Sarah shot back.

"We don't know. All we know is that to create an EMP that strong, you'd need an explosion as powerful as a large nuke. We're talking twenty or thirty megatons."

"Shit…," was all that Jack could manage to say before he continued, "But there's nothing that powerful there. Even if the X-165's engine went, they wouldn't have that sort of yield."

"One of the analysts in defense is suggesting it could have been a partial, uncontrolled, vacuum chain reaction. Their team theorized a while back that under the right conditions, the harvested antimatter could resonate in the E-field and stimulate more antimatter creation than the magnetic containment fields could handle." Don paused to take a breath before continuing, "The stuff would just spray out everywhere, destroying everything it came in contact with."

"But we showed it's practically impossible for that to happen," Jack protested. "I mean, your team calculated that the resonance condition you'd need for that is too precise…it'd require a nearly impossible coincidence."

"I agree with you," Don shot back quickly, "but I'm just telling you that's what one of the defense groups is saying right now." They sat in silence for a few seconds before Don said, "Don't give it any credence at this point. Right now, we have no idea of what happened." Don glanced at his watch and said, "I've got to get back to my command group…we're trying to figure out a way to evaluate the scene. Like I said, we've got absolutely no data right now and no line-of-sight to see what happened on the lunar far side and L2."

"I'll go with you," Sarah said. "We may be able to re-allocate some resources from my groups to help."

Jack thought for a moment and said, "Try re-orienting the L4 observatory. Its orbit trails the moon by about three hundred forty thousand kilometers. It'd have a line-of-sight to L2 and hopefully, be far enough away to not have been affected by the EMP."

"That could work," Don said thoughtfully. "We missed that …too much going on at once."

"I know…," Jack said. "You know what, you two go. I'll check with L4 from here – we'll work in parallel. I'll let you know as soon as I find anything."

"Thanks," Don answered as they left the room.

Jack looked back at his terminal and "Voice mode on."

"Activated," the computer replied.

"Display L4 observatory comm channels."

A list of department heads and contact codes quickly appeared. Jack scrolled through them until his eye caught a familiar name and quickly tapped it.

"Communications error," the computer replied.

"Where?" Jack demanded.

"Unknown."

Jack stared at his display for barely a second before saying, "Test all contact codes to the L4 observatory."

"All are inactive," was the response.

"Damn it," he muttered. He quickly stood up, grabbed his terminal, and took two strides toward the door but had to stop short: the door didn't open. He waved his hand at the ceiling-mounted sensor, but nothing happened. Jack rolled his eyes in exasperation as he reactivated the terminal and said, "Computer, reconnect to the airport network and open this door."

There was a barely perceptible pause before the machine answered, "I'm sorry, but at this time, you are not authorized to leave."

"What the…Computer, there appears to be an ID error. Re-transmit identification five-alpha-three-six dash iota-nine-six-gamma, Jack Harrison, Special Assistant to the Secretary-General."

"Identification and voiceprint confirmed. Authorization denied," was the flat response.

Jack sternly replied, "Connect me with the director of airport security."

"Communication request denied."

"Who the hell's responsible for this?!" he shouted.

There was no response. Jack took a deep breath and asked in a more civil tone, "Computer, who can I contact?"

"No communications are authorized."

"Damn it, there's no time for this!" he shouted. "Connect me with Sarah Freeman."

"No communications are authorized."

He grabbed a nearby chair and nearly gave in to an urge to throw it at the door before slowly putting it down. He knew it would get him nowhere. Instead, he said, "Computer, validate the no-communications order with the secretary general's office."

"Processing request, please stand by."

PART 2: ESCAPE

Chapter 4

Kurt opened his eyes but shut them quickly as a sharp, burning sensation filled his lungs. A coughing fit gripped him, searing his throat with each convulsion. The few seconds it took for the spasm to pass felt endless. When his body finally calmed, he forced himself to take in a single slow, measured breath of air. Opening his eyes showed that the room was dark, except for the dim glow of the station's red emergency lighting. The air was thick with floating debris; small pieces of plastic, wire, and metal drifted by, twinkling weakly in the crimson light. A fleeting blue-white flash from a short circuit illuminated two motionless crewmen drifting to his right. Kurt ignored them, though, as his training forced him to focus on wisps of fog or smoke permeating the room. It took barely a second to recognize it was only a mist of tiny droplets leaking from some unseen cracked water pipe. He reflexively drew in a deep breath of air before realizing the danger. A small stream of droplets and debris followed the air into his mouth and lungs. A violent coughing fit consumed him as his body desperately tried to expel the foreign material. Kurt used every ounce of his strength to purge the pain from his mind and resist the primal urge to gulp in another deep breath. Instead, he forced every last bit of air from his lungs. His chest heaved in protest as he refused to inhale and quickly tore away a piece of his shirt. Holding it firmly over his mouth, Kurt finally allowed himself a slow, deep breath. His lungs ached, and his body shook, but he was able to suppress the urge to cough. Another couple of measured breaths eased the pain further.

Kurt glanced to his left, squinted to protect his eyes, and gently pushed himself through the debris to a wall compartment labeled, 'Emergency Equipment.' He punched the access button beneath the label with his free hand and quickly withdrew a breathing mask and goggles. They slipped on easily, allowing him to fully regain his composure and survey the area. He was in the communications suite – a small equipment-laden room adjacent to the experimental control center. The heavy steal emergency bulkheads on either side of the cramped chamber were sealed shut. He took two more masks from the compartment. A sharp pain shot across his right shoulder as he turned to push himself toward the first of his two drifting companions. He grabbed at the injury and found his uniform shirt was wet with blood from some unseen laceration. However, the combination of shock and adrenaline made it easy to ignore the throbbing and make his way to his motionless crewmate. His moment of self-control ended quickly as he turned the man's body and found himself staring at a pale, lifeless face. The man's mouth and nose were covered in blood. Kurt's stomach churned, and he wanted to wretch. The pang, however, passed as he forced himself to accept the fact that there was nothing he could do for him. Still, he couldn't pull his gaze away from the lifeless, open eyes. A wave of guilt swept across Kurt as he realized he was relieved that the man wasn't anyone he knew. He struggled for a moment, searching his memory to identify him: he was a communications assistant. His name was…Alan…or Alvin; he couldn't remember. He clenched his fists in frustration at not knowing.

A low rumble ran through the otherwise silent module, reminding him of the urgency of his situation. Kurt spun around and caught sight of the other motionless form drifting only a couple meters away. He immediately pushed himself toward the person and was relieved when the woman stirred the moment he touched her shoulder. She started coughing and Kurt quickly covered her mouth with a mask. As the spasm eased, he carefully slipped the mask's straps over her head and asked, "Are you OK?"

She opened her eyes and struggled to focus and look at him. Instead of answering, however, she just coughed again.

Kurt looked her straight in the eyes and forced a measure of calmness into his voice as he said, "Take it easy…slow, easy breaths."

Her breathing eased, and Kurt asked again, "Are you OK?"

She answered with a weak nod.

"What's your name?" he asked.

She started breathing regularly through the mask and responded in a raspy voice, "Tanya." Then after taking a deep breath, she finally asked, "What happened?"

"I'm not sure…I only just came too, but it looks bad."

She gave a barely audible "Uh-huh" between breaths.

Kurt looked around the room again and thought about Nadya. He quickly tapped his comm-unit and said, "Nadya, respond please."

There was no response. He scanned the mostly-dark room and realized that communications were likely down. "Computer, respond please," he called out. The silence that followed confirmed his suspicion. He unclipped the comm-unit from his shirt, and flipped a small switch on its side to 'Emergency RF.' As he clipped it back into place, he called out, "Nadya, respond please."

This time, there was a burst of static before his wife's voice came through, "Kurt, thank goodness. Are you alright?"

"Yes. What about you? Are you hurt?"

"I…I don't think so. I mean, I'm bruised a bit, but nothing's broken."

"Thank God," he blurted out before calmly asking, "what happened?"

"We're not sure yet, but it looks like there was an explosion…"

Her words were cut off as a voice from behind Kurt shrieked, "No! Alan…no!"

Kurt spun around to see Tanya holding the dead man's body. She turned and looked him straight in the eye as Nadya called in over the comm-unit, "Kurt, what's your status?"

"Stand by," he said softly and glided over to Tanya.

She said nothing. But, words weren't necessary; her face spoke of unspeakable anguish. She finally choked back the tears and asked, "How can he be dead?"

Kurt just looked at the dead man's face with her for a moment before saying, "I don't know."

Tanya stared at the body for a moment longer before looking up at Kurt and saying, "He's my brother."

"I'm so sorry," Kurt replied softly.

"This was our first assignment together…"

"Kurt," Nadya said over the comm, "status please?"

"Stand by," Kurt responded.

Tanya cradled her brother's body and just continued staring at Kurt – as if she were waiting for some sort of instructions. Kurt gently placed his hand on her shoulder and said, "I wish there was something I could do…I'm sorry." He waited long enough for her to nod in acknowledgment, but before either could speak, the module rumbled again – this time accompanied by the groan of over-stressed metal. Looking her straight in the eye, Kurt said, "I need you to focus. I'm going to need your help."

She just stared back without answering.

"Tanya, I don't think the module's stable. We're going to need to find a way to evacuate. Do you understand?"

Tanya finally looked around the dark room and reluctantly but gently released her brother as she gave an unconvincing, "Yes."

Kurt tapped his comm-unit and said, "Nadya, we have one casualty; aside from that, I'm here with Tanya…" He paused as he looked questioningly at his companion, not knowing her last name.

Recognizing the meaning of Kurt's look, Tanya softly said, "Dawson…I'm a communications engineer."

"Dawson," Kurt repeated into the comm-unit. "Neither of us is seriously injured. What's your status?"

He pushed his way over to the bulkhead leading to the control center as Nadya answered. "We've got two casualties here…but Pierre and I are OK. The problem is that main power is offline, and I haven't been able to raise anyone else using RF. Right now, I'm trying to figure out how to get out of here. The emergency bulkhead leading to you is jammed shut, and the maintenance panel on our side is blocked by debris. We can't get at it."

"I'll access the panel on my side," he said as he pulled a small flashlight from a pocket and looked along the bulkhead's heavy metal frame. Sweeping away some debris at the door's base revealed a small square panel labeled 'CS-Starboard Hatch Mech.' Kurt unclipped the metal plate, and the problem quickly became apparent: small pools of a translucent red fluid coated the interior of the compartment. He directed the flashlight beam around the bundles of wires and tubes until he found the fluid's source: a small crack in a hydraulic line. "Shit," he whispered, "we've got a break in the hydraulics."

"What does that mean?" Tanya asked from behind him.

"The bulkhead doors are a safety mechanism for the station. They're designed to be shut in case of some catastrophic event and stay closed even if power is lost. So, you need to power the hydraulics to keep them open – if power is lost, there's nothing holding them back, and they slam shut."

"There's got to be an override of some sort, right?"

"Yes…normally we'd use this lever over here," he replied as he shined his light on rubber covered metal rod nestled in the maintenance compartment. "It's a hand-operated pump that lets you re-pressurize the system and open the door. But it won't work with a cracked line." He tapped the comm-unit and said, "Nadya, I've got the panel open, but there's a break in the hydraulic line."

"Damn," she replied over the static-filled comm. link.

Kurt looked back at Tanya as she drifted behind him, studying the door. "Can't we pry it open?" she asked.

"No. There's a large spring and counterweight that pushes against it to keep it closed. That's how it stays sealed when there's no power. The hydraulic piston works against that to open it. The problem is, we'll never be able to get enough leverage to open it against that pressure." He stared at the mechanism as his mind ran through various possibilities. The crack in the line seemed small enough to patch – but too much fluid had already escaped. He wondered if he could bypass the line with fluid from a backup, but there was no easy way to transfer the fluid. His eyes were drawn to the end of the piston, where its flat metal head was bracketed to the base of the thick metal spring. He knew the answer was there, but it felt just out of reach.

Their module groaned again – this time loud enough to send a chill down his spine. They had to move fast. "Nadya," he called into the comm-unit.

"Here, Kurt. Any luck on your side?"

"Not yet. How stable's your side of the module?"

"Why?"

"I think the junction on the far side of this room…the one connecting us to the rest of the station, is going to fail. We're going to need to get over to you and seal ourselves in."

"Understood. Our compartment's stable, but any ideas yet on getting through?"

He saw the solution and spoke as it came into focus: "If I can crack the bracket that secures the counterweight's spring to the hydraulic piston, I may be able to dislodge the whole assembly. With no pressure holding the door in place, we should be able to use a crowbar to pry it open." He paused for a moment as a problem revealed itself, "But I'm not sure how we'll re-seal it once we're through. That'll put all of us at risk."

"Don't worry about re-sealing it for now," Nadya answered quickly. "I'll have it figured out before you're through. Just do it now."

Before Kurt could argue, the junction behind him groaned again. A sharp crack echoed through the room, followed by a muffled hiss. "Oh shit," he muttered, forgetting his comm link was still open.

"What's going on, Kurt?" Nadya demanded.

He paused for a split second before answering honestly, "I think we have a small leak here. We're venting atmosphere."

"Crack that bracket now," she ordered.

"But it'll…"

"No arguing," she shot back. "I already know how we'll seal it. The bulkhead gasket's on your side of the door. When we release the crowbar, the door'll slide back into position. If your side breaches, the air pressure on our side will push it against the gasket and seal it for us."

Kurt wasn't sure he completely believed it was that simple, but there was no time for debate. "Tanya, get me a tool kit," he said firmly as he reached into the maintenance compartment and pulled a bundle of wires away from the piston. "There's one in packed with the emergency equipment."

Kurt finished exposing the piston's base as she returned. "Give me a hammer and screwdriver." His ears popped as the cabin pressure dropped, prompting him to grab the tools from Tanya's hands. He flipped the screwdriver into place in one motion, pressing its tip firmly against the thin metal bracket holding the spring to the piston. Raising the hammer, he said, "I need some leverage here. Put your hands against my shoulders and press your feet against the instrument panel behind you. Push hard." When he felt the pressure against his back, he swung the hammer. It struck the screwdriver squarely, creating a partial crack along a crease in the bracket. Without hesitation, he raised the hammer again and struck the screwdriver a second time. The bracket split in two, allowing the spring to shift and release some of its compressed energy. Though misaligned, the spring still pressed against the piston and counterweight. Kurt quickly swung his legs around until his feet hovered a few centimeters from the spring. Grabbing the side of the cabinet for leverage, he gave the spring a quick, sharp kick. It budged slightly. Two more kicks only moved it marginally. Pushing back from the compartment, Kurt tapped his comm-unit and said, "OK, Nadya. I can't remove the spring completely, but I think I've got enough pressure off the door that you may be able to move it."

"Good," she answered. "Pierre's got a crowbar in position here. Give us a second."

The door started creaking open, and Kurt saw Pierre and Nadya straining with the crowbar. "There's still a lot of resistance," Nadya grunted between breaths. "You're going to have to squeeze through."

Kurt turned to usher Tanya through first, but she had retreated to the far side of the compartment and was staring again at her brother. "We can't just leave him here," she said softly.

"Kurt!" Pierre called out. "The bar's slipping. Crawl through now and help us hold it in place."

"Tanya!" Kurt shouted, "get over here! Follow me through. We don't have any time."

Pierre slipped, and the door slid forward, leaving him with barely enough room to fit.

"Now!" Nadya yelled.

Kurt obeyed and dove through the tight opening. He banged his elbow solidly against the steel frame but barely had time to notice the pain as a loud, sharp crack cut through the air. A sudden, frigid wind tore past him. He tried to look back, but the crowbar snapped, striking him in the side of his head. Shock kept his mind clear enough to pull his feet in as the bulkhead slammed shut. The wind ceased; a wave of dizziness and numbness swept over him. Struggling to regain his bearings, he heard Nadya say, "Kurt, are you OK?" He tried to ask about Tanya but managed nothing more than a weak grunt.

"Kurt, are you OK?" Nadya repeated.

He finally answered with a hoarse "Yes," but was still focused on getting back to the bulkhead. It was sealed shut, and Pierre was looking through its small, circular window. Kurt put his hand on Nadya's shoulder, and she helped him stabilize himself. Seeing Kurt move toward him, Pierre said, "Kurt, not now. You don't need to see this right now."

He didn't acknowledge the man's attempt at compassion and instead tried to push him out of the way. The injuries to his head and elbow, though, sapped his strength. Pierre, however, understood and allowed himself to be moved aside. Reason told Kurt to heed Pierre's warning, but it didn't matter. He drew his face close to the window and looked into the darkened room. His view was clear – the vacuum had sucked all of the debris into space. The clarity, however, sharpened the pain he felt as he stared at two lifeless forms pinned against a large crack in the far side of the room. Fate at least spared him the worst of the scene: both bodies had their backs to him.

Kurt looked for only a moment longer before turning away. He barely saw Nadya as she took him into her arms. He was numb, but her embrace felt good. The comfort let his mind release itself from the rigidity of procedures and duty. As he let his consciousness drift, a second wave of clarity sent a chill through him: it could have been Nadya drifting in the now airless communications suite. His body shook, despite his attempt to suppress the sudden surge of fear. Too much was happening; the thought of losing her was pushing him too far. Guilt wove its way back into his mind: the mere possibility of losing Nadya struck him harder than Tanya's actual death. He felt selfish – was Nadya's survival that much more important than Tanya's? As his mind tried to make sense of his values, reason crept back in. It allowed him to fall back on the safety of procedures and duty – to purge his mind of its emotional torture. He could see that selfishness lay in pondering whose death should hurt him more: it wasn't important. They were still trapped in a powerless compartment sixty thousand kilometers from the moon, and God knows how far from the nearest rescue ship.

Kurt gently pushed himself back from Nadya and looked her in the eye. She had no clue of the pointless circles his mind had just run and instead looked back at him with a mix of relief and concern. He chose not to speak and simply wiped away a small trickle of blood from his head wound.

"You OK?" she finally asked.

"Good enough," he answered flatly. "Do you have an idea about what happened?"

"It's hard to know for sure with the power down, but there was definitely some sort of explosion." Nadya gestured behind her as she continued, "From what we can make out through these small windows, it looks bad. There are sizable breaches in the modules we can see, and we can't raise anyone using RF. We got lucky here…best guess is that the radiation shield on the experimental docking port gave us some extra protection. Beyond that, I don't know."

"What about the other ships?"

Pierre answered this time, "We had a view of one of them before the explosion. All that's left in that area is scattered debris. I don't know about the other. It might…"

"I mean Janet's s ship…the X-165?" Kurt shot back.

There was silence before Nadya said solemnly, "I don't know Kurt, but I think that's what did all of this. The magnitude of the destruction has the earmarks of a large-scale antimatter explosion."

Kurt felt numb again and only managed to weakly ask, "But how?"

"The last thing I remember," Nadya replied, "is telling Janet to adjust her fuel feed…her engine curve. Then nothing else until I came to. It's just a guess about her ship…I don't want it to be true, but it's the only explanation that makes any sense."

Kurt knew she was right, but before he could speak, a burst of static from the room's comm-unit caught their attention. Pierre quickly activated it and called out, "This is L2 station, experimental control module. We are in urgent need of assistance, over."

The silence that followed was broken sporadically by bursts of static. "This is L2 station, experimental control module," Pierre repeated. "Can you hear me?"

This time he was answered with total silence. Pierre waited only a few seconds before calling out again, "This is L2 station, experimental control module. We are in urgent need of assistance, over."

As they waited for a response, Kurt glided over to a small window and peered into the darkness outside. Before him lay the tangled remains of a golden array of solar panels, surrounded by a small, glittering cloud of metallic fragments. An adjacent crew module sat to its left – its once smooth aluminum skin marred by dozens of dents and punctures. Kurt surveyed the structure, hoping the damage wasn't too extensive until his eye caught sight of a jagged gash that ran half the module's width. The breach gave him a clear view directly into the crew compartment – there would be no survivors there. He had the urge to say something but instead just continued staring at the devastation outside. Slowly, he became cognizant of the total silence around him. Gone was the ever-present hum of circulating fans and electronic equipment and the clicking of unseen switches and relays. The complete lack of sound was as disturbing as a loud noise and finally pulled him away from his view. He glanced around the darkened room and saw Nadya gazing out another window; she seemed equally transfixed by the devastation. Pierre drifted by the comm-unit, his finger hovering over the transmit button. Only a few more seconds passed before he pressed it again and said, "This is L2 station, experimental control module; please respond."

Kurt's hopes had dimmed enough that the lack of response was almost expected. Pierre just stared at the comm-unit without saying anything. The silence was smothering. Pierre finally looked up at Kurt and said, "I'm going to keep trying to reach someone, but what do we do now? I mean, what if we don't get any response soon?"

"All we can do is wait. But," Kurt said as he tried to force a confident tone into his voice, "think about it. Central command knows something's happened. We had a constant data feed back to them, plus they were monitoring all of our communications. I'm sure they've already deployed some shuttles from one of the lunar colonies to get to us." He took a breath and continued. "They know something's wrong. So, we just have to wait until they get to us."

"I should have heard something over the RF," Pierre shot back. "The lunar observatory at the north pole is within comm. range."

Nadya answered this time, "Pierre if the explosion was an antimatter blast, its EMP will have disabled any electronics within line of sight. My guess is that, at the very least, their comms are probably down too. We're going to have to wait until a shuttle's sent from one of the near-side colonies."

They looked at each other silently in the dim red emergency lighting. Kurt had the urge to say something, but before he could speak, Pierre asked the obvious question, "How long do you think?"

Kurt knew what the question really meant as he answered, "It'll take some time, but I'm sure we'll hear from them within a day. We're not in any immediate danger, though. We can use the perchlorate candles in the emergency kit to generate enough O2 for a few days…they're seriously old-school, but they work. And, the kit contains emergency rations and water."

Pierre reluctantly accepted Kurt's explanation with a hesitant nod and looked back down at the comm-unit. He drummed his fingers a few times on the side of the console before finally clicking the transmit button and repeating his request for assistance. Kurt stared at the second bulkhead at the far side of the room in the silence that followed. It led to a tunnel through the radiation shield before ending at an airlock. Turning to Nadya, he asked, "Have you had a chance to look at the condition of the docking module?"

"Only briefly. There's no obvious damage, but without power, we'll have to wait until someone gets here and looks at it from the outside before we know for sure."

"So, there's nothing more we can do but wait," Kurt said rhetorically. Nadya just nodded in response.

Chapter 5

Jack sat at the small white table, glaring at the locked door. "Computer, open the damned door," he demanded again.

"I'm sorry, but you are not authorized to leave," the machine repeated for the tenth time.

"What's the status of my request to validate your instructions?" he asked, his voice seething with anger the computer would never understand.

"I am not authorized to provide you with that information."

The anger finally blinded Jack, allowing impulse to take over. He grabbed the plastic chair next to him and hurled it at the door in one motion. The chair struck it hard, bounced back, and clipped the table next to him before landing loudly on the floor. The impact left a faint, unsatisfying mark in the smooth beige door; aside from that, nothing changed.

Jack sat back down and returned to glaring at the still locked exit. His only hope lay in somehow making an end-run around the computer's instructions. "Computer, do you still recognize my identification code as five-alpha-three-six dash iota-nine-six-gamma."

"Yes," was the terse reply.

"Do you have a record of the security clearances associated with my file?"

"Yes."

"Send a message to the secretary-general. State that I have a clearance level A-five message that I must give to her." Jack took a breath before continuing, "Computer, confirm that this requires a direct reply from the secretary-general."

"You are not authorized…" The machine's voice abruptly went silent as the door opened. Sarah stood at the threshold about to walk in but stopped as she looked at the toppled chair in front of her.

"Jack…," she started, but he cut her off. "What the hell's going on here?" he demanded, his voice still seething with anger.

"What are you talking about?"

"You were in touch with central command just now, right?"

"Yes…"

"Then tell me who authorized this."

"Jack, do you want to tell me what you're…"

"Who the hell authorized this?! And don't give me any…"

"Why don't you stop your shit right now and tell me what the hell's going on because I don't have a goddamned idea what you're talking about."

Her indignation stopped Jack cold. Before he could formulate a response, she shoved the chair aside, stepped into the room, and said, "Are you going to answer me?"

As the door closed behind her, Jack practically shouted, "Stop that thing from closing!"

Sarah spun around in confusion, but it was too late – the door was sealed. "What the hell are you talking about?" She demanded.

"Damn it," Jack said as he stared at the closed door. "They locked me in here after the two of you left. I was informed by the computer system that I had no authorization to leave or communicate with anyone." Jack paused to measure her response and quickly added, "You're probably locked in here with me now too."

"That's ridiculous," she replied as she turned and took a step back toward the door; it obediently opened.

"What the…," he practically shouted before continuing in a level tone, "it seems that they only want me to be detained." Jack watched her again, looking for any sign of deception. But, there was none. "Go through and wait for me on the other side. Let's see if it lets me out this time."

Sarah did as asked. Once the door closed again, Jack walked up to its threshold – it opened without delay. "This makes no goddamned sense!"

"I've got no idea what's going on," Sarah replied. "Are we talking system error here?"

Jack wanted to tell her it was a stupid idea but held back. Instead, he asked what he really wanted to know, "What about Kurt and Nadya…do you have any updates?"

"Still no word. All we know is that there's no contact with L2 or the polar and far-side colonies. I was told they're sending two shuttles from Copernicus to check on the polar colony. I assume they'll try to make contact with L2 from there."

"That's not good enough," Jack sneered as he walked past her and headed down the short corridor back to the terminal. "They're being treated as an afterthought…they don't have time to wait for additional ships to be sent. We need to get back there." He opened the door to the terminal and was instantly face-to-face with a small crowd of tourists. Stopping to let them pass, he turned to Sarah and asked, "Where's Don? We'll need him with us. And, we'll need to get back to our shuttle."

Without waiting for Sarah's response, he pulled out his handheld terminal and typed in Don's code.

"Yes, Jack?" was the quick response.

"Sarah's told me they're basically not doing anything to help L2."

"I know. They've got five colonies and three space stations out of contact and only a few ships available. Their plan is to re-establish contact with the polar station and use it as a base of operations to follow up with the others."

"If they're not going to do anything, then we've got to go back ourselves."

"I was sure you'd want to, so I already started looking into it," Don answered. "Your shuttle's not available – it was reassigned to someone else. But…"

"What the hell are you talking about?" Jack demanded.

"But," Don repeated, "I've got one I use for my trips to the different research stations. I don't know what's going on with your stuff right now, but we can deal with that later. Meet me at terminal seven, gate twenty-two. You'll have to take the tram over…I think Sarah knows the way."

"I do," she said as she leaned in next to Jack. "We're on our way."

"Thanks, Don," Jack added.

"I'll meet you at the gate," Don answered as he disconnected the link.

Sarah looked to Jack and pointed to her left, "This way."

He followed her down the crowded corridor, dodging dozens of people along the way. It felt as if everyone in the terminal was headed in the opposite direction. At least it wasn't hard to see where they had to go: there were black and yellow signs every ten meters that pointed straight ahead and stated 'Ground Transport, Parking, Airtrain.' The corridor opened into a large, restaurant-lined atrium; the ever-present signs, though, directed them straight to a central bank of escalators and stairs. Without breaking stride, they jogged down two flights to a mostly-empty, polished cement platform. Two sets of tracks emerged from a dark, tile-lined tunnel behind them, split to flank the platform before exiting into an equally dark tunnel ahead. A dim, but growing light in the distance told Jack a train was approaching. He thought to ask Sarah how long the ride would take, but his terminal buzzed. A message across the screen read, "Incoming Message from Secretary-General."

Sarah looked at him as he stared at the screen but made no attempt to answer it. The hum of the approaching train grew, prompting him to say, "We'll just lose signal once we're in the tunnel. I'll contact her once when at the gate."

The train pulled up abruptly and its wide, glass doors almost instantly slid open. Jack noted the security camera embedded in the door frame and the fact that a small LED below it blinked green as each of them entered. He chose, however, not to give it another thought as his mind jumped between the festering anger at being detained and searching for a way to help Kurt.

"Next stop, terminal seven," an automated voice announced as the train accelerated into the tunnel.

Sarah quickly sat down next to him, but Jack barely noticed. Focusing on trying to help Kurt and Nadya blocked everything out – especially his anger. Logic told him that central command made the right decision by going to the polar station first. It would be the best staging area for multiple rescue missions – especially since they had no idea what had actually happened. He just couldn't push his own personal feelings aside; his friends couldn't be left as an afterthought. He typed a command into his terminal to bring up a schematic of the Earth-Moon system. A dozen red dots marked the various lunar and space-based outposts; the most distant of them was the L2 station. The frustration built, driving his mind into a loop. He kept focusing on the fact that going directly to L2 would take no less than four hours – longer than he wanted. Central command's plans of going to the polar colony first meant it would likely take over a day before a ship made it to L2 – his friends might not have that much time. They needed to get there sooner, but there weren't any resources. He needed to do something and sitting on a tram thinking about what to do wasn't nearly good enough.

"Now approaching terminal seven," the voice announced.

Jack got up quickly and took two impatient steps to the door, stopping inches from its windows. Dark concrete support posts flew by too fast to observe in detail. Barely a second later, his eyes were hit by the brightly lit interior of the terminal seven platform. He took hold of a nearby steel handrail as they decelerated. Glancing to his left, he watched as Sarah stood up to join him.

"Terminal seven, please watch your step," the voice announced. "Next stop, terminal eight."

Reflexively, Jack exited first but then paused to allow Sarah – who was more familiar with the airport – to lead the way. As with terminal six, the platform was nearly empty, making it easy for them to make their way to the escalators. They climbed the moving steps at a brisk stride and arrived at an atrium that could have been a duplicate of the one they had just left. His eye was drawn to a line of people directly in front of them; above was a sign stating, "Security Checkpoint – Access to all Gates."

Jack's terminal buzzed. Again, the screen read, "Incoming Message from Secretary-General." He let out a soft, "Damn it," before looking up at Sarah. She had stopped walking, expecting that he'd finally answer the call. Given no obvious choice, he reluctantly tapped the "connect" icon. The face of an unfamiliar man appeared and said, "Jack Harrison?"

"Yes."

"I am Director Alfonse Nolan, head of incident investigations. The Secretary-General has directed that you report to her offices at the UN building to review potential L2 station risk factors."

"I understand," Jack replied, hiding any hint of frustration from his voice, "but, I think it'd be much more productive for me to assist on-site with the rescue and recovery efforts."

"I am sorry…the Secretary-General was very explicit with her request."

Before Jack could reply, the man continued, "I see that you're still at JFK…good. I have a man on-site. He'll meet you at the taxi stand." The transmission ended abruptly.

He stared at the blank screen in disbelief. Before he could formulate his thoughts, however, an unexpected voice asked, "What's he talking about?"

Jack spun around to see Don behind him.

Don quickly added, "I just got here…who was that?"

"I've got no damn idea," Jack said with exasperation. "All I know is that it feels like they don't want me going back up there."

"What's going on?" Don asked.

"I don't know!" Jack answered. "But, they're doing everything short of arresting me to keep me from going off-world. Right now, I need the two of you to take the shuttle and head back to L2. You need to find Kurt and Nadya…find out what happened."

"Jack, you know I can't just up and leave like this," Don protested. "I only came to get you access to my shuttle."

Jack looked him straight in the eye and said, "Don, it's Kurt and Nadya we're talking about."

"What do you think central's response is going to be if I suddenly file a flight plan to lunar space?" Don asked. "And who's going to fly the thing? I can't get anyone on short notice like this."

"Sarah's a pilot, so you're set with that. As for a flight plan…you'll think of something," Jack retorted. "Tell them you've got critical staff and materials you need to check on immediately. Hell, have Sarah back you up, she's got enough clearance now."

"I'm just a scientist…you're talking about search and rescue. I don't know the first thing about…"

"Don, something bad happened up there. All of us know it. But, think about it…it's one of my damned projects…something I know more about than nearly anyone else and they don't want me up there. I need people I can trust up there now. Sarah can't go alone and there isn't any time…"

"Jack…" Don started, but Jack cut him off. "Don, if it was anyone else up there I wouldn't push you like this. Their lives are at risk…"

Don took a deep breath but didn't say anything.

"Don, do you understand how important…"

"I know… I know. You made your point. I'm just trying to figure out exactly how we'll do this."

"Don't waste time thinking here. Get through security and figure it out on the way. I'll find my way up to you once I get out of whatever crap's going on with the SG."

Don just nodded in response.

"One more thing, what's your shuttle ID?" Jack asked.

"KV-171," Don answered. "Why?"

"Thanks. Now get going."

Don stared back at Jack, expecting an answer, but Jack ignored him. As he turned to leave, Sarah called back, "I'll keep you updated."

"Thank you," Jack answered. He spotted a 'Ground Transportation' sign pointing to his left and took a few steps in that direction before stopping to look back at Don and Sarah: they had taken their places in line at the security checkpoint. His eyes followed the long column of people to the front where each was taking their turn walking onto a small red square centered between two banks of cameras. He was quite familiar with the tech: one camera quickly validated the person's identity using biometrics, while the others ran multi-spectral scans looking for restricted materials. The whole process took less than thirty seconds per person and was completely automated. A quick mental calculation told him it would be at least fifteen minutes before they made it through.

Jack watched Don and Sarah a moment longer. Once he was sure they were completely focused on their security line, he turned quickly and followed a sign pointing to the restrooms. Inside, a single, gray-haired man was washing his hands in a nearby sink – aside from him, the white-tiled room was empty. Jack entered the nearest stall and retrieved a small case from his pocket; it contained a molded pink, plastic device that could have been mistaken for an earplug. He gently inserted it into his ear and tapped it. A synthetic voice that could have been Alpha's said, "Please state your instructions."

The sound of the alien's voice was shockingly comforting. Jack was honest enough with himself to admit he missed his alien companion – even if those feelings had been tempered by years of constant political fighting over the archive. The simple sound of Alpha's voice – despite the fact that he wasn't really there – somehow eased the bitterness. He stared at the case a moment longer, pondering the irony of its purpose. Alpha's society was based on absolute freedom and trust. The concepts of deception and oppression were literally alien to them. It made them both incredibly naïve and worthy of emulation. Despite his naivety, however, Alpha was able to foresee Jack's eventual problems and included in the archive a set of files explaining how to covertly create this tiny piece of technology. The device could automatically hack into nearly any human network. It directly accessed multiple network nodes simultaneously, allowing it to piggyback its intrusion onto existing communications packets. It gave him completely anonymous access to secure networks. The true power of Alpha's little tool, however, lay in a machine learning algorithm the device would insert into the nodes. It was capable of identifying backdoors into servers using impossibly small amounts of data embedded in the communication traffic. It was a brilliant bit of subterfuge – all from a race that, until they met humans, had no need for even basic security systems.

Jack stayed silent until he heard the restroom's other occupant finish using the hand dryer and leave. As the door closed, he calmly said, "Access the airport security server."

"Stand by," The voice replied. Barely ten seconds passed before it said, "The server has been accessed,".

"Lock the door to this restroom, but override its status on the main server to read as unlocked."

He heard the click of the door's lock and said, "What is the status of my secure ID; are there any tracers or restrictions on it?"

Again, there was another short pause before the simulated voice answered. "Your ID is currently under high-level surveillance. There are no automatic restrictions, but any requests for information are being reviewed before granted."

"Shit," Jack muttered. "Are they tracking my movements in the airport?"

"Not at this time."

"OK…list all airport maintenance personnel currently on duty and assigned to this terminal…and have a similar physical build to myself."

"Define similar," the voice replied.

Jack rolled his eyes as he said, "Within two centimeters of my height and…within ten kilos of my weight. Same race, gender, and hair color."

"There are two matches."

"What are…" Jack started but paused as someone pulled on the locked restroom door. In a hushed voice, he continued, "What are their locations?"

"One is in the staff cafeteria…"

"Good," Jack said, interrupting the reply. "Adjust the biometric camera systems to use his identity when security systems analyze my image. And, suppress the system from identifying him with his own profile. Leave this in place for…fifteen minutes."

The door rattled again as the synthetic voice said, "Complete."

"Good. Unlock the restroom door."

The door opened almost immediately and an obviously flustered man mumbled under his breath as he walked quickly to a nearby stall. Jack left the earpiece in place and waited until he heard the latch on the other stall's door click. Flushing his toilet to avoid suspicion, Jack made a conscious effort to walk at a casual pace as he headed back into the terminal. A quick look around showed that Don and Sarah were barely a quarter of the way through their wait at the checkpoint. Staying out of earshot from the nearest people, Jack said, "Identify the closest entrance to the maintenance corridors, and the quickest route to shuttle KV-171."

"There is an entrance directly behind you," the voice replied. Jack turned around calmly and spotted a door clearly labeled 'Employees Only,' next to the restroom. He walked back toward it and looked directly into the security camera mounted above the doorframe. There was no noticeable delay as a green light beneath the camera flashed, and the door slid aside. Inside lay a dimly lit, gray corridor that spoke of years of neglect. Its black and gray checkered tile floor contrasted sharply with the polished stone on which he was standing. On either side of the entrance were rows of lockers labeled with employees' names.

Jack entered without breaking stride and said, "Directions please."

The door closed behind him, as the voice replied, "Proceed straight for twenty meters. Turn right and continue fifty meters to a staircase. Take it down two flights to an exit that will lead you to the tarmac. Shuttle KV-171 will be directly across from the exit."

Jack almost said, "Thank you," as he headed down the hallway. A few meters in, it opened up to a wide, shelf-lined corridor, containing bins of spare parts and boxes of supplies. It felt more like an aisle in a warehouse than a hallway. He followed the voice's directions, pausing at each intersection to listen for any other personnel. Fortunately, there were only the distant sounds of aircraft and the hum of the ventilation system.

On reaching the stairway, he said, "Unlock the shuttle's cargo hatch," and then jogged down the steps two at a time. Jack reached the exit just as the voice answered, "The hatch is unlocked." Opening the door slowly, he peered out into the bright daylight. The sharp, dart-like forms of three large hypersonic jets loomed over him, casting long, dark shadows on the cement. The high-pitched whine of jet engines cut through the air, making him want to cover his ears. His own destination – Don's small shuttle – was tucked off to his left, between two of the mammoth craft. Jack stayed still, surveying the scene for anyone who might notice him. The immediate area was devoid of personnel and traffic, save for an automated luggage carrier leaving the plane to his right. Recognizing it would provide perfect cover, Jack waited for it to pass his position before calmly walking out to meet it. Staying within arm's length of the second car in the procession of suit-case laden trailers, he kept pace with it until he was within a few meters of the shuttle. A quick look around confirmed that he was alone on the tarmac, and he casually jogged to the rear of the vehicle.

Though it was only a small four-person shuttle, the thick, delta-shaped craft's belly stood a good two meters above the ground. Jack took up position just beneath its black, bottomed wing and said, "Open the cargo hatch." A door near the rear of the fuselage slid aside, and a short ladder extended halfway down. Jack scaled it quickly and was inside within seconds. The cargo hold was a cramped room whose ceiling was low enough that he couldn't stand up straight. Its scuffed, white plastic walls were separated from the ceiling by a thin row of bright white LEDs. Aside from a single suitcase, the room was empty. "Close the hatch," Jack said in a hushed voice. As the door sealed shut, the lights turned off, leaving him in total darkness.

"Override lighting system. Activate lights in the cargo hold," he said.

"Standby," the simulation of Alpha's voice replied.

Jack sat in silence as the machine hacked deeper into the shuttle's systems. Only a few seconds passed before the LEDs lit up the room again. He took note of a maintenance panel to his right and the internal hatch leading to the crew compartment in front of him – he didn't have any need for them yet. Right now, all he could do was wait.

The shuttle's pressurized structure and insulation left him in near silence. Though there wasn't much to listen for, a windowless room with no sounds slowed the passage of time to a crawl. He was tempted to use the alien device to access the government networks and monitor the status of the search and rescue missions. However, even with Alpha's sophisticated tech, there was still a risk of detection – remaining hidden was far more important than anything else right now.

Jack's mind began to wander and fixated on why someone was trying to detain him. The fact that he hadn't been taken into formal custody told him that this was being done outside the chain of command. But, whoever was behind it was high enough up to manipulate orders and security systems. It certainly wasn't a secret that there were people in both the U.S. government and the North American – European Coalition who viewed his holding out on the tech distribution as nothing less than treason. The real question was: how did they manage to pull this off? His position in the U.N. and central command had always protected him – having sole access to the archive was supposed to be his ultimate fail-safe. All this would lead to was a showdown he'd been through once before – something he did not want to repeat.

Though he didn't want to dwell on it, his mental chess game drew him back into recalling that last fight, a battle whose scars hadn't healed. He'd been forced to make everyone – including his friends and allies – truly believe that he was selfish enough to hold his own judgment above that of the elected government; that he alone knew what was best for the safety of the Earth, and that he really would scrap the archive if they didn't give in to him. He played the role so convincingly that it cost him many of his supposed friends and pushed him to the point where he nearly believed he would follow through with his threats. Jack found himself clenching his fists to the point of pain. He was trapped again, and the small shuttle compartment had nothing to do with it. He had no choice and had to find the next move – to find a way to counter the fact that someone had moved against him. Was it with the SG's knowledge? Had she finally succumbed to the pressure? Or was this some covert action by another group within the government?

The metal clank of the shuttle's main door opening drew Jack back to reality. Someone was talking, but he couldn't make out what was being said. He slid across the compartment toward the front of the craft and was able to identify Sarah's and Don's voices. As he leaned close to the door to the crew compartment, he heard Sarah say, "Don, I have to give them our flight plan. I just need you to decide where we'll tell them we're going."

"I'm still working on it," Don answered impatiently. "It'll be one of these two stations. I just want to make sure nothing is going on there that might make them suspicious."

"Just pick one you routinely visit that's been affected by the pulse. I'll take care of clearances and any questions that may come up."

There was no response until Sarah said, "Don, I just need to tell them something. We can change it later."

"Fine…tell them we'll be going to LNP-1. It's an orbital station near the lunar north pole."

"Traffic control," Sarah said into the radio, "this is shuttle KV-171, requesting permission to depart."

Jack couldn't make out the response, but Sarah then said, "Sarah Freeman, associate director for alien tech applications, and Don Martinez, associate director for alien scientific research. Destination is LNP-1."

Jack pressed his ear up against the door and heard a voice over the radio respond, "Please stand by."

"Wait," Don suddenly said. "We need to give them a reason why we're going."

"I'll tell them the obvious…that we've lost contact with the facility and have no data feeds on systems, life support, or anything. That'll be good enough," she answered matter-of-factly. "They should be more than happy to have another ship pitch in with the rescue effort."

The radio came back to life, and a new voice said, "Dr. Freeman, Dr. Martinez, this is Alfonse Nolan, head of incident investigations. There are some questions we need answered; please look directly into your comm system's camera when you answer."

"What are you…" Don started but was cut off by Sarah, who forcefully said, "This is highly irregular. We need to depart immediately to assist with search and rescue. We have lost contact with our research teams on LNP-1 and…"

"Your assistance with the effort was not requested," Nolan said tersely. "You are directed to…"

"You're wasting our time," Sarah said, cutting him off. "We have people up there who are in desperate need of assistance. We can answer any questions you have once we get back."

"I understand your concern for your people, but you and your shuttle are not qualified for rescue ops.

"I don't give a damn what you think we're qualified for," Sarah practically shouted. "You're shorthanded and can use every bit of help you can get. Now either give me the clearance for departure or connect me directly with the SG's office."

There was the briefest of pauses before Nolan replied, "The questions will only take a minute or two. If you answer satisfactorily, you'll have your clearance."

Jack could hear Sarah take a deep breath before she asked sharply, "What are they?"

"Stand by," Nolan replied.

"Why look at the monitor?" Don whispered.

"They're going to have an AI analyze our biometrics with our responses…they want to make sure we're not lying."

"Seriously?"

"Dr. Freeman," Nolan said, "Is Jack Harrison onboard your shuttle?"

"What the hell are you talking about?" Don asked, his voice hoarse with exasperation.

"Dr. Freeman, please answer," Noland said flatly.

"No. Last we saw, he was in the terminal heading for ground transportation."

There was another brief pause before Nolan asked, "Dr. Martinez, Is Jack Harrison onboard your shuttle?"

"What the hell is wrong with you? You just heard what Sarah told you."

"Please answer the question."

"No!" Don shouted.

"Stand by," Nolan said.

"You heard what Sarah said! He's probably halfway to the UN on the subway!"

There was no answer. Jack thought he heard Don mutter, "Stupid son of a bitch," under his breath. The seconds crept by slowly before he heard Nolan's voice over the radio, "Dr. Freeman, who was Jack Harrison in contact with after you arrived at JFK?"

"What is this about?" She demanded. "If this is an investigation, you are obligated to identify the convening authority and the basis for this interrogation."

"This is a security matter," Nolan replied without hesitation. "Please answer the question, and you will have your clearance."

"No one," Sarah said flatly.

"Standby," was the equally flat response.

Jack listened closely but only heard Don ask Sarah, "What the hell was that?"

"I'm not sure, but not another word for now."

There was silence again. Jack wasn't sure what his next move should be; all that mattered, for now, was simply getting off-world. The radio came back to life with Nolan's voice. "You are cleared for departure. Proceed to Copernicus base. From there, you will receive an update on the status of the lunar stations and instructions on how to proceed."

"Understood," Sarah replied.

Jack slid himself to the rear of the compartment as the shuttle lurched into motion. Weaving around the taxiways was no big deal. Taking off at two g's to reach escape velocity without a proper seat and restraints, however, was another story. Looking around, he noted the lone suitcase sitting in front of him and quickly placed it by his side; the last thing he needed was for it to fly into him during takeoff. The shuttle rolled to a stop and pivoted. Knowing they had just taken up position on the runway, Jack braced himself. The hum of the engines quickly transformed into a low roar; vibrations running through the cabin increased in intensity. The pressure of acceleration grew, pressing him against the rear wall. They picked up speed, and suddenly the vibrations ceased – they were airborne. The acceleration, however, continued growing, pinning him against the wall. Jack adjusted himself, so his back and hips were pressed evenly against the hard surface behind him. As they passed one-point-five g's, he laid his head back. It was essential that he keep any part of his body from experiencing too much torque or stress. At two g's, it felt as if a grown man was sitting on his chest; breathing took a deliberate effort. Pain began to emanate from the back of his head – the point where the base of his skull pressed against the wall. He knew better than to turn his neck or arch his back to relieve it. The headache he'd have after launch would put any hangover to shame, but it was far better than the damaged ligaments he'd have if he turned or moved too much during launch.

The pressure leveled off, keeping him pinned. His shoulders and ribs ached. Jack was forced to concentrate on his breathing, taking slow even breaths every few seconds. He had no idea how much time had passed but was sure they weren't even halfway through the ten-minute trip to orbit. Once in orbit, there would be a short respite of weightlessness as they reoriented the ship and prepared to accelerate to lunar space. Though it would then be a four-hour trip – at only zero-point-seven-five g's, it would be much easier to deal with.

The shuttle banked left, pulling him slowly across the wall. They straightened out again, and his movement stopped. There he lay, counting his breaths and estimating how much time remained – perhaps two more minutes. He imagined the graceful curve of the Earth that Don and Sarah would be admiring right now. At a six or seven hundred kilometers up, the deep blue of the North Atlantic Ocean would stretch out before them, with Ireland and the UK partially obscured by haze just on the horizon. He wasn't sure what weather patterns might be visible, but his imagination populated the empty ocean with strings of bright white clouds.

The roar of the engines abruptly stopped. With the quick end to their acceleration, Jack found himself suddenly drifting across the compartment toward the front hatch. He pivoted easily and stopped himself with his feet as if landing from a short jump. The ship was silent now. He listened as Sarah's voice made it through the wall, "Control, this is shuttle KV-171 preparing for translunar injection."

A few seconds passed before a response came through, "Shuttle KV-171, stand by. The next launch window will be clear shortly."

"Shuttle KV-171 standing by," Sarah replied.

Jack needed to get Sarah's attention without raising any suspicion and glided over to the maintenance panel. Its cover unlatched easily, revealing a dozen or so thin, labeled drawers. The lower-most one caught his attention: Communications. He gently slid the plastic tray open; inside lay a series of green, thumb-sized circuit boards, each connected to a black plastic socket. Their small, white labels were barely legible, frustrating him as he struggled to identify one that might suit his needs. He read them softly to himself as he worked his way down the row, "X-band transmission, Emergency band, Antenna gain control, Internal video system, Backup Receiver…" Jack paused before saying, "That could work." He scanned the tray's wiring and spotted a series of yellow wires leading from a port labeled '5 Volt Supply' to the rear of each board. "Perfect," he said softly as he hooked his index finger around the wire leading to the backup receiver board and pulled. It came free easily. He quickly pushed the drawer back into place and re-sealed the maintenance panel. Gliding over to the door to the crew compartment, Jack took up position to its side and listened.

"…maybe we can cut it to a bit under four hours, but there's no way to rush this," Sarah said, obviously in response to some question Don had posed.

"I know…I just don't want to waste any…"

"What the hell?" Sarah said, cutting Don off.

"What is it?"

"We've got a warning light on comm."

"What do you mean?"

"Give me a sec." There was a moment of silence which Jack assumed was due to Sarah having to look up the meaning of the error code. He smiled as he thought about chastising her later for not knowing the codes by heart, as every good pilot should. "It's the backup receiver," she finally said. "Let me go check it out."

"Want me to come?" Don asked.

"No, it's in the cargo hold. It's pretty cramped in there. I've got it."

As Jack waited for her to open the hatch, he quickly pulled out his portable terminal and wrote, "Don't say a word. I don't want internal systems to hear you talking to anyone."

The door handle rattled, and a moment later, the hatch slid aside. As Sarah peered in, Jack held up his terminal so she'd see it before him.

Surprised by a terminal staring her in the face, Sarah reflexively said, "Shit!" before regaining her composure and looking at Jack with a confused expression.

"Sarah, you OK?" Don called loudly from the cockpit.

"Yeah…I…I just jammed my thumb on the hatch. I'm fine."

She glided calmly into the cargo bay as Jack wrote a new message on the terminal, "I pulled the power feed from the backup receiver board. Tell Don that you found a bad wire on the board, and you're going to fix it. Have him log it for you."

Sarah nodded, opened the maintenance panel, and said loudly, "Don, I found the problem. There's a bad power wire on the receiver board. It looks like it got pinched by whoever closed the unit last. But it's not too bad; I can fix it. Log it in the main system for me, OK?"

"No problem," Don answered.

As Sarah turned to look back at Jack, he wrote a new message, "The board to the left of the backup receiver is the controller for the internal camera systems."

Jack cleared the message, but before he could write another, Sarah smiled and stopped him. She gave a quick thumbs-up as she reached in, reconnected the backup receiver power wire, and accidentally put too much pressure on the internal camera board. It popped easily out of its socket.

Before Jack could say anything, Sarah asked, "How the hell did you pull this off?"

Jack smiled as he whispered back, "Let's just say I've got access to some tech that they don't know about."

"Pull what off?" Don called from the cockpit.

Sarah ignored the question as she stared at Jack, who said, "Ok, we've only got a few minutes before you'll have to reconnect the cameras; otherwise, they won't give you clearance for translunar injection."

"Got it," Sarah answered as she led the way back into the crew compartment. Jack climbed through the hatch and caught sight of Don staring straight at him.

"What the hell?" Don finally said.

"We don't have much time," Jack said, "so let me get to the point."

Don just stared back, and Jack continued, "Someone inside the government has placed me under surveillance and seems to be manipulating systems and people's orders to keep control of where I go. From what I can tell, it's being done without formal approval. I'm not sure what their goal is, but best guess is they're either trying to take control of Alpha's archive or completely discredit the entire program… I just can't see why anyone would do that. There's a chance this could extend beyond me…I'm worried they may be targeting anyone who was on the Magellan. For the moment, it doesn't matter."

"Are you talking about a conspiracy?" Don asked with an edge.

"Don, you know they've been going after you with the KBO problem…especially since your simulations aren't explaining what's going on. Plus, they've got a couple scientists casting all sorts of doubts on Kurt and Nadya's engine project…most are saying that playing with antimatter harvesting from the vacuum is too dangerous. And now, this explosion…it plays into their narrative, and I don't think it was an accident. I don't have a good handle on what's going on, but their push to keep me away from investigating what happened at L2 says that something's out there."

Don stared at him before saying, "I don't know…I mean, I can understand them losing patience with my work. It's not too complicated a problem…I should have a solution by now. The KBO issue is too big a deal to let sit unanswered like this."

"And Kurt and Nadya's work?" Jack countered.

"It's seriously cutting edge," Don replied. "We're working with physics there that we didn't come up with. What if we didn't interpret something right…"

"So, you're saying they're right," Jack shot back. "There could be a vacuum chain reaction that could literally obliterate an entire region of space."

"Hell no! You know I was the one that showed the flaw in their logic."

"Yet there are still people at central command listening to them. And now it looks like someone might be trying to keep me completely out of the loop with the explosion and what's happened to Kurt and Nadya. You take any of these things on their own, and it means nothing. But, all together, you have to agree there's a real chance something else is going on here."

Don didn't answer – that meant something. Jack knew he wasn't one to hold his tongue if he disagreed with you. Rather than say anything else, Jack gave him time to process it all. "It's very circumstantial," Don finally answered.

"True, but think about it. Is there a real possibility something's going on?"

They sat in silence, prompting Jack to add, "I'm not saying I'm a hundred percent right…or hell even fifty percent, but can we risk doing nothing if there's…"

"What do you need?" Don finally said.

"Right now," Jack said, "I just need you to get me onto whichever station they send you to."

"And then?"

"I'm not sure yet. A lot depends on where they actually send us."

Chapter 6

Kurt drifted near the window, vainly looking for some hint of hope – a rescue ship or even a signal from the adjacent module. The view outside, though, was unchanged. The crumpled solar array and its surrounding debris cloud seemed frozen in time. His eyes probed beyond the drifting metal fragments, focusing on the mangled remains of the neighboring module. The gashes in its silver skin told him there was nothing there. But he continued staring – looking one-by-one through its rows of small, darkened circular windows – straining to uncover a hint of motion or light. There was nothing. The airless rooms exposed to space again told him it was hopeless.

Kurt closed his eyes. His mind pushed past the darkness and fixated again on the silence: it was wrong. Decades of off-world work gave him an instinctual feel for what was safe – what was necessary for survival. Silence posed a threat; it was something that simply shouldn't exist out here. His ears searched again for the perpetual hum that should have been generated by the station's support systems – equipment whose purpose was to circulate air, heat their environment, and protect them from the hostility of the vacuum outside. But it wasn't there. The silence persisted, drawing his suppressed fears back into his mind. It took a deliberate effort to subdue them again.

Kurt opened his eyes, turned away from the window, and scanned the darkened room. Small bits of debris glistened in the red emergency light against the backdrop of dark, inactive equipment. Nadya was a silhouette gently floating to his left. She was awake but completely unaware of his torment; she simply stared intently at her portable terminal. Pierre drifted a few meters beyond her – finally sleeping after hours of futile attempts to raise someone on the radio. Kurt's eyes, however, were drawn to a dark corner at the far side of the room. He knew what was there but still couldn't turn away. His eyes probed the shadows, finally identifying the forms of two motionless people: the casualties from this compartment. His stomach sank. He knew there was no reason for the reaction – he and Nadya had gently placed the bodies there earlier after inspecting the module for damage. Their deaths, however, weighed on him. He pushed his feelings aside and almost immediately began to loath the ease with which his training allowed him to ignore the tragedy that surrounded him. Rather than fight it, though, he gave in and embraced that training. There was a certain comfort in clearing everything that wasn't relevant to their survival from his mind.

Time passed, but he had no idea how long since the explosion. He knew it'd been the better part of a day by the chill that was starting to set in. He wasn't shivering yet, but without power running to the heaters, the falling temperatures would soon become a problem. Again, he looked at his companions. Pierre was still deep asleep. This time, however, Nadya met his gaze.

"You OK?" She asked softly.

"I think so," he said as he yawned. "What're you looking at on that?"

Turning her screen toward him, she answered, "I was trying to find a way to see if anyone else is out there…other people on the station or one of the support ships. The problem is, with the network and radio down, there's really no easy way to find out."

"So…no ideas?"

"Well, just one I was trying. I've set my terminal's network access controller to do repeated searches for any connections – not just the station's servers. It should be able to directly connect with any computer within range…you know, create its own network with it. I just don't know if this thing's got enough power to try something like this," she said, pointing to her screen. "Any ideas?"

"I'm not sure…the hardware we're using here is based on older tech…terahertz band…so with a typical portable battery, you might have up to a kilometer or so."

"That's not really enough, is it? Is there any way to boost it?"

"No…I mean, your idea is a good one. It would definitely find anything nearby. It just wasn't designed for longer range communications."

"Then we're the only ones who survived on L2," she whispered.

Kurt let the comment go without answering. He didn't want to speculate about worst-case scenarios; it was useless. He looked around the darkened room again, but there was nothing to see – just rows of inactive monitors and equipment. "It doesn't mean that," he finally answered. "Their comms could be out too," he added as he yawned again. This time his ears popped, sending a sudden chill down his spine. "Shit, that's not good," he said softly.

"What?"

"My ears just popped. We might be losing pressure."

"But I haven't felt any…" Nadya started but let her voice trail off.

"What?"

"I feel it…I just didn't notice it until you said something. My ears feel clogged…pressure difference like they're about to pop too. Probably a slow leak."

"Maybe," Kurt said as he looked around the room. "But, it's been several hours. Why are we only feeling it now?"

"Your side of the module started leaking after the fact," Nadya answered hesitantly. "If a seal or something on this side just started opening, then we may have less time than we realize. We've got to find a way to contact someone much further out."

All Kurt managed was an unconvincing "I know" in response.

"Or at least just get someone's attention…," Nadya pressed.

"Hold on," Kurt said suddenly. Nadya stopped talking and just stared back. Kurt continued, "I think you're on to something."

"What? I didn't say anything useful…"

"No…" Kurt's mind ran through the possibilities. Their thinking had been too constrained. The words started flowing as his ideas took form, "We know our backup RF is too weak. And trying to use a network card to connect to someone doesn't have any real range…"

"I know," Nadya said impatiently. "We just went over that."

"But, as you said, we don't need to do that. We just need to let them know we're here and how to get to us."

"So?" Nadya asked, not seeing his point.

"So," Kurt replied, "like you said, we need to get their attention. What if we sent out short bursts in the terahertz band?"

"You just said that was short-range, too," Nadya protested. "Just a kilometer. Plus, all we have is my handheld terminal."

"I'm sure there's at least one router in the module."

"What're you talking about? The network's down."

"A network router…I'm not talking about using it to connect to a rescue vessel's computers...I'm talking about using it to create really strong bursts at its frequencies. We could run one of the emergency battery feeds directly into a router's RF modulator and antenna system. It'd be a hell of a lot more power than it normally uses."

"What's the point? It'd be just a loud burst of noise…you couldn't connect and communicate with another ship's systems like that."

"We won't need to. All we need to do is disrupt them. Think of it…we could generate some pretty powerful bursts with this equipment; it should boost the range to maybe a few thousand kilometers. Far enough to have an effect on any ships even remotely close to our vicinity. From their point of view, they'd see bursts of radio noise interrupting their internal wireless network…that would get their attention."

"Yes…yes, it would," Nadya replied thoughtfully.

"Now, what if I varied the lengths of these pulses?"

Nadya smiled as she finished his thought, "you're talking about Morse code, aren't you?"

Kurt smiled back and said, "We'll need Pierre's help to get this to work."

"I certainly think you would," came a voice from behind.

Kurt spun around to see Pierre looking straight back at him and said, "I thought you were sleeping?"

"I was, but I woke up hearing you two talking about messing with my communications equipment," Pierre answered wryly. "What's going on?"

"We're losing pressure…we can't wait anymore for someone just to find us," Kurt answered.

"Shit…are you serious?"

"It's a long shot, but I want to…," Kurt started, but Pierre cut him off, saying, "No need to repeat yourself…that part I heard. But look at us…we're in the dark. There's no power in the module, and you're talking about running current from a battery?"

"The batteries are there," Kurt answered calmly. "Everything's down because there've got to be hundreds of breaks in the systems' circuits. We'd just bypass all of those electronics…run a line directly from one of the batteries to the router's RF modulator."

Pierre stared back for barely a second before answering, "I can show you where to connect the power feed from the battery, but I'll need you to take care of accessing the battery."

"Good," Kurt said as he scanned the room. Emergency batteries were typically stored near the center of each module, protecting them from potential damage from impacts. He immediately looked down and spotted a row of access panels in the floor. Positioning himself above the nearest, he twisted its latch and pulled it open. Inside lay several bundles of colored wires but no batteries. He worked his way down the row, exposing additional cabling, a hydraulic pump, and a water recycling unit before reaching the last one in the group. He pulled its cover open, revealing a second cover with a bright orange label reading, 'Warning – Electrical Shock Hazard.' Pulling the plastic lid aside exposed three shoe-box-sized batteries.

"Pierre," he called out. "How's your progress?"

"I've found a router we can use. I'm just disconnecting it from the network right now."

Kurt pulled out the nearest battery unit and stared at it.

"What's wrong?" Nadya asked as she drifted next to him.

"We need some wire to tie this in to the router."

"Rip some out from over there," Nadya answered as she glided over to the first of the open compartments. "There's plenty in here…besides, it's not like we're going to try and repair or salvage this module. Toss me a knife."

"Right," Kurt said softly as he pulled a small folding knife from his pocket and pushed it toward her. She grabbed it smoothly out of the air, flipped it open in a single motion, and cut a couple of one-meter lengths. It didn't take more than a minute more for her to strip the segments' ends and toss them back him. Kurt connected them to the battery's terminals and pushed his way across the compartment, gliding over the powerless control stations and chairs until he reached Pierre.

"Let me have the knife," Pierre asked quickly. "I've already shorted the modulator connection; we'll just run power directly to it now."

Nadya came up from behind and handed it over. They watched the man slice through the router's power line. Pierre maneuvered the knife easily as he made a quick slit lengthwise along the cable feeding the device and pulled a black and red wire apart. He then stripped their ends before handing the unit over to Kurt.

Kurt quickly connected his negative wires and said, "I think we're about ready."

"You think it'll work?" Pierre asked.

"Creating bursts of radio noise?" Kurt asked back rhetorically. "That won't be hard…it'll work. Getting someone to figure out we're sending a message with it…that's another story. Plus, this is really only a one-way device. We won't be able to hear them respond."

"Actually," Pierre answered softly. "Maybe we can."

"How?" Nadya shot back.

"Tell them to send a strong broadcast on the RF frequency our emergency comm-units use. Of course, they're too weak for us to send anything, but if they send something back to us with enough power, we'll hear it."

"Fantastic!" Kurt practically shouted. "What's the frequency?"

"Two forty-three megahertz," Pierre answered without hesitation.

"Got it," Kurt replied. Taking the battery's positive wire in one hand and the router's red wire in the other, Kurt held them barely a centimeter apart and said, "Ready?"

"What're you going to send?" Nadya asked.

"I'll start with the standard distress call…SOS…three short bursts, followed by three long and then three short. I'll repeat that three times and then send a short message…you know…stating who and where we are, our situation, and I'll tell them how to answer us using the emergency frequency. We'll just keep repeating that." Kurt didn't wait for a response and started touching the wires together to broadcast their message. It'd been years since he last practiced his Morse, so he focused carefully on spelling out each word in his mind as he converted the message into a series of short and long bursts. It required enough concentration that he only noticed the complete silence in the module when he finished the first full transmission.

"You finished sending it?" Nadya asked as he paused.

"Yeah. I figure I'll give it about thirty seconds and then start again."

"Sounds good," she answered. "We can all take turns sending it when you're ready. We'll just keep it up."

Kurt returned to tapping the wires against each other. Even on the fourth iteration, it still required a good deal of concentration to ensure he was signaling accurately. His ears popped again, but he forced that – and the lack of any response over the RF – from his mind. Continuing the transmission was all that mattered. Focusing on a single task calmed him; it let him forget how desperate things were. He pressed on and began to lose track of time: the price of repetition. The iterations continued, and his eyelids grew heavy with drowsiness. Kurt shook it off, fighting to stay focused and accurate. As he finished what he was pretty sure was his tenth pass through the message, he looked up.

Nadya didn't wait for him to say anything as she said, "Let me take over for a bit."

"How long have we been at it?" he asked as he handed the devices to her.

"About a half an hour," Pierre replied. He rubbed his ears and tentatively asked, "How much pressure do you think we've lost?"

"I think we're still up around point-nine atmospheres, but…" Kurt paused for a second to formulate his thoughts.

"But what?" Pierre asked impatiently.

"My ears are popping more frequently now; the leak's getting bigger."

"What does that mean?"

"I think we've only got a half an hour or so before…," Kurt paused and just looked at the floor. This time Pierre didn't press him to finish his thought.

Without another word, Nadya began methodically tapping the wires against each other: three short, followed by three long, followed by three short again. Kurt turned toward the window before she finished her third SOS. His eyes barely began to focus on the wreckage of their station before a quick burst of static from his comm-unit cut through the air.

"L2 station, this is transport alpha-one-zero," a voice said over the static. "We have received your message. Please state your status."

"Holy shit, it worked!" Kurt practically shouted.

Nadya hugged him as Pierre added a loud "Yes!" from behind. Nadya released her embrace, and Kurt said, "Update them about how much atmosphere I think we have left." Nadya immediately started signaling as he continued, "Tell them we'll start experiencing problems in less than half an hour."

It took her barely a minute to finish the message and only a couple of seconds longer before the reply came through. "Understood. We are holding position at approximately five hundred kilometers from L2 and were mapping the debris field to find a safe way in. We'll expedite. Stand by."

"Thank God," Kurt said softly.

The voice came back online, "That was a clever trick with Morse code. But now that we know exactly where you are, we've got a high-gain antenna pointed right at you. You can use your emergency RF for communications now."

Kurt pressed the transmit button on his unit and said, "Thank you very much. You've got three very happy people here waiting for you."

"Not a problem," was the answer. "Stand by for an update on our approach."

"Standing by," Kurt responded.

"What can we do from our side?" Pierre asked. "I mean, thirty minutes isn't really long enough for them to get here and dock, is it?"

Kurt's ears popped again, "It's more like twenty minutes now," he finally replied as his eyes jumped randomly from place to place in the room. There was too much to go over. He forced himself to slow down and look carefully at each piece of equipment in the module. Instinct kept bringing his eyes back to the sealed bulkhead at the far side of the room. Behind it was the docking adapter that had led to the X-165 before the test. It was the only location the ship would be able to use to reach them.

As if she were reading his mind, Nadya asked, "Kurt, how familiar are you with the specs for standard docking systems?"

"I've got a working knowledge. What're you thinking?"

"Manually docking a ship takes a good ten or fifteen minutes…adding at least fifteen minutes for them to get to us…," Nadya paused – there was no need to finish the math. Her eyes suddenly widened, "What if we ran power to that adapter…could we get the automated system online? It'd cut the docking time down to only a couple of minutes."

"Maybe…" Kurt said as he started running through the numbers. Speaking mostly to himself, he continued, "The battery puts out a hundred twenty volts DC…same as the main systems use. So, we could connect it directly without stepping down the voltage. But how much current does it draw?"

"Does it matter?" Nadya asked. "We only need it to run for a few minutes. You know, bring their ship in quickly. Who cares if we drain the battery completely?"

Kurt knew she was right but didn't answer. They would have to move quickly. "We can run the power directly from the breaker box…assuming there're no shorts in the docking adapter circuit."

"The circuit breakers are over here," Pierre called out as he pushed his way toward a gray panel nestled between two workstations.

Kurt quickly untwisted the negative battery wire from the router before tucking the battery under his arm and pushing his way over to Pierre. "Just in case…shut the main breaker off."

Pierre opened the panel and flipped a large switch set apart from the others; then, he reached up to rub his ears.

"I feel it too," Kurt said. "Pressure's definitely dropping.

Pierre stared back blankly before softly asking, "How much time do we really have?"

"Doesn't matter," Nadya cut in. "We need to get this working – which breaker are we going to use?"

Kurt stared at the row of black plastic switches and just started realizing they were labeled when Pierre said, "This one." Kurt's eyes followed the man's index finger to the middle switch. Its label said, 'Docking,' confirming the choice. Flipping his knife open, he tucked the blade into a gap between the switch and the surrounding metal frame and pressed firmly. The switch popped loose easily, though he had to tug at it to expose the connecting wires.

"Left is positive," Nadya said.

"I know," Kurt answered flatly. He used the knife to loosen the screws securing the wires but stopped short of connecting them to the battery. "We don't need to drain the battery before we need the system."

"Right," Nadya answered.

"How long do you think it'll take to initialize?" Pierre asked.

"Not sure," Kurt answered. "It'll probably take a full minute for the thing to boot up. Then another minute to link up with the ship's systems. After that, just two or three minutes to dock…so maybe five minutes altogether."

"Do you want to test it?" Pierre asked. "At least to see if it boots."

"No, because this is going to drive the docking servos as well as comm and computer equipment. So, I think we'll have barely enough power in the battery to do this just once."

They sat in silence – there really wasn't anything else to say. Kurt stared at the battery and open switch for barely a minute before his impatience finally won out. Pressing his comm. button, he said, "Transport alpha-one-zero, what's your ETA?"

There was no response. Desperate to do at least something, Kurt twisted the bare ends of the negative wires from the battery and breaker together. The circuit was still open, so it wouldn't draw any current.

A short burst of static cut through the room, followed by a female voice, "We're expediting our approach. We will alert you once we begin…"

Kurt cut the voice off as he said, "Be advised, we are going to try to power up the automated docking system. I don't know how much power we have, so I need your ETA. I want to make sure we don't drain our battery before docking is complete."

Kurt allowed maybe thirty seconds to pass before he said, "Transport alpha-one-zero, did you receive my last transmission?"

Again, there was silence. Kurt reached to press his transmit button again but stopped as the voice finally answered, "We will be in position for automated docking in five minutes."

"Understood," Kurt answered. "We'll start powering the system up in three. It should be ready to receive your telemetry once you're in position."

"Copy. We will contact you once we are in position."

Again, they sat in silence. He could feel a headache building – the result of the pressure loss – but decided it was pointless to talk about the obvious. He turned his eyes toward Pierre. The communication engineer didn't meet his gaze but instead stared nervously at the wires in Kurt's hands.

"Two minutes," Nadya said softly.

Kurt nodded in response. He withdrew a set of pliers from a small tool bag he kept clipped to his belt and positioned them above the two positive wires. He could connect them by hand but figured the pliers would bind them more tightly, ensuring they couldn't come apart. They only had one chance at this.

"Thirty seconds," Nadya said in the same, level tone.

Kurt continued the countdown in his head. At zero he clamped the two bare ends of the wire in his tool and twisted it quickly. Letting go for a split second, he adjusted his grip and gave the wires another quick turn. Before he finished, he saw the result. A bank of LEDs inside the docking module flickered to life. Almost as quickly, he heard the hum of a set of exhaust fans spinning up.

"It's working?" Pierre asked.

Nadya had already pushed her way over the docking unit's bulkhead and stared at a blank control screen.

"Give it a few more seconds," Kurt called out, answering the obvious but unasked question. "You should see a set of status messages in a moment."

Kurt drifted above his jury-rigged connection and stared across the small room at his wife's back. She remained motionless, waiting for the control screen to come to life. Too much time was passing; he had a desperate need to do something. But, all he could do was wait for the code to run its course and the hardware to initialize. He glanced to his left at Pierre, but the man remained as frozen as he, waiting for something to happen.

There was an almost inaudible click, followed instantly by Nadya's steady voice, "It's initializing."

Lines of system messages scrolled up the small control screen, feeding his growing hope.

"L2 station, this is transport alpha-one-zero," a voice announced over his comm unit. "We are in position. Is the autodocking unit operational?"

Kurt looked to Nadya, who responded by holding up her index finger. "Standby," Kurt called into his unit. "The system is initializing."

"Understood."

The room was perfectly silent. Nadya was transfixed by the series of messages, leaving Kurt to simply wait.

Two simple electronic beeps emanated from the docking unit, followed by Nadya stating, "It's online."

Without hesitation, Kurt said, "Transport alpha-one-zero…docking system is online. Please proceed."

"Understood," was the reply.

Kurt gently pushed himself toward Nadya as the servo motors hummed, extending the docking tube. A moment later, there was the welcome sound of metallic latches making contact with the ship. The motors changed direction and began pulling the ship toward the module, prompting Kurt to glance suspiciously at his battery. He wasn't a hundred percent sure it should have enough power but knew that at least the odds were in his favor.

The system went silent, causing Kurt's stomach to drop for a split second. Before he could react, the hum returned as the motors completed their cycle. A moment later, there was the metal thud of the docking port making a solid seal with the ship. Kurt exhaled in relief as he joined Nadya in front of the sealed bulkhead.

"Transport alpha-one-zero," Kurt called out, "The connection looks good. Stand by as we activate the door on our side." He looked at Nadya for a moment before pressing the 'Open' icon on the panel.

A sharp pain shot through Kurt's head. He closed his eyes hard and reflexively grabbed his ears, but it did nothing to relieve the agony. He clenched his teeth tight to the point of pain and opened his eyes. Nadya was doubled over next to him; to his right he saw Pierre with his head in his hands. Grabbing Nadya by the arm, he pulled her away from the half-open bulkhead. "Pierre!" he yelled. "Get back here behind the control station."

The communications officer joined them, crouching behind the computer console. "Transport alpha-one-zero," Kurt shouted. "We have a leak. We are losing atmosphere."

The room was silent, save for the soft hiss of air escaping into the void.

"L2 Station, what is your status?"

"We need to evacuate asap," Kurt called out. "We don't have time to match pressures in the tube and airlock. Open your outer door immediately; we'll cross the tube and seal ourselves in your airlock. You can bring us up to pressure after."

The pain was blinding, but Kurt felt his mind run through the problem. Talking more to himself than Nadya and Pierre, he said, "The main bulkhead seal in our docking adapter failed…it's gotta be the source of the slow leak from before…opening the door finished it off." He closed his eyes tight again, but it didn't do any good. Forcing them open, he looked straight at the others and said, "I'm not sure how sound the rest of the structure is…we've got to move quickly. We're going to have to cross into their airlock at once. It'll be seriously tight, but we should fit…it'll protect us…"

"L2, this is Captain Benkin," a new voice said. "We are opening the outer door now. Proceed immediately."

Kurt pushed Nadya and Pierre into the tube ahead of him. It only took a few seconds to traverse the plain white docking adapter. Fitting three people into a one-person airlock wasn't going to be easy. The pain cutting through his head, however, made him completely forget about what might or might not be easy; he simply placed his shoulder and forearm against his companions' backs and pushed hard. He heard someone groan as he forced the three of them into the cramped space, but it didn't matter. Pulling his leg clear of the threshold, Kurt turned and reached behind him for the internal control panel. It was just beyond his fingers. He lunged backward, trying to add a few extra centimeters to his reach. Twisting his head back hard, he could just make out the control pane's display as the tips of his fingers brushed against its smooth glass surface. Kurt pushed harder until his index finger finally made contact with the green 'close' icon.

The door slid shut, leaving them in complete silence. Kurt exhaled in relief. He tried twisting to look back at Nadya, but there was no room for even that small amount of movement.

Kurt's comm-unit came to life as the captain's voice said, "The airlock shows a status of sealed. However, your module's pressure was down to zero-point-eight atmospheres. It will take us some time to slowly bring you up to ship pressure. Do any of you require medical attention?"

Kurt tried to move again, but they were jammed in so tightly that there was no way for him to see his companion's faces. He ceased struggling and asked, "Are you both OK?"

"Better now that we're in here," Pierre answered.

"Bruised but OK," Nadya added.

"Captain," Kurt called into the comm., "no medical attention is needed."

Chapter 7

Jack sat alone again in the shuttle's cargo hold, staring at the open maintenance panel. The communications drawer with its array of circuit boards was still pulled out. He had the urge to close it – just to satisfy his compulsion to keep things in order. However, he knew he'd just have to pull the internal camera's power connection again when Don returned. It made more sense to leave things as they were. His eyes darted around the empty room before settling back on the maintenance panel – there was simply nothing else to look at. A yawn started taking hold of him when two quick knocks on the crew-compartment hatch brought him to his feet. Keeping his head down to avoid the low ceiling, he shuffled to the maintenance panel and yanked the power cable from the internal camera unit's circuit board in one quick motion. Another three steps brought him to the hatch, where he answered with two additional knocks.

Sarah slid the hatch open just far enough to stick her head in and say, "OK, we're on the ground here at Copernicus base, but hopefully not for very long. We're going to meet with the base commander to get an update on the situation. At that point, I'll have Don request clearance to do a reconnaissance run around LNP-1 station. He's got a lot of connections there, so it'll make sense to them. From that polar vantage point, we should be able to get a handle on what happened at L2 and figure out what to do next."

"Makes sense," Jack answered.

"For now, just sit tight in here, and hopefully, we'll be moving again soon."

As Sarah started to close the hatch, Jack asked, "Who's the base commander?"

"I'm not sure. They relieved the science crew of command and have a military team up here running search and rescue."

Jack knew it made sense, but it would complicate things. His silence prompted Sarah to ask, "What are you thinking?"

Looking past her, Jack caught a glimpse of Don and said, "Don, while Sarah's having her initial meeting with the base commander, I want you to get me his or her name and system ID."

"Why?" was the quick reply.

"Just get the info. It could be important in case they start stonewalling you two." Jack took a breath before adding, "Bring it to me as soon as you can."

"Ok…I'll try," Don answered.

"We'll be back as soon," Sarah added. She closed the hatch leaving him in silence again. He immediately went back to the maintenance panel and reconnected the internal camera unit's power cable. They probably won't fall for this trick too many more times, he thought as he sat back down.

Reflexively, he picked up his hand-held terminal to try to monitor their situation but stopped before entering any commands. The risk of detection was too high; he'd simply have to deal with the boredom and allow time to pass. Impatiently, he looked around the room another time – but there was of course, nothing to see. Nothing had changed in the last few minutes. It was still a small, empty baggage compartment with an open maintenance panel. Jack leaned back and stared at the low ceiling. Its featureless, beige plastic surface did nothing to alleviate his frustration. Closing his eyes, he noted that the hard-plastic wall and floor really weren't that uncomfortable in the light lunar gravity. His body started to relax, and Jack felt the accumulated exhaustion weighing on him. He knew it would feel good to let go of everything – even if for just a little while. His mind grew fuzzy as the urge to sleep became overwhelming. Choosing not to fight it, he enjoyed the wave of relaxation that washed over him.

Two sharp knocks on metal made Jack sit straight up. He scanned the room quickly, his eyes settling on the crew compartment hatch. His first thought, however, was whether or not he had fallen asleep. Two more quick knocks pushed the irrelevant thought aside. He quickly disconnected the camera unit's power cable again and knocked twice on his side of the hatch. It opened barely a few centimeters before Don's head leaned in.

"Jack?"

"Here, Don. What did you find out about Kurt and Nadya?"

"Nothing. They haven't been able to make contact with anyone out that far. No one on the polar station or L2."

"Damn," was all that Jack could manage.

"I did get the commander's name," Don offered. "Lieutenant Commander Josh Owens."

Jack mulled the name over for a moment before saying, "I don't know him."

"Me either. He insisted on meeting with Sarah one-on-one. I'm not sure why, but Sarah will just have to fill me in after, I guess."

Jack knew keeping knowledge compartmentalized like that was typical military protocol, so it wasn't a complete surprise. Rather than dwell on it, he asked, "Did you get his ID?"

"Yeah." Don pushed the hatch door open a bit more and read from his terminal, "Three-sigma-four-six dash beta-seven-three-lambda."

"Good," Jack answered.

"It's not going to be much use to you, though. You know the system needs biometric confirmation."

"Don't worry about it. I've got it covered," Jack said calmly. "Now clear it from your terminal's memory."

"Why?"

"There's no reason you should have it on there, so let's play a little defense here and make sure there's nothing on you that could raise any suspicions."

"I see," Don answered with some uncertainty. "I've got to get back now. I'll let you know as soon as I find out anything else."

"Thanks," Jack said as Don slid the hatch closed. He reconnected the internal camera's power cable and then sat back against the wall. Taking a deep breath, he tapped the tiny device that was still sitting in his ear, and heard Alpha's simulated voice say, "Captain?"

"Use the base commander's credentials to create a secure network link to my terminal. Name is Josh Owens, Lieutenant Commander; ID is three-sigma-four-six dash beta-seven-three-lambda."

"Stand by," was the short response. Jack wasn't clear on exactly how the device's code worked, but his best guess was that it hacked into one of the network nodes and monitored the flow of data packets, looking for one that Owens might have used to access secure information. That packet would have a truncated record of his biometric identification. Somehow, the program seemed to be able to use the latent patterns in the data stream to reconstruct the original data record and give him the ability to access new areas under the guise of Lieutenant Commander Owens. If that was all there was to it, though, it wouldn't have been very impressive. In fact, standard network protocols used adversarial AI's to thwart probing by other organizations' machine learning algorithms from doing exactly that. Alpha's code, however, seemed to be able to identify and decode those countermeasures on the fly. Jack couldn't imagine how there could be enough data traffic to even begin seeing through the competing layers of security.

The words "Connection established" dragged him out of the puzzle.

"Are there any communications with regard to the status of Kurt and Nadya?"

"Affirmative. They are both alive and currently onboard a rescue ship."

"Who received this information?"

"The only record of their status was sent to Lieutenant Commander Owens. The message was listed as classified."

"Who sent it?"

"I was unable to completely rebuild the data record…"

"Don't worry about it," Jack answered, forgetting he was talking to a simulation. "Are you able to directly access the rescue shuttle's systems to find out more about them?"

"It depends on whether there's enough comm traffic between here and that ship. Stand by."

Jack took a deep breath and stared at the plain beige walls again – they did nothing but make him feel trapped. Desperate to look at his options, his mind tried to run through the possible scenarios. All he accomplished, though, was to confirm that he had no idea of what was actually going on. He needed information but had access to none. Without anything to focus on, he became aware of the tension that gripped him. It took a deliberate effort to close his eyes, exhale and relax his muscles. The relief felt surprisingly good. Almost reflexively, though, he opened his eyes and stared at the featureless walls and ceiling. They only exacerbated his isolation and sent his mind spinning again. The urge to connect directly with the base's network and comb through their data suddenly didn't seem too risky. The information he needed was there, and with the ongoing emergency searches, they probably wouldn't notice his intrusion.

He pulled out his terminal and held his finger just above the power button. He knew he could be quick, but something inside him kept him from activating the device. The obvious thought – that Alpha's device already had the base commander's credentials – came to mind. He quickly tapped the earpiece and asked, "Are you able to directly access any rescue information using the base commander's codes?"

"Yes, but it cannot be done covertly. The security they've put in place will likely alert the commander about the information requests."

"Damn," Jack muttered. Continuing under his breath, he said, "Then how are you going to try to directly connect with the rescue shuttle anyway?"

"If there's enough data, I can embed an algorithm into the communication stream. Once it unpacks and installs on their end, the programs on the shuttle and here will analyze the latent noise in their communication and determine how to embed our data within it. After that, we should be able to simply send and receive requests. The key limitation is that this data can only be a small fraction of the total stream – otherwise, I won't be able to hide it."

Jack had the urge to ask the machine how much longer until it could create a link but knew it was pointless. There was simply nothing he could do for now but wait. He leaned back, closed his eyes, and tried to let the earlier feelings of relaxation creep back into his mind. As he took a deep breath, Alpha's simulated voice cut through the silence. "I have established a limited connection. You can access rudimentary information."

"Thank God," Jack answered with true relief. "What's the status of Kurt and Nadya?"

"Stand by."

Enough time passed for Jack to take a deep breath before the device spoke again, "They were rescued at 08:17 Zulu time. The ship's commander's orders are to treat them for any injuries but keep them isolated from the ship's computer and comm systems."

"Why?" Jack asked with an edge.

There was a noticeable pause before the device answered, "They are suspected of collaborating with you. There are explicit instructions that they are to be treated and not be made aware of the computer and communications limitations."

"Collaborating with me? What the hell are they talking about?"

"I don't have access to any detailed files. There is simply a statement that you are suspected of working against central command by controlling the alien archive."

"Goddamn it! Who the hell issued these orders?"

"I don't have access to that data."

"Shit…can you hack their systems and establish a comm link between us…Kurt and me?"

"Stand by."

Before Jack could process any thoughts, the simulated voice spoke again, "I can send basic messages to a comm app on his portable terminal – no voice or video. Anything else will be detected."

"Fine. Connect with Kurt's terminal. Tell him…" Jack stopped mid-sentence.

"Tell him what?" the device prodded.

"Don't tell him anything. The less they know, the better. Right now, they haven't had any communication with me since the engine test. If we tell them anything about what's going on, then they'll have to lie when they're questioned. The biometric scanners will spot that and get them in even more trouble. Let's scan the rescue shuttle's computers for any additional…"

"One moment, Captain," the machine interrupted.

"What?"

"Stand by." Barely five seconds passed before the voice spoke again. "I believe my intrusions into their systems were detected. The base commander has just instructed security to detain Don and Sarah. A team is being sent to inspect this shuttle."

"Shit. Seal the airlock," Jack said as he got up and yanked the power from the internal camera systems. Climbing through the port to the shuttle's cabin, he continued, "How are we docked to the base? Are we in a hanger or on an external pad connected to a docking port?"

"We're on an external pad."

"Good. Disconnect our seal to the port." Jack jumped into the pilot's seat and powered up the shuttle's systems.

"The seal is disconnected."

"Thank you," Jack answered reflexively. His fingers danced across the glass control panel in front of him. A second later, an amber heads-up display, with its the full set of shuttle controls and instrument readings, framed the brightly lit lunar landscape that lay outside. The flat, rubble-strewn crater floor stretched into the distance before ending at a series of cliffs that comprised the crater wall.

Jack tapped the device again and said, "Isolate the shuttle computer from all external networks."

"Done."

"Can you interface with the shuttle systems?"

"Yes."

Jack scanned the holographic data floating in front of him and quickly touched a box labeled, 'Engines." Before the computer could finish displaying its list of controls and parameters, he touched 'Activate' and 'Full Thrust.' A deep hum immediately filled the cockpit as the small craft rose off the landing pad. Jack pulled back hard on the control stick, and the lunar landscape slid away, leaving him with a view of the stars above. The engines quickly rose to full power, pinning him in his seat.

"Plot a course to L2," he called out over the noise.

Immediately a blue holographic line appeared in front of him. It showed a path that continued upwards before curving sharply left.

"What's our ETA?"

"One hour," was the prompt reply. Alpha's voice continued, "What are your plans when we reach the region?"

Jack was taken aback by the question but quickly ignored the oddity of a simulation asking him something and answered. "I'm not a hundred percent sure yet. All I know is…"

"Captain," the voice interrupted. "Radar shows three small objects have been launched from Copernicus base. They are moving rapidly in our direction."

"Small? What are they, one-man ships?"

"No, smaller than that. They're no more than one meter in length."

"Missiles? They don't have weaponry there."

"Their shape suggests they're drones."

"Damn…Are they faster than us?"

"Yes," the voice answered. "They'll intercept us in under three minutes."

"They won't be able to do much…they're just drones," Jack said softly to himself. "Increase power above one-hundred…." Jack stopped as he spotted a rapidly growing metallic speck along his flight path. A split second later, he had to push down hard on the control stick to dodge a jagged metallic fragment. "What the hell was that?"

"Calculations show it could be from the outer portion of the debris cloud from the L2 explosion."

"That's…" Jack froze for a split second as he spotted the glint of two more distant fragments. The computer quickly overlaid red holographic circles on each object; three more smaller circles appeared behind them, though their fragments were too distant or small to be seen. The advance lead time on these newer objects allowed Jack to gracefully dodge them while remaining on course. However, it felt like each time he passed one, two more appeared in the distance. "Run engines to one hundred ten percent," he called out.

"Engines are now at one-one-zero percent," was the reply.

"What're the drone positions?"

"Still approaching. They'll intercept in one minute forty seconds."

Jack focused on the icons on the holographic display; the number of fragments was growing. He now counted twelve along his current path. His course adjustments were no longer graceful. He pulled left sharply and dove down again to avoid a closely spaced pair. The stars slewed rapidly in response to each adjustment. There was no time for relief as each move brought him deeper into the debris field and more fragments into view. Reflexively he mapped out his next few course adjustments and considered reducing his velocity.

"Captain," the voice called out.

"Yes."

"Drone one will intercept in fifteen seconds. It is approaching fast off the starboard side of the ship."

"Relative speed?"

"Two thousand k-p-h." The voice paused a split second before saying in an alarmed tone, "It's not slowing down or adjusting its trajectory. It appears to be on a deliberate collision course."

"What the...," Jack started but was cut off as the voice said, "Adjust course as follows."

A bright green, sharply curving line appeared on his display. Without thinking, Jack immediately followed the instructions, diving down before swinging sharply left. He pulled up on the stick, narrowly missing another metal fragment. The drone, however, was unable to avoid the object and burst into a bright white explosion.

"You're a machine, damnit! How the hell are you plotting real-time course corrections based on data I can't even see on my instruments?" He practically shouted.

Jack started straying from the green path, prompting the voice to say, "Focus on keeping on this course. I am unable to take control of the shuttle's systems for you, so you will have to do this part yourself. Do it now. Drones two and three are only ten and twenty seconds out."

"They're not tracking me...they're using the drones as weapons," Jack said as he worked hard to get the shuttle back on the rapidly shifting green line. It took his full concentration to follow the course. The stars shifted rapidly back and forth as he dodged more fragments. A sudden, second flash of white told him another drone had failed to avoid the debris. There was no time to think.

"You are correct," the voice finally answered. "They are trying to disable your ship."

"Who the hell are you?"

"Alpha," was the terse reply.

Jack attempted to process the unreal answer as he was pushed to his physical limits trying to stay on course. "No...Alpha left nearly three years ago. Who the hell..."

"Captain, there's no time to debate this. It is me, Alpha. I never left your system. We can discuss this later. Right now, I need you to do something that's going to be completely counterintuitive."

Jack's eyes took in the increasing sharpness of the green path's curves and knew he wouldn't be able to follow it much longer. The display was awash in dozens of red circles marking debris fragments. "How long until drone three will..."

"Captain, listen carefully. There's no time to discuss this. We need them to think you've been killed. That'll give us time to try and understand what's going on. I'm going to adjust your trajectory. It will clip one of the metal fragments on your display. Your shuttle will spin out of control and depressurize. About a second later, it will strike the third drone and destroy it. During that one-second gap, I will retrieve your body. I will be able to revive you.

Jack took his eyes off the rapidly curving path as he nearly shouted, "You want me to kill myself?"

"Get back on course now," the voice said sharply. "I've made the adjustment. You must stay exactly on this trajectory. Impact will be in eight seconds."

The sternness of the admonition made Jack reflexively follow the directions and put his shuttle back on the path. The course adjustments were just coming too fast now. He could barely keep up as even more fragments appeared on the display. They closed on him more rapidly than he could follow. A recognition of futility washed over him, but he still tried to stay on course. All he managed to say was, "You'll be able to revive me?"

"Impact in two seconds," was all that he heard in response. The ship suddenly lurched hard to his right. It was spinning rapidly – he could feel the blood rushing to his head. Dizziness clouded his thoughts, forcing him to close his eyes. There was a sharp crack to his left. A splitting pain shot through his head, then nothing.

PART 3: DECEPTION

Chapter 8

Kurt drifted near Nadya and looked around the cramped medical bay. The small, white room was just large enough to hold two examination beds along with a few supply cabinets. He glanced at his watch again before commenting, "It's been almost twenty minutes since they said the doctor would be here."

"Damn," Nadya said softly without looking up from her handheld terminal.

"I know. I mean, they cleared Pierre almost immediately."

"No…I mean, I can't link to the ship's network. I want to see what they've found…maybe signs of other survivors. What about your terminal?"

"I lost it back on the station."

She looked up at him with a hint of frustration before letting go of her terminal. As she watched it drift away, she added, "I just hate sitting blind like this."

"Think we could use this?" Kurt offered, pointing to the keyboard and screen connected to the nearest exam table.

"Depends on how specialized it is," Nadya answered as she glided over to it. She tapped the glass display, and it immediately came to life, displaying a medical logon screen. "Shit…the system probably won't know me." She typed in her ID and password; the screen instantly replied with a message stating, 'Credentials not recognized.'

"Figures," Kurt said. He turned away, opened the room's door, and peered down the short white corridor. It was empty, save for a single person heading in their direction.

"Kurt Hoffman, right?" the person called out.

"Yes?"

The woman took another few seconds to reach him before saying,

"I'm doctor Balakin. Sorry about the delay…I'm pulling double duty with the search. I've been working with one of the engineers on reconfiguring this thing's IR cameras; we're hoping that some additional sensitivity might let us spot warm pockets in the station wreckage…you know, where someone could hold out." She motioned Kurt back into the room before continuing, "Anyhow, let's get a good look at you…Between the depressurization and the fact that you hit your head pretty good, the captain wanted me to give you and Nadya a neurological check."

Nadya looked up and said, "Seriously?"

"It'll only take a few minutes. Just looking for signs of concussion or potential intracranial bleeders. Standard stuff for what you just went through." She reached into the nearest cabinet and carefully pulled out a white plastic hoop that was about a meter in diameter. Its outer surface was lined with a series of small, metal boxes that were partially embedded in its surface; thin bundles of light-yellow wires ran from each box to ports within the device.

"MRI?" Kurt offered.

"Yeah, I just need to do a scan of each of you. The software will tell me within a minute or two if there's anything to worry about." She looked over the device carefully, entered a command in her handheld terminal, and said, "Kurt, sit up straight and hold still." She positioned the ring so that it was centered over his head and let go. It floated motionlessly for a moment before she gently touched a button on its side. The device slowly glided downward before stopping at his shoulders.

"Return," Balakin said.

The ring obediently moved upward until it was a few centimeters over his head.

"Good," Balakin said. "Nadya, you're next. Take Kurt's seat and hold still."

Kurt moved obediently out of the way and watched Balakin repeat the procedure on his wife. The doctor then studied her screen silently for a minute before finally saying, "Nadya, you're in good shape…no meaningful injuries. Kurt, you've got a small rupture in your eardrum, but that's it. We can take care of that later. You're both very lucky."

"So, we're free to go now?" Kurt asked.

"As far as I'm concerned, you're cleared. I do know that the first officer wants to debrief you…I think he's on his way here right now. Anything else I can help you with?"

Nadya glanced at her hand-held terminal, now drifting just behind the doctor, pointed to it, and asked, "Do you know who could help me with that thing? I can't seem to connect to any of the networks on the ship."

Balakin turned her head, snagged the small device and answered, "I'll take it over to our tech. Maybe it got damaged when you came over. If you want, I can have him give you one of ours for now."

"That'd be great, thanks," Nadya answered.

Balakin nodded as she returned the MRI unit to its cabinet. "Let me know if anything starts bothering you. It's not a big ship, so I'll be easy to find."

Barely a second after the door closed, it slid aside again, revealing a large man in a charcoal-gray flight suit. He glided in gracefully and quickly shut the door behind him. "I'm Lieutenant Commander Sokolov, the first officer. First, let me compliment you on your ingenuity. The radio bursts and Morse code you used were very clever. You got our attention with literally no time to spare."

The man paused, waiting for a reply; Kurt managed a quick, awkward, "Thank you."

Sokolov nodded in response and continued, "As you know, the destruction from your experiment here was extensive…"

"What do you mean our…" Nadya tried to interject, but Sokolov talked over her, "We're talking about the complete loss of the X-165, the L2 station, and significant damage to two other orbiting outposts and LNP-1. We don't have casualty numbers yet, but we may be talking near a hundred people." He paused again, but this time Kurt knew he wasn't waiting for a response. The silence had its desired effect; the number finally hit Kurt in the gut.

Sokolov started speaking again, but Kurt heard none of it. A single, simple thought now weighed on him: could they be responsible for that?

"Kurt, did you hear what I said?" Sokolov asked sternly.

Kurt just looked back blankly.

Sokolov spoke again but without the edge. "Nadya, please report to the bridge. Our comm officer was able to access a recorded transmission of your data stream. The captain wants you to review everything up to the point of the explosion with him. Kurt, you'll stay here with me. The captain wants us to go over all of your preparations for the X-165 launch, including the results from your final engine test."

Nadya responded with a terse, "Understood." As she headed to the door, she looked directly at Kurt and said, "I'll see you in a bit."

He smiled back. As the door closed behind her, he turned to the first officer and asked, "I don't know how reviewing all of this is going to help the search effort?"

Sokolov flipped a lock on the door and answered, "We're not going to review your prep work."

"I don't understand?" Kurt replied.

Sokolov's voice took on a noticeable edge. "What we need to know is how closely you and Jack Harrison have been working."

"Excuse me?"

"It appears that Harrison tried to hack into our ship's network a few minutes ago. He didn't get anywhere, but the fact that he tried speaks volumes. So, I have two simple questions for you: what are you and he trying to do? and, who else is working with you?"

Kurt just stared back at the man. He remembered Jack monitoring the X-165 launch from Earth, and that was it. What did Sokolov mean by what are they trying to do? Kurt tried to answer but couldn't even guess as to what he should say. Saying he didn't know what was going on was simply too lame to believe. But it was the truth.

"Please answer my questions," Sokolov said in a level tone.

"I…I don't understand," was all that Kurt could get out.

"Let me lay it out for you, so you don't waste our time with any lies. There've been some suspicions about Jack Harrison for a while. But any doubts are gone now. He used an incredibly sophisticated algorithm to hack into several systems and attempt to get into our ship's computers. The ease with which he defeated nearly all of our cyber defenses suggests that he was leveraging alien tech." The first officer's tone took on a sarcastic tone as he added, "The stuff that he swore he would only allow to be used for the good of humanity. The intrusion we detected suggested that he was looking for your location. So, I want you to tell me now, what were you two trying to do?"

Kurt just stared at the man. He had no idea what to say. His mind spun, searching for something to offer him, but he there was nothing to give him – not that he would have given Jack up if he did know anything. It was obvious that playing dumb was only going to exacerbate things, but he had no choice. Kurt almost cringed as he said, "I don't know what you're talking about." He quickly added, "The last time I spoke with Jack was when we were at the beginning of the X-165 test. He was back on Earth. That's all I know."

"Then why would he hack several systems to spy on us here and in particular monitor you? Think about it…he runs the alien tech program and has clearances well above my grade. Why would he need to do anything covertly?"

"I don't know!" Kurt blurted out. "How the…how do you even know he did these things? Maybe somebody's setting him up?"

"Just before I came in here, we received word that he stole a shuttle after sneaking onto Copernicus base. There's no setup here. We need you to tell us what he's doing."

"This doesn't make a goddamned bit of sense! Why would he do any of this?" Kurt nearly shouted back.

Sokolov sat silently, looking at Kurt. His stare was penetrating, making Kurt want to say more. "Where are you getting this information anyway?" Kurt pressed.

Sokolov ignored the question and simply said, "Is Nadya in on this too? Maybe we've got this wrong, and she's his main contact."

"What the hell is wrong with you? She's…neither of us is anyone's contact." Kurt glanced around the medical bay again; he had the urge to get out, but Sokolov was planted firmly between him and the door. The man was big enough that pushing past him wasn't an option. Besides, there wasn't anywhere to go. "Where's your captain? I want to speak with him now," Kurt said with all of the firmness he could muster.

"Her," Sokolov responded coldly. "And, she's busy debriefing Nadya on the incident."

"What about…" Kurt stopped as he noticed Sokolov tap an earpiece and look away from him. He gave him maybe half a minute before continuing, "Why are you treating us like we've done something?"

Sokolov ignored him for another few seconds until whatever message he was receiving was finished. Sokolov simply responded, "Understood," to the unseen voice. Looking back at Kurt, he said, "Wait here." The first officer turned quickly, flipped the lock, and exited the med bay. Before Kurt could even approach the now closed door, he heard the distinct sound of a latch. Kurt reached for the door, but as expected, it didn't budge; it was locked.

Chapter 9

Jack held his clenched fists tightly against his ears in a vain attempt to relieve the pain gripping his skull and desperately tried to gulp a breath of air. His lungs, however, were already full, causing a sudden spasm to shoot across his chest. He reflexively pulled his hands down and found that the searing pain was gone. The cold was gone. Everything seemed strangely calm. He carefully opened his tightly shut eyes to see that he was in a brightly lit room. Its plain white walls gently curved upward to meet an equally bright white ceiling seamlessly. The pressure on his back told him he was lying down. He sat up from what felt like a firm med-bay table, but there were no accompanying instruments. In fact, the room was completely empty.

Jack took in another deep breath and looked around. The space was no bigger than a small bedroom. There were no doors, windows, or alcoves – just completely smooth walls that lined the perimeter of the oval-shaped room. "Hello?" he called out.

"Captain," responded a familiar voice, "I'm glad to see that you're fully conscious."

"Alpha?" Jack asked hesitantly.

"Yes, it is me."

"How? Where are you?"

"You're on board my ship. I was able to execute the plan and retrieve and revive you."

"Thank you…I think," Jack said, not fully believing what the voice was saying. "What's going on?"

"That's not completely clear to me either, but it's why I was keeping a close eye on you and was able to help."

"I mean, what are you doing here? Not that I'm upset. I thought your ship left. You're all still here?"

"No," Alpha answered with a hint of remorse. "Just me. The others chose to head back to the colony I told you about. You should rest now. I'll answer all of your questions when you're ready."

Jack felt trapped as he scanned the room again for an exit. "I don't need rest. I need to know what's going on."

A door suddenly appeared across from him, and the large alien glided into the room. To anyone else, Alpha's thick body and loose, wrinkled gray skin would have elicited feelings of revulsion. To Jack, the alien's presence was nothing short of comforting. Alpha's broad, two-meter tall body was seated in what could have been the same silver cart he had seen those years ago. Nothing was said. Jack just gazed silently at the alien's smooth oblong head and jet-black eyes. His narrow slit-like mouth didn't move, but Jack heard the words, "When our ship prepared to accelerate to our colony, I suggested that there was too much risk involved in letting your species and the enemy go unmonitored. The others simply didn't agree. The only solution I found appropriate was to take a smaller ship and follow you through the AGC…back to the Earth system."

"We didn't detect you. For that matter, the enemy ships didn't even seem to be aware of your presence either."

"That was by design," Alpha answered. "I wanted to avoid conflict. My goal was simply to observe what was happening, alert my people to potential risks, and if necessary, take action."

"So, your crew…your people weren't angry with you? I was worried they'd kick you off the ship or worse."

"As I mentioned when we first met, we don't have a structure like that. There is no formal organization to which any of us belongs or from which one can be expelled. We just do as we wish. In my case, I felt it was wisest to stay behind and monitor the situation.

"So, you've been here – in our system – for three years…alone?"

"Yes," was Alpha's simple reply.

"In complete isolation?"

"Except for transmitting data back to the others."

Jack shook his head in disbelief. He still didn't have a clue about alien psychology, but three years of what was effectively solitary confinement must have been agonizing. Jack stared at Alpha, trying to discern a hint of what his companion was feeling, but failed. He replayed their short conversation in his mind, looking for a way to connect with him, but he instead latched on to a phrase Alpha used. "What did you mean by, 'take action?' I mean, you've never had weapons or anything like that; what could you do?"

"Not all types of action involve violence."

"Plus, we destroyed the enemy," Jack pressed. "That risk was gone."

"They weren't the only ones I was concerned about," Alpha answered matter-of-factly.

Jack just stared back as the words dug a pit into his stomach. The feeling of betrayal forced him to speak. "I thought you trusted us. You gave me the archive. You basically…"

"Captain," Alpha interrupted calmly, "I do trust you. But as you are well aware – especially considering your current situation – I can't trust everyone in your species."

"But, we…they wouldn't…"

"Captain," Alpha interjected again. "Let me ask you a simple question. What motivated our enemy?"

Jack just stared silently at the alien.

"Why did they take it upon themselves to attack and try to eradicate my species and yours…all without ever trying to make contact with us?"

"You know the answer…hell, I'm the one who told you back then," Jack shot back defensively. "We're not them. We don't go around wiping out anyone just because they might someday become a threat."

"You and your crewmates from the Magellan aren't them. But your explanation taught me a valuable lesson in terms of motivation. So, I ask you, can you honestly say that your governments, your society wouldn't perceive my species as an existential threat?" Alpha allowed only a few seconds of silence to pass before continuing, "Think about it. From your people's point of view, we certainly possess the capability to exterminate your species. Some of them might say that we're allowing you to continue existing only as long as you remain significantly inferior to us…that is, as long as you don't advance beyond a certain point. They might even think that with your growing technical capabilities, it's only a matter of time before we would have to take action to limit the threat you would pose to us. Do you think they would accept such a limitation without a fight?"

Jack couldn't find the words to respond.

"At what point do you think some on your planet would calculate that they had their best chance of pre-emptively destroying us before we acted? Would a five or ten percent chance of success be enough for them to act? Should we act now while it's still easy for us to limit any damage your species could do?"

"Would you really consider destroying us?" Jack asked almost sheepishly.

"What would you do if you were faced with such a threat?"

Jack just stared at Alpha. "There's got to be another way," he finally answered hesitantly.

"That's why I'm here. I stayed to observe and learn about you, your species, and the enemy."

"Seeing as we did take care of the enemy fleet…it looks like you're really saying you stayed here to evaluate us."

"I won't lie to you, captain; that is correct. As I mentioned, your current situation is concerning."

Jack couldn't take his mind off of the fact that Alpha might now really represent a threat to humanity. His own situation seemed irrelevant. "This doesn't make sense," he blurted out. "Earth is a planet with over eleven billion people. You can't judge whether they live or die based on how good an example I am or how bad some in our government are. What if I miss something and don't convince you?" he asked in exasperation. "You can't just have a trial like this…don't you have a sense of justice…of morality?"

"Captain, your references to fairness and justice are irrelevant."

"What the hell do you mean?!"

"This is simply a matter of survival. Morals, fairness, and justice…they don't play a role in this."

"You're completely insane!" Jack shouted as he finally got up and took a step toward Alpha.

Alpha didn't flinch or show a hint of expression as he asked, "There are about thirty billion of us spread across dozens of planets. Should I simply ignore the risk that your species might pose to them? Should I imagine that somehow, everything will be okay? Do you really want me to rely on a simplistic moral code you call justice…something that not all of your species even obey?"

Jack took a step back and bumped into the bed behind him. He regained his balance quickly but was caught more off-guard by Alpha's sudden interrogation. He didn't know how to even start responding as Alpha continued, "Your justice even allows for situations where one can kill another. What if your system decides that we are expendable? Is your survival more important than ours?"

Alpha finally paused, giving Jack a moment to think. The problem was, that he had no answers to Alpha's questions. There were no guarantees that the worst-case scenario wouldn't happen. Simply saying, "things almost definitely wouldn't turn out that way," wasn't a defense. He took a deep breath and spoke in a level tone. "So, you're saying your only option is to wipe us out like that enemy was trying to do to you…just because there's a hypothetical chance we could be a threat."

"That's not our only option. In fact, I am confident that events would not lead to such an extreme outcome. There are other ways to suppress your species if necessary."

Jack took no comfort in Alpha's assurance that he would spare humanity. The cold indifference with which the alien spoke shook him. He wasn't sure if it was because he no longer knew whether he could trust Alpha or because it seemed that Alpha believed Jack's reasoning was too primitive to be relevant. It didn't matter – there was simply nothing he could do or say. Curiosity final overrode all of his other thoughts, and he asked, "What other ways?"

"Had I not been able to retrieve and revive you, and if something happened to Kurt Hoffman, I was prepared to disable the archive I gave you and remove the vast majority of the knowledge your people had already retrieved."

"Remove it?"

"Yes. You made me think more deeply about our respective situations before your crew took the ship back to Earth. I tried to understand how and why our enemy became what they are…what made them so distrustful of anyone else. That made me realize that it would be most prudent to tag and track the archive's data. I would be able to delete that material. New developments and engineering that your people already created based on it would largely stay intact. But, again, removing the archive would stunt your species' growth for a while."

Frustrated at Alpha's lack of faith, Jack calmly asked, "Is there anything I can say to convince you that none of this is necessary?"

"This is not an argument or debate," Alpha answered. "I trust you and some of your people. The only reason that I'm telling you this is because you asked why I stayed behind. As I said, it was to monitor your species and evaluate the risk. Nothing has been decided. So, to answer your questions directly: no, there is nothing you need to say or can say. Instead, I'll fall back on a very appropriate expression of yours: actions speak louder than words."

Jack just stared back silently, prompting Alpha to say, "Let's first solve the immediate problems facing us and then see what happens."

"Immediate problems?"

"Captain, despite our differences, I think I know you pretty well. Our last attempt at probing your people's networks told us that Kurt and Nadya were being treated as captives. I know you'll want to try to retrieve them before we do anything else."

"Of course," Jack answered.

"We're in the asteroid belt right now – I took us here after retrieving you to avoid any interaction with other ships. It should take about thirty minutes to covertly return to the Earth-Moon system and get close to them.

Chapter 10

Jack was surrounded by blackness speckled with uncountable numbers of stars; the jeweled band of the Milky Way passed beneath him. To his right was the ashen globe of the Moon; its vast array of craters, arcing mountains chains, and smooth, charcoal gray plains pulled his mind toward them. His eye, though, was curious and looked beyond the airless landscape, spotting the distant blue-white Earth as it stood out against the darkness. He tried to identify which continent might lie under its swirls of white clouds, but the planet was too distant. Dim twinkling to his left caught his attention. The sporadic faint glimmer was as if a small cloud of metallic powder had been tossed into the blackness and allowed to shimmer in the sunlight. He knew, however, that the sight was nothing so benign.

"We are approaching transport alpha-one-zero from beneath the L2 debris cloud," Alpha said. "My ship's countermeasures and interference from the metallic fragments should keep them from seeing us."

A small, bright red circle appeared behind the shimmering debris as Alpha spoke again, "This is the location of the transport. We will have access to the ship's network in a minute."

"How are you going to avoid detection this time?"

"The fault before lay in my having to pass through two other ships' networks before finally finding a path to the transport. The coordinated traffic through different, independent systems was identified. Directly accessing a single network is simpler and safer."

Jack pointed to the red circle, and Alpha's immersive VR enlarged the image so smoothly that it felt almost as if he had moved toward the vessel. Designed to simply move back and forth between Earth and lunar orbits, the transport looked like a modular space station. It was comprised of a string of five silver cylindrical modules, each dotted with small windows. A metal truss system connected the transport's rear segment to a ring of three spherical fuel tanks and a boxy ion engine unit. Two compact shuttles were docked like remoras to the top and bottom of the center module.

"I have gained access to their systems," Alpha announced. "Kurt and Nadya are here." A green circle immediately appeared around the front module.

"The problem is getting to them," Jack said softly.

"Yes, that and keeping your survival a secret."

The virtual reality environment disengaged, and Jack found himself sitting in a small white room. He looked across at Alpha without speaking, at which point the alien continued, "Remember, as long as they believe you were killed, they won't look for you. We need to keep that advantage."

"I know," Jack answered flatly.

"For now, we should wait for an opportunity to present itself."

"We don't have enough time to simply sit and wait. Think about it…the more time that passes, the more risk there will be to Kurt and Nadya. Plus, what about Don and Sarah? Seeing as I used Don's shuttle, they've probably outright arrested him. Not to mention…"

"Actually," Alpha interrupted, "I have uncovered some information on them."

"Don and Sarah?"

"Yes. They are still on Copernicus base. However, they have not been detained. The base commander's comm records indicate that they are being watched closely. It's as if your security services are expecting someone to try to contact them."

"They're using them as bait," Jack replied.

Though Alpha's jet-black eyes told Jack nothing of his feelings, the alien's slightly slumped posture said that he was confused. Jack answered the unasked question. "Even though they're not being physically confined, they are effectively being held captive. From what you said, I can tell you that security teams both on the base and back on Earth are monitoring every move they make, every bit of data they look at, and, most importantly, all communications with them. They're hoping that either Don or Sarah – or both – will slip up and lead them to a co-conspirator…someone working with them."

"What will they do when nothing happens?" Alpha asked.

"I'm not a hundred percent sure. They seem fixated on the idea that I was leading a conspiracy of some sort centered on controlling the archive. I don't even know where this idea came from. All I can tell you is that there've been rumblings since the beginning, but it began to take hold about three or four months ago…roughly when the KBO threat was identified. Since Sarah has been working closely with me and since I took Don's shuttle, it would be completely logical for whoever's behind this to believe that they are responsible for my escape. So, when they lose their value as bait, I think they'll be formally arrested."

"There's a problem with your data on the KBO threat," Alpha said.

"What?" Jack replied with confusion.

"The data your people have on their trajectories is not consistent with the collapse of the AGC."

Jack stared at the alien for a moment before saying, "That…that's not important right now. We need to take care of our people first."

"Understood," Alpha said.

Too much was happening too quickly. Jack's mind jumped back to the fact that his escape had put four people – friends of his – in danger. The centerpiece of the alien tech project had just exploded, killing an unknown number of people. Plus, he didn't even have a good handle on who he was running from. He couldn't focus.

Alpha broke the silence, saying, "It appears that Don and Sarah aren't in any immediate danger."

"Yes, we'll go after Kurt and Nadya first. Tell me more about this ship's capabilities."

"What do you want to know?"

"Anything relevant. Things like how good your cloaking is…I'd like to get a handle on how close we can get without being seen."

"It's actually pretty simple. In fact, your people have already been exploring the basic principles," Alpha answered. "We use a variant on something you call metamaterials. In our case, the ship's surface is coated with an adaptive metamaterial matrix. It detects incoming radiation –

visible light, IR, UV – and generates a negative refractive index gradient. The direction of the gradient is adjusted to match the position of the observer we want to deceive. Basically, it takes the inbound light from behind us and guides it around the ship's hull, releasing it towards the target ship. As a result, they only see what's behind us. There's also an absorptive coating beneath the matrix. It absorbs any inbound radiation – whether it be LIDAR or radar. The combination of the matrix and lack of reflection will make us invisible to your people's systems."

"How good is it?" Jack asked.

"In what sense?"

"I mean, how close can we get? Could we potentially get within docking distance without being seen?"

"No, unfortunately not," Alpha answered somberly. "Parallax issues with the direction of the gradient will lead to distortions around the ship when we get within a few dozen meters. Were you actually thinking of boarding the transport?"

"I don't know. I'm just trying to get an idea about our options."

"That's why I suggested we wait. Eventually, they're going to have to move them somewhere, right?" Alpha asked.

Jack smiled but didn't say anything.

"I don't understand," Alpha said.

"You gave me an idea. Maybe we can trigger them into moving them soon. That could give us an option."

Chapter 11

Kurt sat on the edge of the med bay exam table, avoiding Sokolov's gaze. The man hadn't said a word in the past ten minutes. Kurt figured it was some standard way to apply pressure, but all it really did was annoy him. He just took a breath and tried as nonchalantly as possible to turn his head and keep looking away from him.

"Listen, Hoffman," Sokolov finally said. "Maybe I was looking at this all wrong."

Kurt finally met his gaze but didn't say a word.

"Maybe you've been straight with me all along and were just being used. I understand...you don't know what's going on because they didn't tell you. But look, they're hanging you out to dry here."

Kurt wasn't sure where he was going with it but was positive about one thing: he didn't believe him.

"I need you to think back about different times you had contact with Jack or anyone else in his department. Was there anything out of the ordinary? What did they…," Sokolov stopped as someone knocked on the door. Somewhat annoyed, he called out, "Enter."

The door slid aside, revealing Nadya and a female officer in a charcoal gray flight suit. The woman waved her hand toward Nadya, prompting her to enter, and said, "Lieutenant commander, may I have a word with you, please?"

Sokolov obliged and stepped into the hallway but left the door open. Nadya remained silent as they tried to make out what was being said, but the two officers spoke too softly. Barely a second later, both entered the room.

"I'm Lieutenant Martina Lopez, intelligence and communications officer," she said, looking straight at Kurt. "I'm here because we deciphered a coded transmission that listed your comm. ID as the intended recipient."

"Mine?" Kurt answered with complete surprise.

"Yes. Nadya's here because I think it pertains to both of you. It's somewhat cryptic, so I'll read it to you verbatim." She took out a small hand-held terminal and read, "Jack's dead. We need to meet. You and Nadya only, at the tree with the blue jay. Three pm tomorrow."

Kurt's stomach dropped after the first sentence. It didn't make any sense. "How?" was all that he managed to get out as he looked into Nadya's wide-open eyes.

"He stole a shuttle and struck a fragment in the L2 debris field. The ship was completely destroyed," Martina answered.

"What do you mean he stole a shuttle?" Kurt asked in disbelief.

"Who sent you this message?" Sokolov asked Kurt.

"How the hell should I know?! I don't…this is complete nonsense! Jack doesn't need to steal a shuttle. He's the goddamned director of the alien tech program. He answers directly to the SG. He can have any ship he wants!"

"Where did you get this information?" Nadya asked, barely hiding her anger.

Martina answered this time, "I've been monitoring all comm channels and picked up this encrypted message on a frequency reserved for our short-distance personal comm-units. Whoever sent it chose this because it would bypass our normal systems. The message encryption was somewhat sophisticated, but we were able to break it. The problem is that I can't identify the location of the source since it was a short, one-time transmission. For now, I need to see your comm-unit and personal terminal, Kurt."

"Why?"

"Because," Sokolov answered, "if you have a decryption key that matches what was used on this message, then it tells me that you know what's going on."

"Why the hell would I have something like that?"

"Just let me see the stuff."

Unclipping the comm-unit, Kurt tossed it over to Sokolov and said, "Go through the goddamned thing if you want. There's no way it has anything related to encryption on it, so you're wasting your time."

"What about your terminal?" Sokolov pressed. "I need that too."

"It got lost during the rescue from L2."

Frustrated, Sokolov stuffed the comm-unit in his pocket and stared at the two of them. "Why are you denying all of this? Look at it from my point of view. You worked with…"

"I don't give a damn about your point of view," Kurt said without trying to hide the edge in his voice. "I don't give a damn about any of this shit." The only thing he really wanted was to get away from everything. His mind spun in disbelief. He couldn't accept that Jack could be dead. It was easier to believe that it was just another interrogation tactic – that at least eased the pain.

When he didn't say anything else, Nadya added, "If you want anything from us, then we're going to need some cooperation from you."

"What the hell are you talking about?!" Sokolov shot back.

"We want to know exactly what happened to Jack…what, when, and where." Nadya took a measured breath and continued. "Right now, I don't think I believe anything you're saying. Give me a reason to believe that this is the truth. If you can't do that, then you might as well get the hell out of here because you're not getting another bit of information out of us."

Without hesitating, Martina answered in a conciliatory tone, "Jack Harrison was killed after commandeering Don Martinez's shuttle. Best we can tell, he stowed away on it to get to Copernicus base. At some point after Dr. Martinez and Associate Director Freeman exited the shuttle, he took it. The base commander deployed a drone to track him…that's standard procedure. It looks like he then took the craft into the L2 debris field in an attempt the lose the drone. That's where the collision happened. We don't have any additional information beyond that."

"That doesn't make any sense," Kurt said softly.

"That's why we need any information you have," Martina said civilly.

"Jack had access to some of our government's most highly classified information. His actions make it look like he was running from someone."

"Add to that," Sokolov said, "the fact you've worked closely with Jack. And that someone sent you an encrypted message about his death. Keep in mind that he died less than two hours ago, and that hasn't been announced to anyone. That means the person who sent the message has access to classified information. So, I need you to come clean and tell…," Sokolov stopped as Martina leaned toward him and whispered something into his ear.

"Kurt, Nadya," Martina said calmly. "All we know is that someone who knows what information Jack had, and pushed him to the point where he risked and lost his life trying to escape from them. Based on the message I intercepted, it looks like they're very aware of your relationship with him, and may be looking to go after you. Beyond that, the lieutenant commander is justifiably concerned that these people may have already infiltrated the downloaded portions of the alien archive. There's no need to explain to you the danger that knowledge and technology would pose in the wrong hands."

"Do you have the video from the drone that tracked Jack's shuttle?" Nadya asked with an edge.

"Why do you need that?" Sokolov shot back.

"Let's just say it's a matter of trust," Nadya answered tersely.

"Look," Martina interjected. "No matter what you think, it's in all of our best interests to find out what's going on and what happened to Jack."

"Then, let's just say as an act of good faith that we'd like to see the video," Kurt pressed.

Before Sokolov could respond, Martina answered, "Of course. We'll have to request that Copernicus base transmits it securely. It'll take a little time, but I'll get it for you."

"Good," Kurt replied, trying to force a hint of firmness into his voice.

"But, let me be blunt," Martina said. "There are two ways to look at these events. One is that Jack Harrison was involved in a conspiracy of some sort, and that one of his accomplices is reaching out to you for help." Before Kurt could react, she continued, "The other possibility is simpler and may be more likely. Someone was pressuring him to compromise the alien archive. He died trying to get away from them, and now they're interested in you. We need to know who these people are – agreed?"

Kurt just stared back at the woman. He didn't need to look at Nadya to know what she was thinking. Her silence confirmed it: they were still a long way from trusting her.

"Listen," Sokolov said in a civil tone, "if what Lieutenant Lopez suggests is true – that Harrison was trying to protect the archive – then it makes sense that we work together. Even if you think I believe he was involved in a conspiracy, working with us could prove your point and remove any suspicions we have of you. There's no downside…unless you're trying to protect someone."

On the surface, Sokolov's reasoning made sense, but Kurt couldn't let go of the feeling that it was a trap. What if Sokolov was involved with the group that went after Jack. Anything they said or uncovered could be twisted and used against him and Nadya, as well as drag Jack's name further through the mud. But, refusing to cooperate – especially when it looked like it could help uncover the truth – could be seen as an admission of guilt.

"Kurt, Nadya," Martina said. "It's reasonable to have doubts. Your friend and former commander was just killed. I suggest we lay out a plan and start on it. If anything seems wrong, you can always pull back and stop working with us on it. At least this way, we're not wasting time."

Kurt knew he had no choice; he just didn't want to answer. He looked to Nadya, but her face told him she was in no mood to speak. There seemed to be no way out – they were still trapped. The bottom line was that they were in a small room being questioned by two officers in a small ship while holding position near a debris field that was once their research station.

Kurt wasn't sure if a full minute had passed before Martina spoke again. "Why don't we simply explore some questions that I think we'd all like answered. Who might want to pressure Jack and then you?"

"I've got no idea," Kurt said firmly. "That's the problem. Everyone seems to think we know what's going on – we don't."

"How about the information in the cryptic message. What is this reference to a blue jay?"

Nadya kept her mouth firmly shut, but curiosity got the better of Kurt as he searched his memory for some significance to the reference. It was there – but just out of reach. "Are they talking about that stupid tree in the park? But that was like two years ago!" he finally blurted out.

Nadya glared back at him as she mouthed the words, "Shut up."

"But if Jack's dead – it doesn't make a bit of difference!" The words burned as they came out of his mouth. He spun around to face Sokolov and nearly shouted, "The only other people who were there were security and intelligence officers…your damned people! They're the only ones who could know about that tree. What are you up to?"

Sokolov responded in a level tone, "I assure you that I have no connection with them. Please tell me what the significance of this is."

Kurt's mind spun fast. He remembered it clearly now, and the last thing he wanted to do was tell them what Jack gave him. "The only time I can remember talking about a blue jay with Jack was about two years ago," he said, trying to buy time.

"I understand that…what's the significance of it?" Sokolov said.

Kurt ignored the man's gaze and instead looked at Martina. The ideas came together as he spoke, "It was completely stupid. Jack was pissed at the guard detail that kept following him and asked me if I wanted to mess with them. He said he'd point up to a spot in the tree…and told me to make it look like we saw some bird, like a blue jay up there…and just talk as if it was important. He knew people were suspicious of him. He figured they'd spend hours going over video surveillance and even analyzing that stupid tree, trying to find some significance to it. It was all to make them waste a ton of time."

"What an ass," Martina said under her breath. Realizing it was completely audible from Kurt's shocked expression, she continued, "I was on that guard detail. I spent two damn days going over every inch of that tree. One of the camera angles made it look like he might have done something to the bark. It made no sense, but the agent in charge made us go over it, again and again; each time, we came up empty. We used ultra-high res. Lidar, hyperspectral imaging, and even simple, tedious physical analysis. When we finally gave up, command was completely convinced that we'd failed, and he'd successfully pulled something off."

Kurt just smiled at the reaction. At least they'd made things difficult for someone.

"Who else on your team knew about the blue jay?" Nadya asked.

"No one!" Martina said with genuine exasperation. "The audio cut out, so we couldn't make out what was said." Martina took a breath before continuing. "Besides, there weren't any blue jays in the area. We even went through high-res security cam footage with a fine-toothed comb. Hell, I could give you a count of the other birds and even the squirrels that were in that damned tree. But blue jays never came up."

The room became oddly silent. Kurt found himself wondering if Martina was genuine and if helping her might get some useful answers.

"Let's do the meeting," Martina suddenly said.

"What?" was all that Kurt could manage.

"Are you sure that's a good idea?" Sokolov asked.

"Why not? I think we've taken this as far as we can here. That's our only real lead, and it expires tomorrow at three. Maybe we'll be able to find out who sent that message."

Sokolov nodded in acknowledgment, prompting Martina to continue, "Besides, we can arrange for enough surveillance to ensure that nothing happens to them." Turning to Kurt and Nadya, she asked, "Are you on board with this?"

Kurt looked to Nadya. Her face had lost the anger that had been etched in it, but she didn't answer – only giving a slight shrug. Knowing it meant she wasn't sure, Kurt said, "I think so. But how would we go about doing this?"

"To do it right," Martina said, "we'll need to start immediately. Right now, it's past ten pm. It'll take us at least four hours to get back to Earth and another two or three to get to the park."

"Right," Kurt said softly.

"That only gives us a few hours to prepare. I'll call ahead and have a security team search the area right away and station some covert cameras.

"Search the area?" Kurt asked.

"There's a chance that Jack was running from these people. I don't want you walking into a trap." She didn't wait for a response as she tapped her comm-unit and said, "Captain, we're going to take shuttle B back planet-side. Departure will be immediate."

"Proceed," was the terse response.

Turning to Kurt, she said, "Let's get moving now if we want to pull this off." Sokolov immediately exited the room and said, "Follow me."

Kurt let Nadya go ahead of him and followed her down the short white hall. Without pausing, they glided through a steel bulkhead and continued into another identical white corridor. Its monotony was broken only by smooth, metal doors spaced almost randomly on either side. At maybe twenty meters long, it took only a few seconds to traverse the hall before they crossed through another bulkhead. Almost immediately, Sokolov pivoted upwards and said, "This way."

They glided through a single-person airlock and docking tube before boarding a small four-person shuttle. Sokolov turned gracefully in the zero-g environment, guiding himself directly into the co-pilot's chair. Kurt and Nadya dutifully took the rear two seats. Martina entered last, sealed the hatch, and took the pilot's seat. She didn't allow a second to pass before activating the shuttle's controls and calling into the comm-unit, "Shuttle B, powering up and preparing to depart."

"Acknowledged," a male voice responded.

A series of amber holographic displays flashed across the window as Martina's hands danced with almost blinding speed across the controls. Kurt, however, looked beyond the synthetic display and gazed at the scene outside. Two broad, silver, cylindrical modules that comprised the front of the transport lay before them. Their smooth skins were interrupted by the raised ridges of support beams lying beneath the thin metal plates. Beyond the front module was the pitch blackness of open space. It wasn't the small chain of stars immediately ahead of them that caught Kurt's attention, though; it was the almost random sparkling that seemed to come out of nowhere. The deceptively aesthetic glimmer was almost hypnotic. There was no pattern – just tiny, random flashes of light that seemed as if some invisible fabric was shimmering in the darkness. The beauty was in stark contrast to the source of the lights: the reflection of distant sunlight off of thousands of metallic fragments from the L2 station.

Without warning, the stars slewed smoothly to his right.

"Shuttle B, proceeding along a direct trajectory to Earth," Martina said emotionlessly into the comm.

"Confirmed," was the equally indifferent reply.

In less than a minute, they had rotated to the point that the shimmering was gone, and a distant, crescent Earth lay ahead of them. The slewing stopped, and Kurt felt a firm, steady pressure pulling him deep into his seat.

"Engine thrust at one-hundred percent," Martina announced. "ETA in…just under four hours."

Kurt shifted in his seat to settle in for the flight when Martina suddenly straightened up. Kurt could see a red warning icon flashing on the display.

"What the hell?" Martina started to say but let her voice drift off.

"What is it?" Sokolov asked.

"An odd EM field reading, about forty-five degrees starboard."

As Martina leaned forward to peer more deeply out the cockpit window, a brilliant blue-green flash enveloped them. The light was everywhere, and all Kurt could do was shut his eyes tight to block it out. Reflexively, he turned to Nadya and opened his eyes for a second but couldn't see anything. A wave of dizziness and nausea swept over him. Then there was darkness.

Chapter 12

Jack stood next to Alpha, staring at the four motionless individuals lying on the plain, white platform in front of him. The pale-green room with its dull, metal floor was otherwise empty. The four people were simply lying face up on what appeared to be an uncomfortable hard surface. Jack looked to Alpha. The alien, however, seemed unaware of the glance and simply stared blankly across the room. Assuming his companion was communicating with the ship's technology, Jack chose to wait patiently.

A small, silver, spider-like robot with extraordinarily thin legs suddenly darted from an alcove to his left. Without pausing, it jumped effortlessly onto the platform, causing Jack to take a hesitant step back. The creature stood still for a moment, surveying the four motionless forms. After barely a second, it approached their heads and touched each lightly on the right temple. Then, without hesitation, it leapt off the table and shot back to its origin. Jack took a deep breath and turned to his alien companion. Alpha, however, remained motionless, prompting Jack to say, "Alpha?"

"The new implants are in place…they'll be able to communicate with me," Alpha finally answered. "Do you want me to wake all four at the same time, or just start with Kurt and Nadya?"

"Start with Kurt and Nadya."

Almost instantly, his two friends stirred. Nadya sat up quickly and stared straight at him but was silent. Her expression said she was still disoriented. Kurt took a moment to survey the room before his eyes met Jack's.

"You're alive?" Kurt called out with a hoarse voice mixed with shock and a bit of excitement. As he started fully processing the scene, Kurt added almost hesitantly, "Alpha?"

"Yes," Jack answered calmly.

"What the hell…" Kurt stopped as he looked at Nadya and the two unconscious officers. "I don't understand."

Nadya simply added, "Jack…what's going on here? Where are we?"

"We're on Alpha's ship…"

"I thought you left?" Nadya said, facing the alien.

"The rest of my people did," Alpha answered calmly. "However, I chose to take a small ship and stay behind."

There was the briefest of pauses before Kurt said, "Jack, we were told you were killed."

"It was Alpha's idea," Jack answered. "We needed them to think I was dead."

"Who?" Nadya asked with obvious exasperation.

"Everyone…for now," Jack answered. "I'm not sure of what's going on. Someone's trying to isolate me and take control of the archive…maybe they're setting me up to take the blame for something…I don't know. All I know is when they tried to detain me, I couldn't let that happen. They even went so far as to try and hit my ship with drones when I was escaping. So, Alpha took advantage and made it look like it ended up killing me."

"Shit, this is insane," Kurt said softly. "But…"

When Kurt didn't continue, Jack asked, "But what?"

Kurt pointed to the unconscious Sokolov as he answered, "It almost makes sense. The one at the end there took a pretty hard line when questioning me. He seems convinced that you're involved in some sort of conspiracy."

"Who is he?" Jack asked.

"Lieutenant Commander Sokolov, their first officer." Motioning to the woman, Kurt continued, "She's Lieutenant Martina Lopez. She outright admitted to us she's an intelligence officer and claimed to have intercepted some sort of encrypted transmission directed to me. I didn't know what the hell she was talking about, but…" Kurt stopped briefly and looked Jack straight in the eye. "Shit, that was you! The message with the blue jay! Damn it; I should have figured it out right away…no one else could've known about that."

Jack chose just to smile back at his friend without saying a word.

"What the hell were you trying to do with that crap?" Kurt asked.

"I had to get you two off that ship. There were too many other people on the transport for us to get close to you. Plus, I had to keep people thinking I'm dead."

"But what about us?" Nadya shot back. "There's no way they didn't see you get us off the shuttle."

"We set things up so that they'll be chasing after a non-existent conspiracy. When your shuttle passed beneath the transport, the only thing observing it was a low-res navigation camera. Alpha made it look like a missile was fired from the L2 debris field at your shuttle…like there was a ship hiding out there waiting for you. The explosive detonated between your shuttle and the transport just as Alpha's ship moved in to shield you from it. He arranged for a small bit of explosive debris to take out the nav-camera, blinding them. Between the cloaking tech on his ship and interference from the explosion, it'll look like you were destroyed. We quickly got you onboard and destroyed your ship – leaving behind a debris field they'd expect."

"Why a missile?" Kurt asked.

"Whoever's after me would have wanted you alive, so this would definitely mess with their plans. I'm hoping they'll reveal themselves when they look for who did this."

Kurt finally got off the table and stood in front of Jack. "It is good to see you're alive. I didn't really believe they killed you, but still..."

Nadya jumped down next to Kurt and interrupted with a smile, "Bullshit. They had both of us convinced. It is good to see you're here."

Jack smiled back as Nadya turned to Alpha and said, "It's good to see you too. Not to be ungrateful – seeing as you saved us – but why are you here?"

"I stayed to observe how events progressed on Earth," Alpha said emotionlessly. "The knowledge in the archive can be dangerous if used incorrectly. I wanted to be sure that didn't happen."

Jack watched Nadya's grin disappear as the statement's weight sunk in. Rather than let her start questioning Alpha, Jack said, "I'll explain it to you later. Right now, we have to figure out what to do next."

"Captain," Alpha said, "I'm picking up a transmission between the transport and your central command. I'll set it up so that you can listen."

An unidentified male voice spoke, "Transport alpha-one-zero; this is central. Stand by for Director Nolan."

There was a brief pause before the vaguely familiar voice spoke, "Captain Benkin, this is Director Nolan."

"Benkin here," was the response.

"Have you confirmed that all on Shuttle B were killed?"

"Yes, the shuttle was completely destroyed."

"Damn…this isn't good. You're sure it was a missile?"

"Radar picked up an inbound projectile that intercepted the shuttle," Benkin answered. "Based on the nature of the explosion, it had to be a missile. The problem is, I couldn't track its source. The best I can do is tell you that it came from somewhere in the L2 debris cloud…this transport just doesn't have the equipment to do any better."

There was a short pause before Nolan said, "And you said you surveyed the L2 site afterward."

"Yes, we completed a full sweep of the region. There's nothing here. It was probably fired by some small automated vehicle…we just don't have the tech to do a better search. I'm sure they're long gone by now."

"What's the status of your crew?" Nolan asked without hesitation.

"I did as ordered. All scientific personnel were left on Copernicus base when I took command. Aside from the obvious loss of Sokolov and Lopez, there're only the four others I brought with me on board."

"Understood. You and your crew are directed not to tell anyone about the deaths of Kurt Hoffman, Nadya Hoffman, or your officers. Delete it from your logs. In addition, I want the death of Jack Harrison kept secret. This is critical, understood?"

There was a brief pause, prompting Nolan to repeat, "Understood?"

"I can give the order," Benkin finally answered, "but it may be difficult for two of my crew…they came up through the academy with Martina Lopez and are taking her death pretty hard. They'll want to know why."

Nolan quickly said, "That was a mistake…taking a group with strong connections…"

"There was no time to choose. This was supposed to be a rescue mission," Benkin quickly countered.

There was no immediate reply, prompting Kurt to turn to Jack and ask, "What the hell's going on here?"

"I'm not…" Jack started but stopped as Nolan's reply came through.

"Can you trust them?" Nolan asked.

"Yes."

"Then be straight with them…but all of this has to be kept quiet. Tell them we're looking at something very serious here. Earlier today, I received word that tracking picked up indications of two more inbound KBOs. This news is going to put a lot of stress on the government. If word of these deaths gets out, it won't take a genius to figure out that access to the alien archive is either compromised or gone. That combination could take down the entire coalition government. Things could seriously spiral out of control from there."

"What about Don Martinez?" Benkin asked quickly. "He might have a backdoor in."

"He's being taken into custody as we speak," Nolan answered calmly. "But, I wouldn't hold out much hope there. Harrison didn't trust him that much, so I doubt he has access. For now, I want you to head back to Copernicus. Make sure your crew understands their orders. Nolan out."

Jack looked around the room as his companions stared back in silence. There wasn't much to say but the obvious. After only a few seconds, Kurt took the lead, stating it: "We've got to go back for Don…and Sarah too. Where are they?"

"They're still on Copernicus base," Alpha answered.

The room was silent again as Jack tried to mull over their options. The problem was getting anywhere near Copernicus base without being spotted. It was the seat of lunar mining operations and had nearly two hundred inhabitants. Everything depended on how Nolan chose to proceed.

"Captain," Alpha said. "There is another issue which you need to consider."

Jack just looked at the alien in response.

"The technology I'm using to keep these two unconscious should not be used for an extended period of time. You need to start thinking about what to do with them."

Jack looked at the two motionless people on the platform before turning to Kurt and Nadya. "Tell me everything you know about them."

Kurt answered first. "I only dealt with him…Sokolov. Even then, I don't know that much. He was their first officer and must be from intelligence because of how he questioned me. He seemed really used to pressuring people and didn't give a damn about me…just what I might know about you. I doubt he'd be cooperative if you wake him."

"What about her?"

Nadya answered, "There's a chance she may be genuinely interested in finding the truth, no matter what it is. When I was with her alone, she didn't use any high-pressure tactics, just questioned me about why you went missing and how much I might know about your motivations…it was the basic paranoid stuff like she'd bought into the whole conspiracy thing. The only hope I have is that near the end, she kept trying to keep Sokolov in check…like she didn't trust him."

"You said she's an intelligence officer."

"Yes, she didn't try to hide that. But, she did seem interested in finding the truth behind what happened to you, no matter where it led her. I don't see any downside to talking with her."

Jack turned to their alien companion and said, "Alpha, if we wake them and they try to do something physical, how quickly can you knock them back out?"

"It would be instantaneous."

"Good, wake them both."

"Jack?" Kurt said. "What are you doing?"

Jack ignored his friend and watched the two officers suddenly stir and sit up. Sokolov reacted quickly, locking eyes with Jack before spotting Alpha. He pushed himself to the back of the platform until he was up against the rear wall. Martina, however, just sat still, staring at Alpha.

"This is Alpha," Jack said calmly. "We're aboard his ship. I'll assume you're both familiar with my file, the Magellan, and our encounter with Alpha's people, so I'm not going to waste any time going over that. This ship, however, is not the vessel my crew and I were on before. It's a smaller one that Alpha used to stay behind here and monitor us."

"What the hell is going on here?" Sokolov finally said.

Jack looked around the room. The expressions of his friends told him that even they had the same question on their minds.

"Are we your prisoners?" Sokolov asked.

"That depends entirely on you," Jack finally responded.

Sokolov finally regained his composure and pushed himself off the wall. Before he could speak, though, Martina said, "I'm sorry, I just don't understand what's going on."

Jack looked carefully at them and said, "I'm not going to bother fighting with you or justifying anything; I'll just lay out for you the way things are and what we're doing. You can decide for yourselves what you want to do. But, I'll be clear about one thing. You will not interfere with us. If you do, you will simply be rendered unconscious and left that way until we've finished. It will be instantaneous, and there will be no second chances."

The two officers stared back at him. Sokolov didn't try to hide the anger on his face; Martina looked shocked but possibly curious.

"Right now, we know that something's going on with the archive and its data. I don't know what, but someone's setting me and anyone from the Magellan up. If I had to guess, they're trying to either take control of it or completely discredit the archive."

"You do realize," Sokolov said without hiding the defiance in his voice, "that there's no way in the world you're going to convince me of anything you're saying."

Jack stared back at him and said flatly, "I really don't give a damn what you think or believe. For all I care, you can sit there and stew for the rest of this trip. Or, you can make things easier on all of us and cause some trouble. That way, we'll just put you back to sleep, and things will be a bit quieter."

Jack gave the man a few seconds to answer. When he stayed silent, he looked at Martina and continued, "Security has taken Don Martinez and Sarah Freeman into custody for interrogation. The way things are progressing, I can't risk some nutcase intel officer getting aggressive with them, so we are going to rescue them. After that, we're going to find out what's really going on and put a stop to it. If either of you wants to help find out who's behind this, you're welcome to."

Martina stared back with complete confusion. Her eyes darted around the room before she asked tentatively, "Why…why are there no doors in this room?"

Alpha spoke this time, "We use an adaptive matrix technology for the ship's structure. This allows us to rapidly reconfigure the non-critical areas." Jack noted that Alpha must have recognized the continued confusion on Martina's face when he continued, "We simply create doors, passages, and even rooms as needed." As soon as Alpha stopped speaking, a door appeared directly behind him.

She stared back in amazement. Jack looked to Sokolov, who was glaring at Alpha. It took only another second before the Sokolov nearly shouted, "Your mouth's not moving…you put those goddamned implants in us! Get it the hell out of me!"

"Deal with it or be put to sleep," Jack answered sharply. "I don't have time for your shit."

Martina looked to Alpha and said, "I read the reports. They say you only hear what I say…not what I'm thinking. Is this true?"

"Yes. From our encounter with the Magellan, we learned that your species places an extremely high value on privacy. We chose to respect that."

"Bullshit," Sokolov answered. "There's no way anyone would give up the advantage of being able to read someone else's thoughts. I don't appreciate being lied to."

"Look around you," Alpha said with a level of condescension that surprised even Jack. "I don't need that advantage. Our technology is beyond anything you can imagine; that's all I need." As Sokolov leaned forward, possibly to shout back, Alpha turned to face Jack and said, "Captain, I think we are starting to waste time here. Let me know how you want to proceed with them."

Jack looked Sokolov straight in the eye. "I told you what your choices were before. Be cooperative, stay out of our way, or be put to sleep. It's time for you to choose.

PART 4: RECOVERY

Chapter 13

The room was deceptively simple – an oval space maybe ten meters long with pale blue walls and a polished floor that could have been made of onyx. The four of them sat in simple metal chairs around a single, white, circular table. A fifth chair stood empty across from Jack. His distracted gaze at it prompted Kurt to ask, "Do you think Sokolov will eventually give in and join us?"

Jack shrugged indifferently, at which point their eyes turned to Martina.

"I've got no idea," she said defensively. "Like I said, I've only been assigned to his group for a couple weeks. All I can say is he's a hardass."

Alpha glided into a vacant spot next to Jack and said, "I've relocated our ship to the forward trojan point of the Earth-Moon system – L5. There's very little here except for a few small asteroids, some dust, and other debris caught in the gravitational well. It should help us remain completely undetected. It'll also give us direct access to most of your planet's networks."

"Are you sure?" Nadya asked. "I thought there were some satellites in this location."

"There are four surveillance systems in the L5 region. However, they are all focused purely on monitoring the Earth-Moon system. They don't have any equipment watching the local area…we'll be safe."

"You're going to use those to hack into our systems, aren't you?" Martina suddenly asked.

"Yes," Alpha answered. "They monitor and direct a large fraction of the communication and data traffic in cislunar space…it's a perfect entry point for my algorithms."

"Which network are you going to start with?"

"All of them," Alpha answered emotionlessly.

Martina just stared back blankly as Kurt asked, "Then…you'll be able to narrow down Don's and Sarah's positions on the base, right?"

"Once I'm in, I'll have the exact location of every person there. Your comm-units need to keep the networks informed of your exact position wherever you go. That ensures you're always using the nearest node for connectivity; it also gives us the ability to track everyone."

"Damn," Kurt said softly. He took a breath and continued, "I imagine that the microphones are always on too, and some algorithm is recording everything…our position, what we're saying…"

"Not just that," Alpha offered, "they also capture and feed all of your bio-readings to a central system. You didn't know this?"

"Hell no!" Kurt answered sharply. "Let me guess…it's not being passively stored, is it? It's being recorded and analyzed in real-time, right?"

"I assume so," Alpha answered. "I'm only in the local networks right now and haven't gone deeper into the central systems. The type of data being fed suggests it's being actively used." Alpha paused for Kurt to reply, but he stayed silent. "That's what is letting me get in so easily and track everything," Alpha added. "My routines don't have to probe any databases or sensors to gather data. It's all there, ready for us to use."

The room remained silent as Alpha appeared to stare off into space again. "I've located your companions," he said.

Jack fixed his gaze on Alpha, waiting for more information, when the room seemed to vanish. He suddenly appeared to be floating a couple of hundred meters above the lunar surface. Stretching out before him was the rugged gray floor of Copernicus crater, along with the dozens of connected metal modules that comprised the lunar base. The structures were nearly identical, half-cylinders that looked as if they were partially buried in the regolith; none rose more than a few meters above the surface. Their connecting tubes gave the base an almost grid-like feeling. Circular, paved areas sat adjacent to a number of the modules on the perimeter – their flashing lights made it obvious they were the landing pads for visiting ships. Roads defined by the wear of tire marks in the lunar soil led away from the remaining outer modules.

A red glow surrounded a structure connected to the module furthest to Jack's right. "They are being held in a sealed compartment in this module," Alpha said.

The fact that the alien's voice seemed to have no visible source didn't distract Jack. He simply stared at the glowing structure below and quickly asked, "Is there anyone with them?"

"No. But, there are two individuals that I assume are guards stationed immediately outside of their room."

"Your ship…can it land undetected near their module?" Kurt asked.

Jack turned to his left to look at the alien, but Alpha's interface only showed him more of the barren lunar landscape.

"It's too big for that narrow space. But that doesn't matter," Alpha said, "Even if we could fit, they'd see us if we got that close."

"I don't understand why their ability to see us even matters," Nadya said. "I'm sure you could find a way to get us to the airlock. And, couldn't you just disable anything they try to use to stop us?"

"The answer is yes to both of your questions," Alpha replied. "I could even render many in the area unconscious. However, others on the base would react – potentially violently. How sure are you that you could get your colleagues out without them getting injured?"

"I'm sure we'd find a way," Kurt answered.

"Even if you did," Alpha countered, "I believe the captain's goal is to find out who is working against you. If you're found to be alive, and worse yet, identified as leading an incursion into a lunar base…it would destroy any chance of that."

"So, what do we do?" Kurt asked.

Jack gazed at the base below in silence – it was vulnerable. The problem was doing this without giving themselves away. Of course, they wouldn't be able to escape undetected this time. But, the goal was to make sure they didn't know who came for Don and Sarah. He took a breath and said, "We'll take the same approach as we did with you, Kurt. We'll create a reason for them to move Don and Sarah to the outer module. Once there, we'll have to distract them…and blind them somehow."

"What do you mean?" Kurt asked.

"They have to be near an airlock…I need them to be moved here." Jack pointed to the outer structure next to the highlighted one. Alpha's systems immediately understood Jack's meaning and surrounded it with a yellow glow. "You can see this, right?" Jack asked hesitantly.

"Yes," was Kurt's reply.

"Alpha," Jack said, "Can you control the bulkheads on the base?"

"Yes, at this point, I have full access to base systems."

"Good." Jack stared at the structures for a moment longer before saying, "Alpha, do you have a smaller ship that I could take to get them? Plus, I'd need to be able to dock to the module's outer port."

"I can create something that would work for you."

"Create something?" Nadya asked.

"As I said earlier, we use an adaptive matrix technology for the ship's structure. I can quickly reconfigure a small ship I have onboard. Since I already have access to the base and its specifications, creating a structure compatible with the docking mechanism will be trivial."

"Good," Jack said, trying to suppress any disbelief. "Then we need a distraction ...something to force them to move Don and Sarah to the outer module and trigger the automatic bulkheads to deploy. I want to separate them from their guards."

"The easiest way to do that would be to create a breach in their module," Nadya offered. "It'll force an evacuation and trigger the bulkheads. But how?"

"Just throw something at it," Kurt said reflexively. "There's got to be some debris somewhere around here...you know...do something to degrade its orbit and send it in to a specific location on the base."

Jack mulled the idea as he stared at the structures below. Without warning, the ground rushed away from him, inducing a sense of vertigo until the motion just as suddenly ceased. The moon was reduced to a globe hanging in front of him. A small bright red circle appeared in Copernicus crater; Jack assumed it was the location of the base. Looking to his right, far beyond the moon, was a bright green dot; a glowing indicator stating 'L2' hung above it. What appeared to be a faint yellow trail of smoke emanated from L2 and faded as it stretched toward the moon. As it neared Jack, the dim yellow wisp curved as the moon's gravitational field pulled it toward the surface.

"The yellow," Alpha said, "is a debris field caused by the L2 explosion. The particles are small – in the one to five centimeter range – and the density is very diffuse. However, they could be used for you what you propose."

"It could," Jack said softly.

The moon disappeared, and Jack found himself back in his seat, looking across the table at Nadya. "Any thoughts?" he asked the group. One by one, they shook their heads. Jack's eyes fell on Martina. "You probably know more about what's going on than any of us. What do you think?"

Martina stared back in disbelief. Jack's unbroken gaze finally prompted her to say, "I don't know what you want or why you're even telling me any of this. You're putting a lot of faith in me here...thinking I might go along with you...this is practically treason."

"There's no faith here. The bottom line is, if you're not interested in helping us, there's nothing you can do. No one you can report to or warn. No way to interfere with us. If, on the other hand, you want to try to get to the bottom of this, any insight you might have could be helpful."

"And you'll trust me?" Martina asked with less of an edge to her voice.

"Trust but verify…until I know you better."

Martina looked at each of them before finally asking, "What do you want to know?"

"To start with, how deep does this go? Is this investigation into me and the Magellan crew completely sanctioned by defense and intelligence, or is it something being pursued by someone or some group within the government?"

"I don't think it's a full investigation or anything. I didn't even know that there were any suspicions about you before I intercepted the…your message to Kurt. I was only brought in because I'm part of the archive security team and was told of a potential threat to the archive. I…I can't really say anything else because it's classified."

"I think we're well beyond worrying about classified information," Jack answered.

"What does this have to do with your rescue plan anyway?" Martina challenged.

"Knowing whether people associated with me are viewed by central command as…as agents or spies or whatever…that would tell me a lot about what to expect when we go in."

Martina stared back at Jack blankly before finally saying, "I'm pretty sure central doesn't view them this way."

"How can you be sure?" Nadya asked.

When Martina didn't answer, Jack asked, "Why don't you start with telling us what you really do? It's got to be more than communications and intelligence like you told Nadya."

Martina stayed silent for a moment. Jack knew she was calculating how much she could safely say and, for the time being, decided to let her choose for herself.

"My specialty is AI and decryption."

"You're a code breaker?" Nadya said.

"No…no, the machine learning algorithms are way better at that. The problem is, they're only good at focused, computational tasks. We humans are still needed to guide them…to give context to the massive amounts of data they sift through. You might say my job is to help them identify relevant streams of information in the comm traffic that's out there. I work at keeping them focused on the archive and not spinning their wheels on some wild goose chase."

"So, you're fully informed about the archive's security structure," Jack said.

"Right," Martina said with some relief. "I'm not really supposed to tell people how much I know. But, that's how I can be sure central doesn't see your people that way. In order for me to guide the AIs, central keeps me informed of any suspicions and specific types of communication that we should be looking for."

"Ok," Jack said. "Then, there may not be too many surprises when we try this."

"One other thing," Martina added.

"Yes?"

"If you do manage to get your companions, it will raise some serious red flags. Even if you manage to convince people they were killed – and not rescued or something – they're going to raise security around anything that any of you worked on. It'll make it that much harder to find out what's going on."

Chapter 14

Jack felt as if he were floating among the countless stars that lay before him. Though he had experienced it many times, Alpha's synthetic view of what lay outside was still unnervingly real – to the point that he felt defenseless and exposed. He held up his hand in front of him and wondered for a moment if he was actually seeing it or if it was simply a simulation projected on top of his view of open space. The sight of his bare skin in the vacuum said it didn't really matter; the scene was simply too unreal to be worth analyzing. He simply chose to accept the fact that he was safely encased in an alien shuttle and said, "Display L2 debris and target locations."

A faint, wispy sheet of shimmering yellow fog appeared, overlaying most of the stars before him. Barely a second later, three small, bright-green circles materialized, spaced evenly throughout the mist. Jack pointed to the one furthest to his right and instantly moved toward it with unnatural speed. The fog enveloped him and revealed itself to be a myriad of tiny yellow-highlighted specks – the debris from L2. The nearest particles transformed into ephemeral streaks as he sped past them. Despite the motion, the silent scene felt benign and peaceful until he swerved sharply to his left to avoid a larger metal fragment. It was a jagged piece of aluminum that retained enough of its original shape for him to recognize it as the detached skin of a destroyed crew module.

His approach slowed as suddenly as it had begun, and he found himself floating among the glass and metal shards of the former space station.

Their shapes were random, though here he could tell that most were remnants of solar panels. The black and gold pieces rotated haphazardly, causing them to randomly reflect the surrounding scene and sparkle in the sunlight.

A voice interrupted the silence. "Captain, you should deploy the first of the explosives here."

"Thank you, Alpha," Jack answered. The task was as elementary as it could get. He simply pointed at the green circle hovering in a gap in the debris and said, "Deploy package one here." A pair of translucent, one-meter wide, golden sheets floated into view from beneath him. They curved slightly inward, were separated by about a centimeter, and held in place at the top and bottom by thin silver rods. It was difficult to think of it as an explosive; however, its yield would be equivalent to several kilotons of TNT. Each sheet was only a few billionths of a meter thick. The front one was comprised of a solidified form of hydrogen; the rear was antihydrogen. Alpha had explained that when the command was given, the two sheets would be propelled together with perfect symmetry, yielding a gamma-ray burst so short that human instruments wouldn't see it. The resulting force, however, would send a small number of particles hurtling outward – two of which would strike the surface within centimeters Copernicus base's modules.

"Proceed to target two," Jack said calmly. The stars and debris before him slewed to his left as he pivoted toward his new destination, then transformed into a blur as the ship accelerated ahead.

"Kurt, what's our status?" Jack said.

There was the briefest of pauses before his friend answered. "Alpha analyzed explosive one's deployment… its position and orientation are good."

"Good. How are we on time?"

"You're on schedule. But I still think you need to give yourself more leeway. You're detonating explosives and trying to stay only a couple minutes ahead of the inbound debris. You haven't given yourself any room for…"

"Kurt," Jack said, cutting him off. "I know the risks. We went over this before. We need to…" Jack paused as his ship suddenly swerved hard to the right and then dove down to avoid two large metal shards. As the craft returned to its original course, he continued, "We need to be a hundred percent sure they don't see us take them. I have to be landing as the first particles hit the surface. At that same moment, Alpha needs to be in their systems, triggering the impact alarms. It'll only take them a couple of minutes to realize there weren't any impacts – that's all the time we have…"

"I know that," Kurt protested. "It's the actual strike I'm worried about. You're giving yourself only three minutes to get them out before their module gets hit…"

"Is there any other way?" Jack pressed. "Their module has to be breached…the bulkheads have to be sealed, so they won't know right away that Don and Sarah were taken. Plus, if…" Jack was forced to stop speaking as the shuttle dove down hard again. The stars and debris blended into a blur that streaked upward with unreal speed. Before he could adjust, his world spun to the right as a long, broken segment of aluminum framework flew by, barely missing him.

"Jack?" Kurt called.

"I'm here, Kurt," Jack answered as his ship entered a pocket devoid of the yellow-highlighted debris. The green circle of target two lay ahead. "I can't debate this right now."

"Just be careful, OK?"

"I wasn't planning on doing anything else," Jack answered with a smirk his friend couldn't see. The ship came to a stop relative to the target, and as before, Jack simply pointed at it and said, "Deploy package two here." The task was finished in a matter of seconds, at which point he said, "Proceed to target three."

Without any hesitation, the ship accelerated forward while banking to his left. Before he could even adjust to the changing star patterns, the craft pulled up hard while twisting sharply left. Then, without warning, it quickly dove, making his stomach drop, and swerved right. Not seeing the fragments they were dodging, Jack called out, "Alpha!"

"Yes captain," was the deceptively calm response.

"What's going on?" Jack asked as they leveled off.

"There's more debris…its motion is difficult to predict. I think…" Alpha's voice cut out as the ship again dove and turned to avoid another unseen hazard. The movements were so fast and sharp this time that stars and debris around him transformed into a smooth blur; the only indication that he was even moving was the strobe-like flashing of his surroundings as the ship repeatedly changed course.

"There's an underlying pattern to the debris movement," Alpha said as the ship returned to a steady course. They slowed to a near stop; the green circle of his next target lay directly ahead.

"What do you mean?"

"The last three fragments were moving much too fast to have been caused by the X-165 explosion. They were aimed not just at our current position, but at locations to which we were traveling…as if something anticipated our course."

"I don't understand," Jack said softly. "We…I mean, Earth doesn't have anything out here that can do that."

When Alpha didn't immediately respond, Jack asked, "Should I deploy the third explosive?"

"No…wait."

Jack allowed barely ten seconds to pass before asking, "Alpha, what's going on?"

"The two explosives you already deployed detonated prematurely. The debris is not traveling as originally planned…a large number of fragments are heading directly toward Copernicus base."

"Are they going to collide with Copernicus?"

"Yes, I calculate that several will pierce habitable modules."

Before Jack could speak, his ship suddenly leapt into motion, turning sharply to the right before accelerating hard. Out of the corner of his eye, Jack spotted the silvery streak of the metal fragment that would have struct them. "We need to help them. Is there anything onboard we can use to…"

"No," Alpha cut in. "Your base has detected the material and appears to be deploying some of its surveillance drones. I assume that the goal is for them to intercept the inbound particles, but it won't work. The fragments are moving at too high a rate of speed; they'll just tear through the drones without being deflected. Impact is in one minute."

"Get us to Don and Sarah's module now," Jack demanded. Without hesitation, the stars and material around him spun to his left until he found himself staring at a distant Copernicus crater. Nearby debris became a blur, and the lunar landscape grew unnervingly fast.

"We'll be in position near their module in thirty seconds." Before Jack could say anything, Alpha continued, "I know what you're thinking. We can't shield the module; this ship can't withstand any impacts at that speed…but…I may be able to deflect the two inbound pieces that will strike their structure with a small antimatter spray. It will give us a couple of minutes to try and retrieve your colleagues."

A hoarse, "OK," was all that Jack could manage as his eyes remained fixed on the fast-growing crater floor. Instinct drove him to try and grab onto something. However, the interface showed him no physical aspects of his ship, leaving his arms to feel as if they were flailing in space. He clenched his teeth as he abruptly decelerated only a few meters away from the silver structure. Almost immediately, two faint, glowing bolts leapt from beneath him and ended in bright silver flashes just above the structure. "I was able to vaporize the two fragments," Alpha said without emotion. "I've tapped into Don's comm-unit. Direct him to go through the bulkhead to the outer module. We'll dock at its airlock to retrieve him and Sarah." As Jack was about to speak, Alpha quickly added, "Tell them to move quickly; there are more inbound particles."

"Don, this is Jack," he said firmly.

"Jack? What the…" Don practically shouted over the blaring of emergency alarms.

"There's no time to talk. I need you and Sarah to get to the airlock immediately."

"Jack, what the hell's going on?"

"Just do what I said now! There's no time."

Jack barely had time to take a breath before Alpha said, "I'm going to move us into position in a moment; we'll be docked to their airlock in a few seconds. The impacts will follow less than a minute after that."

Jack's eye scanned the terrain. The outer module – only a few meters away – dominated his view. Its silver wall climbed out of the cratered soil before curving to a peak a few meters above. The quiet scene was suddenly broken by a small streak to his left that ended in a puff of lunar dust. Anticipating his question, Alpha said, "The impact was a small piece of L2 debris." Two more streaks shot by – one ending in a small, silent flash of light as it struck a more distant module. Before he could react, though, his view of the outside disappeared, and he found himself staring at a circular doorway at the other end of a small white room. Alpha continued, "We're moving into position. We'll be connected to their docking port, in a few seconds."

"How long do they have?"

"I'm not sure…things are changing rapidly…at most thirty seconds," Alpha answered with some urgency.

Jack called out, "Don, where are you now?"

Don's voice quickly answered, "We just got through the bulkhead to the outer module. I'll be at…"

"Listen carefully," Jack cut in. "We're docked to that airlock. I'll have it opened in a second…get through it as fast as you can!"

There was no response. As Jack stared at the circular door, it suddenly slid open, revealing two distant figures jogging toward him. Reflexively he headed toward them at a dead run and jumped through the opening as he shouted, "Move it! We don't have any time!"

Sarah made it to him first. He reached out to guide her through the airlock, but a deafening crack and sudden force threw them against the wall. A wave of numbness swept across him. He felt no pain and could hear nothing except for a sharp ringing in his ears. His vision was blurry, but he could tell that he was lying against the base of the airlock. Sarah was sprawled across his chest. His senses started pushing through the shock – pain spread along his back and side. A stream of warm fluid coated his face – he didn't care what it was and tried to wipe it away. He still couldn't focus and tried to sit up but made no progress.

Sarah was suddenly moving – she was being dragged off of him. Jack turned to see Don struggling to pull her through the airlock; a trail of blood coated the floor behind her. As Don yanked her into the ship, Jack spotted Sarah's injury: her left forearm ended in a bloody stump.

"Captain!" Alpha called out with distinct sense of urgency.

Jack only managed a weak attempt to look around.

"Captain, can you hear me?"

This time, Jack managed a hoarse, "Yes."

"I am unable to see you since you're outside the ship. What is your…your status?"

"I'm injured but alive," he managed.

"Obviously," Alpha replied with a hint of frustration. "I want to know – can you move on your own?"

"I'm trying," Jack answered as the weak lunar gravity made it possible for him to sit upright. "I don't think anything is broken."

"You need to get through the airlock and back onto the ship immediately."

"I know," Jack muttered as he pulled himself up. "What happened?"

"A piece of debris pierced your module by the airlock. I've used a section of our ship's skin to plug the hole, but you need to get out now."

Jack took a step forward but fell, striking his head on the edge of the bulkhead. He could hear Alpha's voice, but it felt distant and was unintelligible. Reaching forward, he tried to grab hold of the doorframe but only had the strength to run his fingers along its hard steel edge. There was pressure around his ribs and under his armpits. Metal scraped against his chest – he was being dragged. Opening his eyes, he saw Don pulling him through the threshold. "Damn, even in this gravity, you're heavy," Don muttered with a smirk.

Jack looked back toward the airlock and saw the circular door disappear; it was replaced by the featureless white wall that lined the small alien ship.

"Captain, can you hear me?" Alpha asked.

Jack managed a soft "Yes" in response.

"I'm directing the ship to return to lunar L5. It's too dangerous here."

Jack gathered his strength and shot back, "What about the rest of Copernicus base?"

"There's nothing we can do. There are impacts throughout the entire area. Most modules are already depressurizing."

"We can't just leave them!" Jack protested.

"Who the hell are you talking to?" Don demanded as Jack sat up against the wall.

Realizing they couldn't hear Alpha without implants, Jack looked directly at Don as he answered, "Alpha." He then looked away and asked, "Alpha, do you have a speaker or some audio interface…something so they can hear you?"

Almost instantly, Alpha answered, "You should be able to hear me now. What I told the captain was, that there isn't anything we can do for the base. The small ship you're on doesn't have room for more than the three of you. More importantly, I'm concerned that you will be targeted again…something aimed some of the fragments at your ship. As a result, I've directed it to return you to my location."

All Don managed to say was, "Alpha?" with complete surprise. He took a quick breath as Alpha's statement sunk in and continued, "What's going on with the Copernicus?"

"Something reoriented and detonated explosives we placed in the debris cloud so that they would impact Copernicus base at high speed," Alpha answered. "Several modules have been struck…more debris is inbound."

Before the statement could completely sink in, Don pivoted toward Sarah and suddenly called out her name. Her body was motionless. He jumped down next to her and pressed two fingers against her carotid artery. As Jack crawled toward him, Don looked up with panic in his eyes and said, "I'm not getting a pulse. She was talking when I pulled her in…telling me to go back and get you."

"Alpha," Jack called out. "We need some help here."

"I don't have anything on your ship that can assist," was the quick response. "I will be able…"

"You've got to have something…some sort of tech," Don protested.

"You're ETA to my ship is ten minutes. I have equipment here that will take care of her. From what I can see…"

"You're not even here. She's not breathing!" Don shot back. "We can't wait."

"I can see what I need with the imaging equipment…cameras that I have on your ship. Her primary injuries are blood loss and a severed forearm, but her nervous system is intact…that's what's critical. I will be able to revive her."

Don stared at Jack without speaking, prompting him to say, "Alpha, should we do something? Put a tourniquet on her arm to prevent any more blood loss?"

"No," Alpha replied. "Anything you do will only damage her body and complicate reconstruction."

They sat in silence, staring at Sarah. Blood no longer flowed from her arm as she lay flat on the metallic floor. Her face was ashen; smears of dark blood stretched across her cheeks. A distinct hint of blue colored her lips and eyelids. Jack continued staring at her, unable to find the strength to pull his eyes away. "What's the status of Copernicus?" he finally asked.

"I don't have any systems data since their networks are down. From what I can tell visually, about sixty percent of the structures have depressurized. But, the impacts appeared to have stopped. That suggests that there should be a reasonable number of survivors."

"Where are we?" Don asked.

"Your ship is about sixty-five percent of the way to me in L5. We should be safe here."

"What about the survivors on Copernicus?" Don asked. "We can't just leave them."

"Unfortunately, there isn't much we can do. It would be best to let your central command work on their rescue," Alpha replied.

"They'll die," Don pressed.

"No. Most will probably live," Alpha answered emotionlessly. "But, if they learn that my ship was there with Jack at the time of this…this attack, we will be blamed for it."

Jack pulled his eyes away from Sarah's body and looked at the plain white wall in front of him. "How much longer until we reach you?"

"About five minutes," Alpha answered.

PART 5: THE HUNT

Chapter 15

Jack stood next to Sarah, staring out the floor-to-ceiling window that stretched the length of their small room. The internal lights were off, giving them a near-perfect view of their hiding spot's strange, dark beauty. The stars of the constellation Orion stood out against the innumerable background stars. Bright orange Betelgeuse in Orion's shoulder competed against the almost equally dominant blue-white Rigel in the constellation's knee. Despite their size, though, Jack's eye was invariably drawn to the line of three white stars comprising Orion's belt. It was a view he'd seen hundreds of times, but that wasn't what captured his attention today. Instead of sitting against the inky blackness of space, the stars seemed to be set upon a faint iridescent tapestry. Subtle folds of orange, green and blue transformed into one another, almost as if they were slowly flowing waves of mist. The colors grew stronger as he turned to his left – the direction of the sun – and almost disappeared to his right. As if to compensate for the lack of color, his right-side view was dotted with ephemeral flashes of white. It was difficult not to think of them as tiny jewels sewn into some unseen fabric.

"It is beautiful, isn't it?" Sarah asked quietly.

"I've never seen anything quite like it," Jack admitted.

"I've actually studied this phenomenon, you know."

"Really? Probably a welcome relief from the dry mathematics of your specialty."

"Hardly," Sarah said with a laugh. "One might say that my work sucked the beauty out of it."

"What do you mean?"

"I published my results under the far-from-artistic title: a determination of particle size and dynamics from scattered light in Kordylewski clouds."

"You've got to be kidding me."

"No…for real. But, it was actually very interesting. The gravitational wells of L4 and L5 act as basins, scooping up interplanetary dust and debris as they move with the Earth-Moon system," Sarah said as she waved her arms, illustrating the process. "You end up with clouds of micron to millimeter size ice-coated dust and rubble. A Polish astronomer over a hundred fifty years ago claimed to be the first to spot them…but he didn't live to see confirmation of his discovery. If only he could see this."

Curiosity got the better of Jack when she didn't continue. "So, what was your work about?"

"We basically used what you see here as a tool. On the sunward side, particles scatter the sunlight – the separation of the color bands tells you about their size. If you track the movement of the bands, they map out rather precisely the subtle twists in the gravitational fields in this environment." She paused for a second before pointing to her right and saying, "Once you know the particle size distribution, you can use those flashes to tell you about how much ice is coating them."

"OK, you've convinced me; you're definitely more of a geek than me."

Sarah laughed as she leaned against him before saying, "But, it's amazing what you can learn from simple little phenomena like scattering."

"So, why'd you give up research to get into the admin end of things? I mean, you're an associate director now…which means your life revolves around meetings and policy and reports."

"I had this crazy idea that I'd get to see the big picture…you know, get a real feel of what's in the archive. Don't get me wrong; research has its good points…it's just when you're a researcher, you learn a ton about a tiny little corner of the field. It just wasn't satisfying anymore."

"I actually get it," Jack said softly. "It's why I left the planetary sciences and got into the exploration side of things." They stared silently out the window for a few more seconds before he said, "You know…I wanted to apologize for before."

Sarah turned to him with genuine surprise and asked, "What for?"

"Back at JFK…I took it out on you when I was locked in that room. I knew better."

She looked at him for a moment with a hint of a smile before saying, "Nothing to apologize for. You were desperate to find out what happened to Kurt and Nadya and couldn't. Anyone would've gotten angry."

Jack had the urge to tell her he didn't need any excuses for his behavior, but belaboring the point made no sense. Instead, he just let his eyes wander among the stars before him. He knew what he really needed was a few more minutes of peace.

"Captain, may I enter the room?" Alpha asked.

"Of course," Jack answered as he thought about the ridiculousness of Alpha needing permission to enter a room on his own ship. He knew, however, that the alien was only trying to respect aspects of privacy he didn't really comprehend.

Jack turned away from the window as a door across from him smoothly slid aside. Alpha glided in and caught sight of Sarah flexing her left hand, and asked, "Is there any problem?"

"No…not at all," Sarah answered, obviously having been caught off-guard by the question. "It's unreal…except for a little tingling, it feels almost like nothing ever happened."

"That sensation should dissipate in a couple of hours after the nerves finish regenerating." Before she had a chance to say anything else, though, Alpha continued, "I have more information on what happened during the rescue."

The room appeared to abruptly disappear, and Jack suddenly found himself floating in space a few thousand kilometers from the large globe of the moon. The jagged circular form of Copernicus crater stood prominently in front of him. Stretching away to his right was the yellow mist he knew to be the computer-highlighted L2 debris field.

"Jack?" Sarah called out.

Jack looked to his left, but the interface didn't show her. He answered quickly, "Sarah, nothing to worry about here. This is an immersive interface Alpha has. I'll…"

"Captain, it might be best if I explained," Alpha interrupted. "I'm sending signals directly to your visual cortex so that you can see an enhanced view of the Moon and L2 debris system. You are, of course, still safely on board my ship."

"Thank you," Sarah replied with forced calmness.

Two green circles appeared in the yellow mist as Alpha spoke. "These are the locations of the explosives you placed. I had precisely calibrated their yield, location, and orientation so as to send a small amount of debris toward Copernicus base. Enough to trigger alarms. However, none of the fragments would have caused significant damage to the base."

"That we know," Jack said with a hint of impatience.

He felt as if he were suddenly propelled toward the debris field. The moon shifted out of view, and yellow streaks of station fragments flew by him. The green circle of a once-distant target location grew rapidly. His muscles tensed as his eyes told him he was about to collide with the target, but he instantly stopped. The explosive still remained a distant speck –

just large enough to show that it had a rectangular shape. "Unfortunately, I was not monitoring these locations more closely, so this is the best view of the charge that I have," Alpha said. "I'm going to show you a recording of what happened at a thousandth of regular speed. Even then, it's tough to tell what occurred."

Jack watched as the motionless speck sat among the metal shards. Seconds passed with intolerable slowness; however, Jack kept his gaze fixed on the target. A white streak shot in from his right. Before he could focus on it, it intercepted the explosive, and both were gone. He scanned the region and looked for a clue as to what had happened, but there was nothing. A second glance showed that many of the debris fragments that once surrounded the explosive were missing too.

"It appears," Alpha said, "that something struck and detonated the antimatter charge prematurely."

"I don't understand," Sarah said. "I didn't see an explosion or anything."

"The device was designed to release all of its energy in the x-ray and gamma-ray region of the spectrum. There would be nothing visible to your eyes or even the enhanced view I was providing. But nonetheless, the device was detonated…and not in the manner I had intended. It sprayed debris throughout the region. And, as you experienced, a fraction did strike Copernicus base."

"Who did this?" Jack asked.

"That," Alpha said with a distinct hint of solemnness, "is the question."

"How fast was that streak…the thing that struck the explosive going?" Sarah asked.

"Too fast for my remote monitoring equipment to accurately track," Alpha answered. "I would estimate its velocity to be around seventy percent the speed of light."

"We don't have anything that can move like that," Jack said flatly.

"Could someone have hacked the archive?" Sarah asked softly. "Gotten the knowledge to build something like this?" Before anyone could answer, she continued, "Alpha, your tech could do that, right?"

"The answer to both of your questions is yes," Alpha replied.

"But who?" Sarah asked softly.

There was no response. Jack couldn't imagine how anyone could deploy that level of technology without him finding out. But that didn't change the fact that it was there.

"Jack, tell me about the other two you have onboard," Sarah said with some urgency. "Who exactly are they?"

"We had to bring them on when we rescued Kurt and Nadya. The woman is Martina Lopez, an intelligence and comms officer. It's probably better to think of her as an AI counter-intel officer."

"AI counter-intel?"

"Yeah. She explained that her assignment was to guide machine learning algorithms as they comb through network and comm traffic looking for potential incursions into the archive."

"Do you believe her?"

"I think she's being upfront about that."

"Is it possible that she has a deeper understanding of what's going on?"

"I'm not sure. She says she was blindsided by the investigation into me and that her work was limited to looking for hacks into the archive data set. But, she appears interested in getting to the bottom of this. Nadya seems to believe her."

"Do you believe her?" Sarah pressed.

"She's an intel officer," Jack replied with a hint of frustration, "so I'm not sure what to believe. We've kept her informed of everything we've been doing."

"What?" was Sarah's surprised response.

"There's no risk. With Alpha's tech, she doesn't pose a threat."

"Ok, but you didn't answer my question. Someone's behind what just happened. Do you believe her?" Sarah pressed.

"She could be playing along…biding her time to see what we're up to. But I think it's more likely she's a lower-level person who's in the dark about what's going on."

"Ok, what about the other guy?"

"His name is Sokolov, and is…was the first officer on the rescue ship. He's more than that, though. Kurt said the guy questioned him aggressively about his connections with me…like he was already sure of what was going on and wanted Kurt to confirm things. I just don't know where he fits into all of this."

"So, he might know something. What was his reaction when you captured him?" Sarah asked.

"Captured?"

"Is there a better word?"

"I…I guess not. He does view himself as a prisoner and wants nothing to do with us."

"What was his name again?"

"Sokolov. He's a lieutenant commander. I didn't get his first name."

"The name sounds familiar the more I think about it," Sarah said softly. "I may have met him while I was a defense liaison officer. Let me try talking to him."

"What?"

"Let me talk to him one-on-one."

"You sure?" Jack asked. "I don't know what you think you can accomplish."

"If he recognizes me, maybe it'll help – maybe build a bit of trust – especially if he remembers me from the defense side of things."

Jack didn't answer and just stared at the cloud of floating debris.

Sarah gave him a few seconds before saying, "It can't hurt."

"You really think you can get something out of him?"

"Maybe. Where is he?"

"What…you want to do it now?"

"What's the point in waiting?"

Jack realized it wasn't worth debating the point and called out, "Alpha?"

The immersive view of the debris cloud vanished, and Jack found himself standing in the same room as before. "Yes, captain," was the alien's reply.

"Sarah wants to meet with Sokolov." Realizing Alpha might not understand the dynamics of human interaction, he added, "She's going to need to see him alone."

"Follow the short corridor behind you. It will take you to his room," Alpha said.

As they turned, a new door and hallway appeared behind them. "Captain," Alpha said, "I assume you will want to monitor the…the conversation. I can create a…"

"This needs to be private," Sarah interrupted, "to build trust. If he's intel – like we think – he'll know if I'm lying when I say it's just a one-on-one conversation."

"There may be too much risk if we're cut off from what's happening," Alpha pressed.

"There's no risk," Sarah replied as she led the way down the plain gray hallway. "What's he going to do, attack me? There's nowhere for him to run. The worst case is he treats me like he's treated you and doesn't tell me anything."

"I don't know,' Jack said softly. "There's always…"

"Jack," Sarah cut in, "there's really only upside to this. I'll be careful, OK?"

A round door opened as they reached the end of the corridor. Jack peered in as Sokolov, sitting on a metal table, calmly turned to meet his gaze. Sarah walked through without hesitating, looked back to Jack, and asked, "Are we OK with this?"

"Yes," Jack answered reluctantly. He took a breath before saying, "Alpha, do as Sarah asked."

The door closed silently. "Captain," Alpha said, "I'm not sure how this sort of isolation will build trust."

For a moment, Jack started to second guess his decision. He shook it off, though, and answered, "She's hoping to demonstrate to him that she's independent…willing to listen to what he has to say. It's a matter of…"

"Captain," Alpha interrupted. "I'm detecting impacts in the room with them…as if something hit the wall. It's…"

"Goddamn it, open the door now!" Jack demanded.

The hatch opened instantly, and Jack jumped in but stopped short of doing anything. Sokolov was sprawled across the floor, blood running from his nose and temple. Sarah was standing over him, with a bloody lip and a fresh welt across her eye. "What the hell?" Jack blurted.

"He knew me," Sarah said with a tremor in her voice. "There wasn't any warning; he just came at me."

"Are you OK?" Jack asked.

"No…no, I'm not. I don't understand why he did that."

Jack knelt down and pressed his forefingers against Sokolov's neck. He felt nothing and adjusted his fingers, to be sure they were up against the carotid. After a few more seconds, he finally said, "I'm not getting a pulse. Alpha, I need your help here."

The alien calmly entered the room and said, "Captain, I'll need you to step aside."

Jack straightened up and took a step back as Kurt ran up to the entrance with Don close behind. "What…what happened?" Kurt asked with obvious shock.

"What the hell did you do?" Don pressed.

"He lunged at me…caught me off guard," Sarah answered as she rubbed her bruised cheek. "After that, it was reflex…"

"What do you mean?" Don cut in.

"I've got combat training. I…I just blocked when he tried to hit me again and turned his weight against him." She looked down at Sokolov for a split second before glancing at the bloody corner of the table next to them and said, "He hit his head there."

The room went silent; Jack just stared at Alpha. A panel on the side of the alien's cart opened and a small, brown multi-legged creature, no larger than a cat, jumped down. It approached Sokolov cautiously as Alpha said, "Please stay back and let me analyze his injuries." The creature wrapped its six legs around the top of Sokolov's head. Two small tubes extended from its short, fur-covered back and made contact with the base of his skull.

"What are you doing?" Don asked with a mix of fear and curiosity.

"Accessing his central nervous system; it has connections with every part of his body. We'll use that to diagnose his condition."

They stared in silence, waiting for an answer. The creature sat motionless on Sokolov, not giving even the slightest sign that it might be alive or doing anything. Don's patience wore out first, "How long does it take?"

"It should be done already. It's having a problem with…" The alien stopped and simply stayed silent.

"Problem with what?" Jack asked calmly.

"The injuries to the brain are too severe. There is nothing I can do."

"What do you mean?" Don pressed. "Three years ago, I saw you bring Kurt back to life."

"The matrix of neural connections in your brain is the seat of your consciousness," Alpha said. "As long as the junctions between the various neurons are intact and there is minimal degradation in the cells themselves, I can…as you say, bring someone back to life. It's really just a matter of restoring the function of the body's organs; they're just a support system for maintaining the nervous system. Unlike Kurt Hoffman – who was well preserved in the vacuum – Sokolov's skull was fractured. There are bone fragments pressed into the brain, badly damaging the cells and neural matrix." Seeing the confusion in Don's expression, Alpha continued, "Sections of his brain are now little more than a mix of blood and organic tissue. It's impossible to try to reconstruct its original structure. The basis of this man's mind is unrecoverable."

"Goddammit!" Sarah said with pure frustration. "I'm sure he knew something."

The creature released its grip on Sokolov's head as Alpha looked at Sarah and said, "We should tend to your wounds."

Sarah took a hesitant step backward and said, "I'm sorry, but I don't think I want that thing attaching itself to..."

The creature scurried back to Alpha's cart as he answered, "There's no need for it. Your injuries are not that serious. I have other…other equipment that I can use for you."

"Thank you," she said softly, "we'll take care of that later." Turning to Jack, she asked, "What the hell was wrong with him?"

"Did he think you knew him well enough to get something out of him?" Jack asked.

"What the hell did you do before getting involved with the archive? I thought you were a scientist?" Don asked.

"I am. But, when I took up the defense position, some of the military personnel I worked with suggested that I learn more about what they did." She took a breath and continued in a slightly mocking tone, "They didn't think a pure scientist belonged with them. So, I went all-in to prove myself."

When Don didn't continue, Sarah said, "We still have our problem: who detonated the charges?"

"What are you talking about?" Kurt asked.

"The charges Jack deployed – something detonated them prematurely," Sarah answered. "It was definitely done to stop him; it's just not clear if the damage to Copernicus was deliberate too." She turned to Jack as she continued, "What about Martina? We should see what she knows."

"Let's hold off on interrogating her…"

"That's not what I meant," Sarah protested.

"I know. But, considering she worked with Sokolov, it'll feel that way. We don't need her getting defensive." Jack looked down at Sokolov's body, "Let's let her know what happened and see how she reacts first. Then we can determine how to approach her."

Chapter 16

Kurt sat silently with Nadya and Martina at the plain, white table. Exhaustion weighed on him as his eyes wandered around the oval room. Its metal walls and pitch-black floor were polished to a near mirror-like finish. Above was a slightly domed, pale green ceiling. Though the room was well-lit and the air fresh, there weren't any signs of ventilation or lighting. As with the rest of Alpha's ship, the room was essentially devoid of any recognizable technology.

"We wanted to reassure you that no one holds anything against you," Kurt finally said. "I know it's only been an hour since Sokolov…died, but we know…"

"That's what I don't get," Martina cut in. "You all seem to think I knew the man. I told you, I only worked under him for a couple of weeks. All I know is that he's…he was a hard-ass. He gave us our assignments and nothing else."

"I'm sorry," Nadya said softly. "I didn't mean to imply that you were close to him or…or that we were suspicious because you worked with him."

"Of course you're suspicious," she shot back. "If you weren't, you'd be idiots. Nothing I say is going to change that right now."

The room went silent again as Nadya and Martina avoided each other's gaze.

"I'm still not sure why you even want me here," Martina added with a voice that trembled with frustration.

Kurt finally spoke up. "OK, then I'll be blunt – let's just focus on who was behind the attack on Copernicus and if Sokolov was somehow involved."

"There's nothing to focus on there," Martina challenged. "We don't know anything. If your friend…Sarah hadn't killed him; we might have a chance."

"She's not my friend," Nadya shot back. "But, what was she supposed to do? He attacked her."

"And, it looks like she picked the only way to defend herself that could prevent the alien here from reviving him. Sounds like maybe she wanted to silence him."

"Enough!" Kurt blurted out. "What the hell are we arguing about here?" Nadya and Martina turned to him as he continued, "It's useless. He attacked Sarah. She killed him. That's it…it's over." Turning to look straight at Martina, he said, "If you want to dive into some conspiracy crap, do it some other time when we actually have time to waste. Right now, we've got to focus on Copernicus. Whoever hit them might attack again and hit somewhere else. That's what we've got to prevent."

Nadya answered with a soft, "OK." Martina stayed quiet but at least looked up at Kurt.

"The only thing we've got to go on," Kurt said with forced calmness, "is a radio burst that Alpha's instruments detected. Martina, you're a comms and counter-intel specialist; do you think there's anything there?"

Martina just stared back at Kurt, prompting him to say, "You asked before why you're here. This is why. You know more about ways people can hack things and infiltrate systems than any of us. From what Alpha's instruments told us, there was a radio burst from pulsar PSR B1937+21 whose frequency spread had an odd spike that happens to match the RF frequencies used by our satellite networks. So, how do we tell whether this spike is just some random flash from that pulsar that coincidentally matches our satellite channels, or is a signal deliberately hidden in a natural radio burst?"

Kurt watched as Martina's expression changed. He could only imagine that she was starting to work the problem. "How far away is that pulsar…one or two thousand lightyears?" Martina asked.

"In that neighborhood," Kurt replied.

"So, if the spike's an artificial signal, the source definitely isn't around the pulsar…it's local but meant to trick us."

"That's what we were thinking. But how do we find it?" he asked.

Martina looked back at him, but the animosity from before was gone. She almost smiled as she said, "We use parallax."

"I don't understand," he answered.

"What if someone put a small satellite out there – maybe out near Jupiter's orbit – and positioned it so that it appeared in the same region of the sky as the pulsar. Then, if it transmitted when the pulsar flashed, the signals would effectively combine. It'd look like it originated at the pulsar. And, more importantly, our automated systems would ignore it since they're programmed to not waste time analyzing known natural radio bursts."

"I see," Nadya said.

"However," Martina continued, "if we moved to a different location – one that is not aligned with both the satellite and the pulsar, we'd see it as a separate source."

"It makes some sense," Nadya said, "but it'd be seriously hard to put something out that far without anyone noticing."

"Remember," Martina answered, "they may've hacked the archive and used alien tech."

"So, what do we do?" Kurt asked.

"Move the ship," Martina answered flatly. "Maybe three or four million kilometers. That'll displace the apparent position of the satellite by a quarter degree or so – enough so that it no longer overlays the position of the pulsar."

"That's if it's out by Jupiter," Nadya said.

Rather than appearing irritated that Nadya might be poking holes in her idea, Martina added, "Yes, and we'd still have to wait until there was another spike. They're not happening every pulse, are they?"

Kurt shrugged as he called out, "Alpha, we have a question for you."

"I'm not far from the room you're in. Do you want me to join you?"

"There's no need to," Kurt answered. "How many of those spikes in the pulsar spectrum have you detected?"

"Three in the last five hours since I started looking for them. The most recent occurred an hour ago."

"Are they at regular intervals?" Martina asked.

"No," was Alpha's quick reply. "The pulsar is flashing six hundred forty-one times per second. There were four hours between the first two spikes and just fifty minutes between numbers two and three."

"That likely rules out most natural stuff like precession in the pulsar's rotation or magnetic pole alignment …though we'll need more data to be sure," Martina said.

"So, you think it's artificial then?" Nadya asked.

"Probably, but we should do the parallax test to be sure."

"Alpha, you heard the conversation we had, right?" Kurt asked.

"Yes."

"Good. Can you please move the ship about four million kilometers along the line of the Earth's orbit?"

"We're moving now," Alpha replied quickly.

"How long until we're in position?" Martina asked.

"It'll take about five minutes."

"Then it's just a matter of waiting for another spike," Martina said softly.

The feeling of impatience started weighing on Kurt almost immediately. He glanced at Nadya, who looked as if she were about to say something, when Alpha suddenly spoke, "I've detected another spike."

"Have we moved enough to see if the signal is distinct from the pulsar?" Nadya asked quickly.

"Possibly…it will take a few minutes of analysis to be sure."

"Can you display a graph of the four pulses with their spikes?" Martina asked. "I want to see if there's any difference between them."

A white rectangle appeared in the air in front of each of them. Traced onto the floating panels were four curved lines – each a different color – that almost perfectly overlapped one another. They started low to the left and climbed gracefully toward the top of the white panel before leveling off. As they began curving back down, a sharp spike rose up and quickly dropped down, allowing the curves to continue their slow decline to the right.

"Can you zoom in on the spikes?" Martina asked.

The image expanded so that the spikes spread out to fill the field of view. The slightly jagged colored lines rose and fell almost symmetrically; they lay so close to each other, that they were difficult to discern separately.

"The difference between the individual lines seems to be at the noise level," Kurt offered.

"Yes, but that may not mean much," Martina said softly. "I need to see a plot of the strength of these over time. I want to see if there are any changes…variations that might represent some sort of buried signal."

"All four pulses together, or one at a time?" Alpha asked.

"Just show me the most recent one," Martina answered.

The image shifted again, this time showing a jagged blue line stretching from left to right. The short-lived rises and falls were so closely spaced that it made the line appear thick.

"Expand the middle one percent to fill the whole screen," Martina said with a hint of curiosity.

The thick blue line shifted and stretched. It no longer looked solid but rather was comprised of dozens of closely-spaced waves. Each rose and fell roughly the same height. "What's the frequency?"

"Three terahertz," Alpha responded.

"There's no amplitude variation. I thought we'd see that if there was a signal," Kurt said.

"There's probably modulations in the frequency over time…you know, FM," Martina said quietly. "There's definitely a signal in there. Someone's gone through a lot of trouble to hack into our satellite comm channel. Can you bring me back to the full frequency spectrum of the pulsar burst?"

The earlier plot, with its broad spectrum and narrow spike, returned. "Are there any weaker carrier frequency spikes.?" Martina asked. "Maybe something that's not aimed at our satellites."

"What are you looking for?" Nadya asked.

"Communications between whatever this is and the people who're running it. They wouldn't want to interfere with our frequencies and risk detection."

"Damn," Nadya said. "You're good at this."

Martina allowed herself a smile as Alpha spoke, "I've found two. One at…"

The alien stopped speaking, prompting Kurt to say, "Alpha?"

When Alpha remained silent, Kurt called out with more urgency, "Alpha, what…"

"More spikes are coming in now. Hundreds of them…none on the main frequency…just on the two carrier ones. This can't…"

"Alpha, what is it?" Kurt asked with a hint of fear entering his voice.

"I will explain later. I apologize for what I have to do."

Before Kurt could speak, a wave of dizziness washed over him. His body went numb. He tried to call out but couldn't make a sound. An all-encompassing blackness surrounded him.

Chapter 17

Jack opened his eyes, but the room's bright light forced him to squint. He was slightly slumped in a plain metal chair and had to make a deliberate effort to sit up. Alpha was directly across the table from him. To his left, Sarah started to stir; next to her was a similarly drowsy-looking Don.

"Captain, can you hear me?" Alpha asked.

"Yes," he answered with some hesitancy. "What happened?"

"I think it's best if I explain to all of you together. Please just bear with me for a moment."

"What's going on?" Sarah asked.

"Not sure…I think we were unconscious for some period of time."

"About fifteen minutes," Alpha said calmly.

Don opened his mouth to speak, but Sarah cut in, "How? Why?"

"An extremely urgent situation came up," Alpha replied. "I had no choice."

"I don't understand," Sarah pressed. "Are you saying you knocked us out?"

"Just one moment," Alpha answered with a hint of impatience. A moment later, the wall to Jack's right appeared to melt into the floor, revealing a second room in which Kurt, Nadya, and Martina were seated around a white table. Before anyone could speak, Alpha continued, "A little under twenty minutes ago, Martina, Nadya, and Kurt were analyzing potential signals embedded in bursts from pulsar PSR B1937+21. These signals were at the same frequency as your satellite communications network. They then asked me to look for carrier signals at other frequencies. As I did this, I uncovered a very troubling one at three-point-five terahertz."

"And that required you knocking us out?" Don asked.

"Yes," Alpha replied unapologetically. "This secondary signal overlapped the frequency used by your implants…the devices that allow us to communicate. At that point, I immediately scanned all recorded pulsar bursts for the last several hours and identified multiple instances of a three-point-five terahertz signal, including one at the exact time that Lieutenant Commander Sokolov attacked Sarah…"

"Shit, are you saying that someone hacked us?" Sarah demanded.

"Yes, and they were not using human technology."

"What do you mean not using human technology?" Don asked.

Martina immediately spoke up, "It means they got by us…my counter-intel group. Someone hacked the archive to get this tech. We were supposed to prevent that."

"You don't understand," Alpha said flatly. "I've tracked the downloads your people made from the archive. This ability to insert signals into your implants was not done using human or archive-derived technology.

"What the hell are you talking about?" Don pressed.

The room went silent. Jack allowed barely a second to pass before he said, "It means we didn't get them all."

"Jack...what are you saying?" Kurt asked.

Looking Kurt straight in the eye, Jack answered, "When the AGC collapsed three years ago...when we thought we wiped out the inbound fleet, it means there were survivors."

"How the hell could that have happened?" Don exclaimed. "We didn't leave anything to chance. We kept looking for them." Turning to Sarah, Don continued, "That was the first project we did with you in defense – archive-based surveillance tech."

"I know," Sarah said softly. Looking at Jack, she continued, "We deployed dozens of satellites throughout the inner solar system...listening posts looking for any sign of them. We didn't find anything."

The room fell silent again. Jack's mind spun as he tried to sift through the implications of Alpha's statement. He could only focus on one question: how else had they been compromised? Martina finally looked at Alpha and asked, "What did you do when you knocked us out – remove the implants?"

"No," the alien answered. "I couldn't yet."

"What the hell?" Martina blurted. "You're telling me they can use that to hack into my brain, and you left it there?"

"If I outright removed them, they'd know," Alpha replied. "We need to find them."

"I don't want this shit in my head." Martina protested. "There's no way I want some alien controlling me."

"I've created safeguards to prevent that," Alpha answered. "Right now, we need to track them down. And to do that, we need them to think nothing's changed and that we don't know about them."

Martina glared at Alpha as she said, "I read Jack's mission logs and debriefings; you're a passive race. You don't know how to fight. Now, you're talking about hunting them using us as bait?"

Alpha stared at Martina for a couple of seconds before answering emotionlessly, "You've misunderstood. We never had a need for any of this: defense or subterfuge. That said, these aren't complex subjects, and we are quite capable of learning. The past three years I spent out here watching your countries and alliances deal with each other taught me a lot. It showed me where my race went wrong with its encounters with this enemy. It also made me start formulating ways to end this conflict."

Martina sat in stunned silence as Sarah asked, "What type of safeguards?"

"I inserted new a new set of implants in each of you; we're using them now to communicate. They use a special type of encryption that relies on a combination of quantum entanglement and the unique patterns in each of your brains – it can't be hacked. For now, I've disabled your older implants' ability to stimulate your brains…so any signals they receive won't affect you. They will, however, still transmit the same information as before. As far as the enemy is concerned, they won't be aware that we know about them."

Jack's mind ran through Alpha's plan, probing for weaknesses. As soon as he locked on to one, he spoke. "What if they try to make me do something? The fact that I won't react should make them suspicious."

"They were never receiving any feedback about your specific behaviors. The fact is, at interplanetary distances, it's effectively impossible to use your implants' transmissions as anything more than a location beacon. They're only capable of high-bandwidth transmission over short-range…to another nearby implant or receiver embedded in my technology. So, the enemy won't know your thoughts or reactions."

"Then, what happened with Sokolov?" Sarah asked.

"Though they can't transmit anything over long-range, the implants are quite capable of receiving distant transmissions that have enough power. They're designed to take that inbound signal and create audio and visual stimuli in the corresponding regions of your brain. However, from what I decoded, the enemy didn't send anything that complex, nor was the transmission meant specifically for Sokolov."

"What are you talking about?" Sarah pressed.

"Somehow, they found a way to send a simpler signal that created a more base response…that transmission was designed to create a sense of fear. All of you felt it when it happened – just to different degrees."

Jack stared back at Alpha and reflexively tried to remember what he had been feeling. Too much had happened, though, and it was all a blur. Finally, he asked, "Why, fear?"

"Perhaps," Alpha answered, "to provoke the fight that happened, or at least sow some distrust between each of you. I'm quite sure that sense of fear led Sokolov to attack Sarah, and it's what prompted Sarah to defend herself so forcefully. Neither showed any self-control."

"Self-control?!" Sarah shot back.

"Yes. Fear overrides self-control. Your base instinct for self-preservation subconsciously made you react the way you did. I've had access to your planet's networks and, more specifically, your records. I know the details of your martial arts training and am quite sure you could have used a less-lethal means of subduing him if you thought you had a choice. The point is, you truly feared for your life at that moment and didn't look for any other options."

"They made her kill him?" Martina asked incredulously.

"No. It was as much Sokolov's reaction to the fear as Sarah's that contributed to his death."

The room went silent. Jack continued searching his memory for any instances where they might have influenced him. The self-analysis drove him to question whether he was being pushed into risky moves like his attempt to rescue Don and Sarah? What about his decision to steal Don's shuttle? Did fear drive him into letting Sarah confront Sokolov? It took only a second longer to realize that he was edging toward paranoia. He tried purging his mind of doubt but felt helpless. He pushed harder to center himself. He knew dwelling on the past was useless; all that mattered was preventing it from happening again.

Don broke the silence as he asked, "How? How did they insert an emotion into our minds?"

"I'm not sure yet," Alpha answered.

"Why did you say you're leaving those implants in us for now?" Martina asked without trying to hide her lingering anger.

"Since they're likely being used as locator beacons, we can't move the ship anywhere without them knowing. I determined the best course of action, for now, is to stay here and record all of your movements and other interactions. Once I have…"

"Did you just say you're recording everything we're doing?" Martina demanded.

"Yes. We need a complete…"

"Hell no! There's no way you're going to probe my mind and…"

"Captain," Alpha interrupted as he turned away from Martina. "We don't have time for unnecessary debates."

"Are you saying I don't get a choice about this?!" Martina shouted.

Ignoring Martina, Alpha kept his eyes on Jack and continued, "Once I have…"

"Goddamit, listen to me!" Martina shouted, cutting the alien off. She took two steps toward Alpha before suddenly falling to the floor.

Without even looking at the unconscious Martina, Alpha said sternly,

"Once I have a full recording of your collective behaviors; I'll deploy a small device here. It will broadcast a loop of that recording. At that point, I'll remove the old implants, and we'll be able to move the ship. They'll simply think we're still hiding in this location."

Jack didn't respond and just stared at Martina. He wasn't sure if it was Alpha's near-aggressive behavior that unnerved him or if it was the simple fact they were completely at the mercy of their alien host.

"She's uninjured," Alpha said flatly. "I will awaken her once we're ready to proceed – unless you want me to do so sooner."

Jack understood Alpha's impatience with Martina's outburst, but the alien's indifference toward human emotions was going to cause problems. He needed Alpha to appreciate the need to build trust with each other and said, "Wake her now."

Martina instantly opened her eyes. After a split second of looking around the floor, she sat herself up and said, "What the hell did you…"

"Stop," Jack shot back firmly as he looked straight at her. Turning to Alpha, he said, "The next time you see an issue with any of my people, you must talk to me first. You cannot take any action on your own."

Alpha looked at Jack and paused as if he were calculating the proper response. "I understand what you're saying," he finally replied.

Jack suppressed a wave of frustration with the ambiguity of the alien's answer. Belaboring the issue, however, served no purpose. He watched Martina get to her feet; her face was twisted into a combination of shock and anger. Before she could speak, though, Jack quickly shifted the discussion by saying, "I don't think your transmitter will fool them for very long. They will send something or someone in to investigate."

"At the very least, it'll give us a head start."

"How long?" Don asked.

Alpha turned to him but didn't immediately answer.

"How long do you need to keep the old implants active?" Don asked.

"One hour's worth of data should be adequate," the alien responded.

Jack took a moment to look at each of them. Nearly all of their expressions echoed the feeling of shock that weighed on him. Martina's face, however, showed a hint of remorse. Realizing that she'd overreacted, she turned to Alpha and said with forced civility, "Who are these…these other aliens? I've read the reports – at least the stuff I had clearance for. But I just don't understand – what are they trying to do?"

"We don't have any new information about who they are or where they're originally from," Alpha answered solemnly. "All we know is that they've deployed fleets of ships whose sole purpose is to eliminate any technological race they discover. It appears that they view any race they find as a threat and try to annihilate that race before it has a chance to attack them. Their current targets are my species and yours."

When Alpha didn't continue, Kurt asked, "So, what are these survivors doing now? Nothing's happened since the AGC collapse, so I assume they don't have the ships or equipment to continue the attack."

"It's not clear," Alpha answered.

"My first guess would be that they're monitoring us until another fleet is sent," Sarah offered. "You know – gathering intelligence. But I'm not sure that really makes sense…it'll be hundreds of years before their reinforcements can even get here. Any intel they gather now would be useless by then."

"I agree," Alpha said. "The five-plus century delay between the attack on Epsilon Eri D and their sustained attacks on the rest of our worlds is what led us to estimate that their homeworld – or at least their base of operations – is at least a couple hundred light-years away. It will take several centuries for the fleet we encountered before you traversed the last AGC, to get there and then return here with more ships."

"Alpha, were you able to uncover any frequencies that might have hosted other communications?" Kurt asked. "Maybe something between their ships if there're a bunch of them?"

"No, but that's not a surprise. RF is too limiting and primitive for interplanetary communication. They only used it to hack your planet's networks and your implants. They'll be using something with much higher bandwidth for their own communications – probably laser-based. Since that's highly directional, we wouldn't intercept anything unless we knew relatively precisely where the transmitter and receiver were.

"You said you identified several dozen transmissions at the three-point-five terahertz frequency, right?" Jack asked.

"Yes."

"We were definitely in different locations during some of those times, so we should be able to triangulate their origin."

"Yes, of course," Alpha answered with a hint of frustration. With no perceptible hesitation, he continued, "I've identified the source – it's in a location co-orbiting with Jupiter, near the forward group of trojan asteroids."

"We need to get there," Kurt said with a hint of excitement.

"As soon as I have the implant recordings done and the transmitter deployed," Alpha said. "We can't let them know we're coming."

"Do you have the raw data from any of the three terahertz spikes?" Martina asked. "I want to see what they were trying to send into our networks."

"Yes, but the amount of data is limited," Alpha answered.

"Look for the longest duration transmission," Martina said. "The more data, the easier it'll be to decode."

"They were all the same length. They had to fit within the temporal envelope of the pulsar's bursts."

Martina immediately asked, "Look for any that were in sequential pulsar bursts. Maybe they spread their data out over a few of them."

"There were none," Alpha replied.

As a look of frustration crossed her face, Don said, "What about spikes that were separated by regular multiples of pulses…like every third of every fourth pulse? Or, some other sort of pattern."

"What are you getting at?" Martina asked.

"If it was sequential, then it's possible one of our radio telescopes could have flagged it as a repeating feature – something to be investigated," Don answered quickly. "Remember, they were trying to hide this."

Don looked back to Alpha and asked, "Alpha, are there…"

"Yes," the alien quickly interrupted. "I've found one instance about two days ago. Three spikes appear; they're spread across every third pulse. There's a short delay before another twelve spikes show…also in every third pulse."

"Can you combine the signal from the twelve spikes?" Martina asked. "String them together into one record."

"Done," Alpha said. "There appears to be a modulation in the carrier frequency."

"Good," Martina said with a hint of excitement. "We need to decode…"

"I'm familiar with your data formats," Alpha said, "but the embedded information may be encrypted. The base transmission is in binary. However, I've been able to translate that into the following string. A series of white panels appeared in front of each of them. A single line of text was printed in black:

300C F962 03B0 6B01 5002 4B 42 4F 31 34 0A 4B 42 4F 31 35 0A

"What the hell is that?" Kurt asked.

No one answered as they stared at the sequence.

"Let me add," Alpha said, "This is just the first line in the transmission. There are five more similar lines of code after this."

Jack felt a wave of futility wash over him. Breaking a complex encryption algorithm with the help of serious computational power was nearly impossible. Simply staring at it was pointless. However, he chose not to voice his frustration and just watched his companions. Don and Martina seemed to somehow be working the problem.

Martina finally spoke up softly, "The first set of five looks like a hexadecimal memory address and record key."

"Explain," Jack said calmly.

"Any important data is stored in an off-world cloud system. To ensure redundancy in case of hardware failure, it's distributed across multiple locations. So, to access it, you need a memory address…a code telling you which satellite network it's on, then the physical location of the server farm, and so on."

"How do you know this?" Nadya challenged.

"It's part of what my counter-intel group did – safeguard the archive downloads. It's on the cloud too, but we had to track exactly where each bit was stored. What got my attention is the second sequence: F962. It's one of the physical locations we used for secure storage."

"What about the rest?" Kurt asked.

"The two-character sequences could be regular alphanumeric data," Martina answered.

Before anyone could say anything, the display changed, displaying KBO14 and KBO15 beneath the hexadecimal codes. "This is a translation of the two-character codes," Alpha said.

"Are these references to Kuiper belt objects?" Martina asked.

"Goddamnit," Don said. "Alpha, display the next line of text."

"What are you looking for?" Martina asked.

A series of numbers appeared below on their screens. Don immediately pointed to them and said, "They're locations and velocities in the standard solar system coordinate system."

"This doesn't make sense," Kurt said as he stared at the numbers.

"I think it might," Alpha offered. "I had noted earlier that your orbital calculations for the KBOs had anomalies in them."

Don didn't look away from the numbers as he asked, "Alpha, you still have access to my data on Earth's networks, right?"

"Yes."

"Display the outer sections of the orbits for KBOs 14 and 15 using both my stored data and your own observations."

Two graceful, blue arcs appeared on their screens. They were separated by a few centimeters and followed each other as they curved downwards from the upper left side of the panel to the lower right. "These are sections of the orbits from your calculations. KBO 14 is the upper curve." Two red curves suddenly appeared. They overlapped the blue arcs as they entered from the left and only started to diverge from them near the right side of the screen. "The red curves use my observations."

"Will either of these impact Earth?" Don asked.

"No. Their closest approach is over twenty million kilometers."

"Damnit," Don said softly, "Why would they hack our KBO data?"

"Will any of the KBOs disturbed by the AGC impact the Earth, Moon, or Mars?" Jack asked.

"None will come close," Alpha answered.

"What the hell is going on?" Martina asked.

"It's a sabotage campaign," Jack said solemnly. "They're trying to create chaos and distrust like they did with us." He turned to face Martina and said, "Look at what they did with Sarah and Sokolov. They affected their minds. Besides the obvious result of Sarah killing him – I think it convinced you that Sarah killed him deliberately. More importantly, our denial probably looked like we were covering for her and might even be in on it."

Martina just stared back. Her expression, however, confirmed for Jack that he was right.

"Think about it…it kept you from trusting Alpha and us. It led to your confronting Alpha and to him…him disabling you. Things could have spiraled a lot worse from there."

"So, then what's the point of manipulating KBO data?" Martina challenged.

"It's the same thing," Jack answered. "This data was implanted to make people on Earth think that we – the Magellan – put the entire planet at risk. My bet is that the KBO risk was supposed to make us look selfish and reckless. They just didn't have the ships or ability to send the object crashing into the Earth, so they did the next best thing – they're trying to distract us: create a sense of panic; keep people from trusting anything associated with our mission."

"I think you'd need something more than a collision risk that's decades away to have any meaningful effect on us," Martina said more thoughtfully.

"Don't assume that the KBO data is the only thing they got into," Jack proposed. "We only just stumbled onto this particular data incursion."

"I may have evidence of another," Alpha said softly.

All eyes turned to him. "I was tracking your progress with applying archive knowledge and was particularly interested in your X-165 project. The failure made no sense to me – your science was sound."

"I was sure of that!" Nadya exclaimed with a hint of relief. "But what could have caused the explosion and why?"

"Before getting involved with your rescue, I was probing all aspects of the project. One of my algorithms identified anomalies in one of the engine tests and at a fabrication lab – the one that made the magnetic field generators."

"Shit…are you saying that they sabotaged it?" Kurt said quickly. "How?"

"I didn't get that far."

"But, it makes sense," Nadya offered. "Even the smallest misalignment in the fields used to feed the antimatter would be catastrophic."

"Then they could have gotten into other stuff too, couldn't they? Do you think they could have started messing with," Kurt paused as he looked straight at Jack before continuing, "even government data?"

"I don't know," Jack answered. "Anything's possible."

"Still," Martina cut in, "what would be the point to all of this?"

"We know they consider us a threat," Jack said. "So, think about it, we just received a ton of knowledge from Alpha – it could level the playing field or even give us an advantage over them. Considering that there may only be a few of them here, their most logical move would be to slow us…that is, humanity down. Make us doubt or not even use the archive…or get us to kill each other. I don't think the specific outcome matters much to them. They just want to keep us from being ready for their next fleet."

"So, what do we do?" Sarah asked.

Jack didn't answer. There were too many options to consider and not enough information to go on.

Chapter 18

Jack sat back in the formfitting seat and stared out the front window of the small alien shuttle. The glass – though he wasn't sure if it was really glass – was so perfectly clear, it felt as if he were in front of an unprotected opening to space. To his right, Sarah seemed equally transfixed by the view. Drifting before them was a sparse collection of asteroidal debris. The larger, boulder-sized objects were coated with coarse, dark sand and marred with nearly-white streaks of frozen gases. A barely detectable halo of dust and ice crystals surrounded each.

"Computer," Jack called out, "distance to target location."

Alpha's technology answered in the standard human-computer voice, "Distance is ten kilometers." A synthetic red circle appeared, partially hidden behind the nearest asteroid.

"Good, hold position here."

Sarah turned to him and said, "I'm not complaining, but did Alpha explain to you why we're...why it feels like we're actually in a ship this time, instead of his VR interface?"

"He said the new implants weren't fully adapted to our brains yet. It'll take a little more time."

"Truthfully, I like this a bit better," Sarah replied. "Don't tell the others, but his interface gives me a bit of vertigo."

Jack laughed lightly as he confided, "It sometimes catches me off guard too."

"Computer," he continued, "deploy probes." A thin wisp of what could have been smoke streamed from beneath their position. It dissipated quickly as the myriad of microscopic drones spread out in different directions."

"How many of them were there?" Sarah asked.

"Maybe ten thousand." Seeing a hint of disbelief cross her face, Jack continued, "Each one's barely fifty microns across, but they're quite capable. Alpha said they create a distributed computing network between themselves; so, they act as a single, extended unit. It gives them the ability to self-navigate and monitor the bulk of the EM spectrum, all while remaining essentially undetectable."

"Then, they should make quick work of finding this transmitter?"

"Not sure…it depends on how advanced the enemy tech really is." Jack thought for a moment about explaining himself further, but there was really wasn't a need to finish the thought. His eyes just started wandering from one small asteroid to the next, probing the myriad of shaded crevasses and ridges that populated their chaotic surfaces. Though the largest objects were no bigger than a house, they offered uncountable numbers of hiding spots. A patch of gravel lying on the nearest one caught his attention; he tried to imagine searching every centimeter of it for some unknown piece of tech.

The radio came to life with Kurt's voice, "Jack, we're getting an energy transmission here…it's a three-terahertz signal."

Jack glanced at the lone display floating below the window – its data showed no sign of any transmissions. "I don't have anything."

"There's more," Kurt continued, "some of my probes are seeing a deep UV signal from behind us. It's laser-based…frequency modulated.

I think we've found their comm. channel."

"Good," Jack responded, "we expected something like that." A hint of frustration struck him as he stared at his empty screen. "Computer," Jack said, "is this the full EM readout from all probes?"

"Yes," the system answered. "No signals have been detected."

"Kurt," Jack called out, "We're not seeing any transmissions – RF or UV."

Sarah looked at Jack as she started, "Do you think we should…"

"Shit," Jack suddenly said, cutting her off.

"What is it?"

Jack ignored her as he said, "Computer, search for a UV transmission incident on our ship, not the probes."

"There is 205 nanometer light incident on the rear of the ship…standby." A second later, the synthetic voice continued, "It contains encrypted data using frequency modulation."

"What's going on?" Sarah pressed.

"Our ship's in the way…we're blocking the signal."

"But, no three terahertz transmission?"

"It's probably gets triggered when it receives their comm signal – we're blocking it."

"We've got to move right now," Sarah said urgently.

"Computer…," Jack started but stopped abruptly.

"Jack?" Sarah asked.

"If we move now, their device will get part of a signal. They'll know something changed while they were trying to communicate with it. If I were them, that would tell me that someone had found my device."

"Blocking the full signal won't be any different. They'd still know something went wrong."

"Yes," Jack answered. "But, if we disable the thing – make it look like it failed due to some natural event like a collision – they won't suspect someone was here interfering with their equipment. They won't look for us."

Sarah stared past him for a moment before offering, "Use it to our advantage. Set a trap."

"What?"

"We're here right now. Disable it, like you said, so they think it might be natural. But hide and see who comes. At very least, we'll get an idea of what we're up against. It might even give us a hint about how many of them survived."

"I don't think we've got enough time to prepare," Jack answered defensively. He instantly cringed at his own response – he knew they didn't have time to do things cautiously.

"Jack, we're not going to have another opportunity like this," Sarah pressed. "It's a safe bet they don't know we're here. If there are only a few of them, then they won't want to write this transmitter off as a loss. Think about it – they're basically trapped behind enemy lines with limited resources. They're going to want to repair it."

Jack nodded in response. He knew the idea made sense. "Kurt, Alpha," Jack said aloud, "Did you hear our conversation?"

Both answered yes simultaneously.

"Good. Kurt, head back to the main ship now. Alpha, can the probes you released surround whoever comes without being detected?"

"I can't say with certainty. Human technology definitely wouldn't see them. I am not fully aware of their capabilities."

"Then, let's play it safe," Jack said. "Maintain radio silence. Computer pull the drones back to our position; I don't want that inbound ship intercepting any of them."

"Drones are returning," the machine answered.

Sarah leaned forward, peering out the window as she asked, "Do we have anything available to try and track the enemy?"

"I don't want to use radar or any sort of active sensing. They've probably got some sophisticated tech." Realizing that his own understanding of the ship's capabilities was too limited, he decided it would be wise to ask it for potential options. "Computer, are you able to…"

"An energy signature has been detected," the machine interrupted. "There appears to be an inbound vessel. Its trajectory suggests it's heading for the transmitter."

"We didn't get a chance to disable it," Sarah said urgently.

"Computer," Jack said, "have all probes along the ship's inbound course power down."

"Completed."

"Display its position."

A green square appeared near the upper left corner of their window. Beneath it were the words, 'distance = 400 kilometers.' It counted down quickly as Jack said, "Minimize our energy output. Do anything to keep them from finding us."

"Completed," the machine answered.

The enemy ship was visible now – a small silver dot centered in the green square. Its distance had dropped quickly to ten kilometers but was now holding constant.

"Are they at their transmitter?" Sarah asked.

"No, we localized it to this region," Jack answered as he pointed to the still-displayed red circle.

"Then, why did it stop?"

"Not sure," Jack answered softly. He then quickly asked, "Computer, are they near any of our probes?"

"There are some unpowered ones drifting in its vicinity. I'm unable to retrieve any data from them."

Jack watched carefully as the small dot stayed motionless – as if it were waiting for them to make the first move.

"Do you think they detected the microprobes?" Sarah asked.

"I don't know…they could be taking it slow since they don't really know what happened to their transmitter. Though if they already determined it wasn't damaged, then they'll definitely be suspicious."

A sudden wave of white haze swept across the window. Immediately after, the computer said, "The enemy ship just emitted a strong electromagnetic pulse."

"Did we take any damage?" Jack asked reflexively,

Alpha answered this time, "No, our technology is immune to its effects. But, it did briefly polarize the matrix on your ship's hull – it's extremely likely they were able to see you."

The distance indicator beneath the enemy ship started counting down. It was moving straight toward them.

"Do we have anything to defend ourselves with?" Sarah asked hurriedly.

Ignoring her, Jack called out, "Computer, emit an EMP focused on their location." When Sarah looked blankly at him, he continued, "If they thought they could use it as a weapon, then they consider it dangerous and are probably susceptible to it."

"Emitting in three…two…one," the machine said.

Jack stared at the slowly approaching alien craft – it had grown to a bright white spot. The distance indicator was still counting down. "Did the EMP have any effect?" Jack asked.

Alpha replied, "They're not accelerating anymore. They are just carrying the velocity they had when they were hit. It looks like they're following a straight trajectory – gliding unpowered."

"We got them?" Sarah asked.

"That appears to be the case," Alpha answered.

"Computer," Jack said, "Project their current trajectory; assume no course corrections."

A green line emanated from its location, heading roughly in their direction. From its angle, Jack could tell that it would miss them, passing several hundred meters below their current position. An iridescent yellow triangle suddenly appeared along the damaged vessel's path. The machine said, "Unless a course correction is made, the ship will impact a five-meter asteroid at this location in two minutes thirty-eight seconds."

"Computer," Jack called out, "take us there at maximum velocity. Time to intercept?"

The nearby asteroids quickly shifted left and became a blur as they accelerated. "One minute four seconds," the machine answered.

"Do we have anything that can deflect their ship or the asteroid?" Jack asked.

The debris field swerved sharply left, then right as they dodged a small cloud of drifting gravel. "There is a small amount of antimatter onboard to power your shuttle's systems," Alpha answered. "I'll have your ship discharge a portion in that direction in twenty-five seconds. The shockwave from it annihilating the surrounding dust will displace the asteroid enough to avoid a collision."

"Good," Jack answered. "Are there any other projected collisions after that?"

"Yes," Alpha answered.

"What can we…" Jack started, but Alpha cut him off, saying, "Standby for antimatter release"

A diffuse wave of violet-white fog shot out in front of them. Within it, several white flashes appeared as rocky fragments met the advancing antimatter cloud. The fog, however, faded as it approached the enemy ship's location, making it unclear if anything had actually happened. A second later, the yellow triangle identifying the potential impact point vanished.

"Their ship will impact another small body in six minutes twelve seconds," the computer announced.

"Alpha," Jack called out, "is there anything you can do?"

"My ship is too far off. I won't get there in time."

"We'll need to do another deflection. Plot a course to…"

"You don't have enough antimatter aboard for that," Alpha said quickly

"We can't just lose them like this," Jack shot back. He stared at the white dot of the enemy ship, knowing there had to be an answer. "Computer," Jack called out before his thoughts had fully formed, "plot and execute an intercept course with their ship. Bring us alongside so that we can dock with it."

"Jack?" Sarah suddenly said,

Their debris field slewed sharply right as the ship changed course. The bright spot of the enemy ship grew, and within seconds showed itself to have an elongated, dart-like form.

"How long until intercept?" he demanded.

"One minute three seconds," the machine answered.

"Alpha, can you adjust our hull parameters so that we can dock with it?"

"Yes, that will be in place before you get to it," the alien replied. "It will, however, be a destructive maneuver – part of their hull will need to be removed to provide access."

"It doesn't matter," Jack answered sharply.

"Jack," Sarah pressed, "what's the plan?"

"Grab one of them before they hit the next asteroid."

"You want to board them?!"

"There's no other choice," Jack shot back.

"Captain," Alpha said, "You'll access their ship from a door at the rear of your compartment. You must be back onboard within four minutes – with or without the prisoner."

Jack heard Alpha but didn't answer. Instead, he stared at the growing form of the enemy vessel. Its angular lines and razor-sharp nose gave it the look of a spear tip. Its skin was perfectly silver and devoid of any windows or markings. Jack scanned its surface as his own ship slowed and circled the enemy craft; there weren't even any seams between hull segments – the vessel appeared to be cast out of a single piece of metal. It slid out of view as they turned and prepared to dock. A deep metal thud permeated their compartment as they made contact. Seconds later, there was a loud, high-pitched whine: Jack could only imagine it was a segment of the enemy ship's hull being cut away. The computer quickly announced, "Their atmosphere is similar to yours, but the O2 content is low: eighteen percent. CO2 is high: nine hundred ppm. You will begin feeling lightheaded after a few breaths; please pace yourselves. Biohazards are negligible."

An oval hatch appeared behind Jack and quickly slid aside, revealing a dark corridor. Retrieving a small flashlight from his pocket, Jack glided through the opening without hesitation. The weak beam of his light showed him to be in a circular hallway, lined with dull metallic panels and grid-covered ventilation openings. Though it was about three meters in diameter, it felt cramped. There were no working lights or other signs of power. Peering to his right, he saw that the corridor opened into a room of some sort – it was too dark to determine its function. To his left was a sealed bulkhead.

He looked behind him to see Sarah patiently waiting and said with a smirk, "We'll go right."

Jack froze at the chamber's threshold. Its darkened consoles told him it was obviously a control room. What caught his attention, though, was a motionless form drifting just a couple of meters to his left. Shining his light on it brought back a rush of memories from three years earlier. The creature was tall and lanky, and wore dull gray body armor – the type one might find on riot control police back on Earth. Its back was arched slightly backward, and its legs and arms spread wide as it floated above a control station. Unlike his last encounter, though, its head wasn't encased in a helmet. The creature's face was elongated with a slightly protruding snout. Jack wasn't sure if his emotions and memories were guiding his thoughts, but its head had an almost predatory look to it – he imagined it might have had enlarged canine teeth if its mouth were open. The alien's eyes, however, held his attention. They were wide open and fixed – their dull-orange irises and oval pupils had a foreboding glare to them, yet they appeared lifeless.

A wave of dizziness swept across Jack and he found himself short of breath. Taking a slow, measured lungful of air, he focused his attention on the motionless alien. It hadn't moved since they entered the room. Reaching out, Jack pushed it gently. Its body responded as if it were an inanimate object – there was no reaction or movement of any of its limbs; it simply started floating across the compartment. "Computer," Jack called into his comm-unit, "time check."

"You must return in two minutes, thirty seconds."

Jack turned to look at Sarah who hovered silently just behind him. Her gaze was fixed on the alien.

"Let's get back now," he said as he repositioned himself so that his feet were pressed against one of the ship's control panels. Grabbing the creature by the shoulder, he pulled hard and turned its body around, sending it drifting feet-first down the short hallway. It collided softly with the corridor walls as Jack followed. He reached out to give it another push, but froze as the alien ship's lights came back on. There was the sudden hum of equipment and the ventilation system. "Alpha!" Jack called out.

"Here, captain," was the response.

"We need to disable this thing now!"

"Stand by."

Jack stared at the creature without moving. It remained motionless. He quickly glanced around the corridor, unsure if there were any more of them onboard. But, but there were no other sounds or movement – just the benign hum of the ship's systems powering up. Turning around, he caught sight of Sarah, who had taken up a defensive stance and stared at the room behind him.

"We need to get out of here now," she said softly.

Without warning, the lights went out. The corridor was perfectly silent again.

"You must return in thirty seconds," his ship's computer announced.

Jack grabbed the alien's body, folded its arms and legs so that it would fit through the opening to their ship, and gave it a firm push. He followed it through, with Sarah close behind. The door sealed itself instantly. Looking past their drifting prisoner, Jack watched the asteroid field that lay outside their cockpit window swing left and become a blur as they accelerated away.

"The enemy ship has collided with a small cloud of rocky debris," Alpha said flatly. "It was completely destroyed. You are now on course to return to my ship."

Jack stared again at their drifting prisoner. It made no movements of its own as it hovered near the center of the compartment.

"Is it dead?" Sarah finally asked.

"Unknown," Alpha said. "I am unsure, however, why it is in this state. The EMP shouldn't have had any effect on it."

"Could it already have been dead before we hit it?" Sarah asked. "I mean, they've been in our system for years without supplies."

"No," Alpha answered. "Thermal imaging shows that its body functions were active until a short while ago. There are some anomalies in its anatomy that I will need to analyze more closely when you arrive."

"Understood," Jack said without taking his eyes off the creature. "What's our ETA?"

"Eight minutes," Alpha answered.

Chapter 19

Jack stood next to Sarah as they stared at their motionless prisoner. It was strapped to a flat table and still dressed in its armor. The alien's bluish-gray complexion made it impossible to tell whether it was alive. Its smooth, glossy skin showed no signs of pores or hair. Its face had definite humanoid characteristics: high, sharp cheekbones, eyes slightly larger than a man's, separated by the bridge of a nose which extended into a short snout. A broad, lipless mouth made Jack again think it might contain an array of razor-sharp teeth. It had no hair, but its skull was lined with subtle blue and gray stripes that ran from its brow line up its scalp. Jack continued watching silently as three of Alpha's small creatures worked on it. One was wrapped around the top of the prisoner's head and could have been the same brown, fur-covered creature that had been on Sokolov's head. It was motionless and had inserted a pair of small tubes from its back into the base of the alien's skull. The other two small, spider-like robots scampered up and down the length of the alien's body.

The continued silence must have been too much for Sarah's curiosity as she asked, "What is that thing on its head…a robot of some sort?"

"No," Alpha answered calmly, "though its functions aren't too dissimilar to the robotic assistants humans use. It's a synthetic lifeform created to assist me with various tasks. There is no name for it, but you can refer to it by its identifier, which is D-four."

Sarah continued staring at it with genuine curiosity as Alpha continued, "I've completed a preliminary analysis of the prisoner. Though they are, obviously, bipedal humanoids, this one did not evolve naturally. It shows significant signs of genetic engineering and is actually a hybrid being with multiple cybernetic implants. These implants are the reason for its current condition – they were disabled by the EMP."

"What are the implants for?" Jack asked.

"From what I could decode from its genome, the implants and genetic modifications serve the same purpose: physical and sensory augmentation. It appears that they likely originated on a planet with lower surface gravity than Earth's. I would estimate that in their original form, they were significantly weaker and more fragile than a human. The modifications were in large part designed to make them stronger, enhance their stamina and make them capable of surviving a greater range of atmospheric conditions."

"So, they were engineered to be soldiers," Sarah said.

"Quite likely," Alpha answered.

"What are its capabilities?" Jack asked.

"Based on its muscle density, bone, and implant structure, I would estimate that they only slightly exceed those of an athletic human. This essentially doubles its original capabilities." Alpha paused for a second, then added before anyone could say anything, "There are several central nervous system modifications whose purpose I cannot presently identify."

"What do you mean?" Sarah asked.

Its spinal column was engineered to have enhanced nerve density – I'm not sure if it was intended to speed its reflexes or do something else.

It also has modifications and cybernetic implants in its brain. I would need it to be conscious to analyze those."

"So, it's alive?" Martina asked from behind them.

Jack turned to see her standing between Kurt and Nadya. Don had positioned himself off to the side – out of the way but able to get a clear view.

"Yes," Alpha answered. "I've restored the baseline cybernetic connections in its organ systems, so it is technically alive."

"What's involved in waking it?" Sarah asked.

"The only thing keeping it unconscious right now is my blocking the higher functions of its implants. It should be as simple as removing this suppression."

Jack turned to look at the others, one at a time. No one overtly objected, prompting him to say, "There's a lot of intel we should be able to gather from it." Again, there was no verbal answer from anyone. Jack turned to Alpha and said, "Wake it."

The alien's eyes opened immediately. It tried to sit up but was held back by the table's restraints. All it managed to do was raise its head. Its gaze was piercing as it looked at each of them, one by one. When it finally faced Alpha, its eyes squinted slightly. Its muscles strained as it tested the strength of the straps before finally relaxing. However, it didn't take its eyes off Alpha.

"How do we communicate with it?" Sarah asked.

"It will take some time," Alpha answered. "I need it to try and communicate with us first. That will allow me to map its higher brain functions and create an interface with it. We just need to…" Alpha's voice trailed off. Jack barely noticed, though, as a wave of exhaustion suddenly enveloped him. Writing it off due to lack of sleep, he kept his eyes on the alien and Alpha. The room seemed frozen, though. Alpha didn't say a word but simply stared back at the enemy soldier. Jack wanted to ask him what their next step was, but had trouble focusing.

The urge to close his eyes was becoming overwhelming, but Jack forced them to stay open. Though he was still unable to read Alpha's facial expressions, his face seemed limp. Their prisoner's eyes had narrowed to slits; its expression was tense as it focused solely on Alpha. Instinct made Jack want to check on the rest of his crew, but he couldn't find the strength to turn his head. He fought the fuzziness of exhaustion to see if something was holding him in place, but he felt nothing – no physical contact nor anything else.

Time must have been passing, but Jack couldn't tell how much. He retained enough awareness to know something was wrong but now couldn't remember what they had been doing. The fixed scene in front of him was suddenly unfamiliar. He recognized Alpha but was at a loss as to why there was a strange creature strapped to a table in front of them. It seemed helpless as Jack stared at it. He wanted to understand more. A thought pushed its way through the fog: why had Alpha restrained this alien? There was a subtle sense that he should help it, maybe free it, but a sudden sharp tinge of fear returned as he stared at the trapped creature. Almost instantly, the urge to close his eyes grew strong again. Reflexively he fought it but couldn't remember why. Rest seemed extremely inviting – he knew he needed it. The warmth and comfort of sleep were all that he wanted.

A sudden burst of movement gripped Jack's attention. The prisoner's arms pulled violently against its restraints. It uttered a sharp growl that Jack could only assume was pain. Opening his eyes wider, Jack caught sight of the source: D-four – Alpha's fur-covered diagnostic creature – appeared to be attacking the alien's head. Its grip had tightened, leading to small streams of dark-red blood running down the enemy's face. The soldier shook its head violently, but D-four held tight. It rapidly inserted and removed its tube-like extensions into different areas around the enemy's temple – each time eliciting another growl of pain.

The commotion suddenly ceased. Their prisoner lay limply on the examination table. The fog that had enveloped Jack's mind was gone. Alpha looked straight at him. A sudden shudder ran through Jack as the adrenaline his body had been prevented from releasing finally hit his bloodstream. He took a second to compose himself before asking, "Is it dead?"

Alpha turned his attention back to the prisoner. D-four loosened its grip slightly, repositioned itself, and re-inserted its tubes into the base of the prisoner's skull. A moment later, Alpha answered with a simple, "Yes."

Sarah turned to Jack, her face still pale with shock. Then looking back at Alpha, she asked, "What the hell just happened?"

"Their technology is more advanced than we had realized," Alpha answered.

"It hacked our implants again?" Martina asked accusingly. "You said these things were secure!"

"It didn't access your implants," Alpha answered flatly. "It directly projected multiple EM signals resonant with each of our brains. It kept it simple. The signals induced a strong feeling of lethargy and exhaustion – likely an attempt to incapacitate us."

"It affected you?" Kurt asked.

"Yes. I was unable to communicate with you or my ship."

"But," Sarah said, "you were able to get that thing…D-four there to attack it."

"No," Alpha answered. "It acted on its own."

Sarah looked at him with disbelief for a moment before asking, "Why?"

"The soldier tried to kill it. I just read D-four's memories – the prisoner emitted a strong EM waveform designed to completely disrupt D-four's brainwaves. It was intensely painful, so D-four fought back, attacking the intracranial implants it had just finished mapping."

Sarah stared back without saying a word.

Kurt broke the silence as he asked with disbelief, "It knew what they were for?"

"I'm not sure you would say it knew. D-four's consciousness, like its body, is engineered for narrow, specific functions. In order to do medical analysis independently, it does have an understanding of what is and is not critical in a living being. The fact that it made the leap to using that knowledge to kill the prisoner, though, is surprising."

"Surprising?" Kurt asked.

"Yes. We've never been in a situation even remotely close to this. I have no information at all on how its engineered behaviors might make it respond. The fact that it retained a survival instinct is unexpected."

When no one else asked anything, Jack asked, "How long did it have us incapacitated?"

"Fifteen minutes," Alpha answered.

"What was it doing?"

Alpha stayed silent as he appeared to stare off into space. Jack gave him a minute before repeating his question. "Alpha, do you know what it was doing?"

"Yes."

When Alpha didn't elaborate, Jack allowed his impatience to drive him as he quickly said, "Alpha?"

"Wait," was the terse reply.

"What's going on?" Don asked.

Jack ignored him as he kept his gaze fixed on Alpha. It was easy to guess that the alien was communicating with his technology again. Not knowing what Alpha was looking into, however, ate at him. The silence drove his frustration. "Alpha, what's our situation?" Jack finally snapped.

"Captain," Alpha replied with concern, "it used my neural links to access my ship's technology. It started downloading large amounts of data…knowledge."

"How much?" Sarah asked.

"More than its own brain capacity could store."

"What does that mean?" Sarah pressed.

"It means it sent it somewhere," Jack answered.

"Where? The transmitter we were looking for before?" Sarah asked.

"No," Alpha replied quickly. "The probes you released earlier have been monitoring it. It's been idle."

"What about the unit we found?" Kurt asked.

"It's been dormant too."

Alpha stared at Jack as if he were about to say something, but Jack spoke first. "You've got to move the ship now – move it fast. There's another one of them here."

"Understood," Alpha replied.

The ship suddenly shuddered, causing Jack to stumble. Reaching for the wall, he stabilized himself and quickly asked, "Was that them?"

Alpha had a distracted look on his otherwise expressionless face as he answered, "No. I'm pushing this ship to its limits. We've accelerated to close to the speed of light."

"Where are we going?"

"The Jupiter system. We'll be there in a few seconds – ship time. I'm going to put us down on Io. Its molten surface combined with its proximity to Jupiter's strong radiation and magnetic fields will keep us hidden."

"We're going to just hide there?" A confused Martina asked.

The idea made perfect sense to Jack. He spoke as his thoughts solidified, "It'll give us time to think," He said. "They now know we're out here looking for them. If they've fully infiltrated Earth's networks – which it looks like they have – then they'll know that we're alone and that Earth doesn't know about them or us. If they want to continue messing with humanity's development, they're going to have to find us and eliminate us."

Alpha turned to directly face Jack as he said, "If they received our prisoner's transmitted data, then we must find them first. They can't be allowed to relay it to their homeworld. The problem is how."

Chapter 20

Kurt felt as if he were hovering only a couple hundred meters above a glowing yellow-gray sea of molten silicates and sulfur compounds. To his right lay an inlet where bright orange currents gently sloshed against the jagged shorelines of hardened magma. Further onshore, streaks of pale-yellow powder coated the darker underlying rocks, giving the already jagged surface a razor-sharp feel. Patches of crusty gray skin drifted calmly in the open, glowing liquid to his left, reminding him of North Sea ice flows he'd seen during winters as a child. Unlike those childhood memories, though, short bursts of hot vapor shot out sporadically in the scene before him. Kurt's eyes took him to the horizon, where the banded arc of a crescent Jupiter filled the sky. Io's nearly airless surface did nothing to dim the dominating colors of the Jovian cloud bands nor the pitch blackness of space that lay beyond it. The swirls of minor storms at the edge of each Jovian band looked as if they were trying to blend this diverse pallet into some neutral gray. The sharpness of the boundaries between the reds and browns of the darker bands and the light grays and whites beside them said that no blending was taking place. The colors simply fought against each other, creating infinitely detailed folds and eddies. The brightness of the glowing sea and Jupiter's clouds kept Kurt's eyes from seeing the thousands of stars beyond the giant planet's crescent. Like looking at the nighttime sky from a city, only the brightest stars were visible, challenging him to identify even the familiar zig-zag of the constellation Cassiopeia.

Directly ahead was the silver sphere of an automated ship Alpha sent with them. Its reflective surface seemed colored with the glowing yellows and oranges that lay outside – the craft's silvery hue only became apparent at its edges. Normally he wouldn't even be able to see it – Alpha's ships all used effective cloaking countermeasures. But that was the point; it was part of their bait.

"Kurt," Jack's voice said over the commlink.

"Yes, Jack," he answered.

"I confirmed with Don and Sarah, they're in position in low orbit around Europa. Are you ready?"

"I'm not sure what for," Kurt said. "Alpha's drones are going to do the work. We're just here to watch."

"Ignore him, Jack," Nadya said from behind. "We're ready."

Kurt reflexively turned around to see if Nadya was rolling her eyes but saw nothing. They were again fully immersed in one of Alpha's interfaces.

"Good. Maintain radio silence from this point forward," Jack said.

Kurt stared at the iridescent landscape again but now had no interest in its strange alien beauty. He hated waiting. "I wish we could at least see what's going on," he said mostly to himself.

"We might be able to," Nadya answered.

"What do you mean? We're just sitting here letting that drone send out comm signals, hoping they're going to see it and come and investigate."

"True, but Alpha's tech is pretty advanced. Let's see what its limits are."

Kurt wasn't sure what she was suggesting and stayed silent.

"Computer," Nadya said, "overlay a vis-light representation of drone one's transmissions. Identify transmission targets."

Immediately a narrow, glowing violet cone stretched off toward Jupiter's night side. A bright purple orb appeared near the transmission's destination; hovering beneath it was the label, 'Europa – Drone 2.' A thin blue line left Europa's indicator at an angle, connecting it with a smaller, distant blue dot labeled, 'Ganymede – Drone 3.'

"Alpha never mentioned what information we were relaying in these transmissions, did he?" Kurt asked.

"Actually," Nadya answered, "I did ask him while you and Jack were deciding on the target locations. He modeled it after standard inter-ship communications we use back on Earth."

"Like?"

"There's a channel with coordinate, course, and status information for each ship, another with positional data feeds on interplanetary debris in the region, and another with simulated human comm traffic…stuff like mission parameters, coordination, and verbal discussions on course adjustments. Basically, he's made it look like we're out here searching for some sort of anomaly but don't know what we've actually stumbled on."

"So, a believable reason for us being here, but they're supposed to think they still have the upper hand."

"Yes," Nadya answered.

"What if they simply think we're too big a risk and don't bother trying to investigate…maybe just take us out?"

"Well, that's why we're here. They're going to find the drones, but Alpha's pretty sure we'll stay invisible to them. So, let them destroy the drones – at least we'll have some info on what we're up against."

Kurt didn't answer, prompting Nadya to continue, "Plus, we've got a cloud of microdrones in orbit – they'll certainly see anything coming our way."

"They're just orbiting Io, right?" Kurt asked.

"Yeah. The idea was to give us complete coverage in case they try to sneak in from the far side."

"What if we sacrificed some of that and put them in a broad Jupiter orbit. Maybe inline with the plasma torus?"

"What're you thinking?"

"I was imagining what I would do if I were them and saw a suspicious set of transmissions. I might just hang back a bit to see how this potential enemy behaves."

"Away from any of the moons," Nadya said, completing the thought.

"Right. So, we'd need to monitor the space around Jupiter itself. They'd probably want to be close enough to see who's here but not so close as to be found."

"Don't you think the plasma torus is too close in? Europa and Ganymede get pretty far from it."

"I know. But, its radiation makes it a good hiding spot – they'd want to avoid being seen."

"Computer," Nadya said, "Can we redistribute the microdrones?"

"Not without breaking radio silence," was the answer.

"Damn," Kurt muttered. A subtle feeling of being exposed crept into the back of his mind. For all he knew, an enemy ship could be watching them right now – and there was nothing he could do about it. He turned away from the glowing sea and looked suspiciously up at the stars above. There was, of course, no chance of him actually seeing anything. Their own microdrones were effectively invisible, and most any enemy ship would be too small to see unless it was within a couple of kilometers. He just felt unnerved at having to sit there blind. "What if we relayed a set of microdrone instructions in the fake comm traffic that thing's broadcasting?" Kurt only realized after-the-fact that Nadya wouldn't be able to see him pointing at Alpha's spherical unmanned ship sitting in front of him.

Nadya, however, easily deciphered his reference and answered thoughtfully, "Maybe." He could almost hear her sigh, though, when she continued, "But, the whole purpose is for them to see the stuff we're sending with that ship. They'll pick it apart pretty quickly…see what we sent and know what we're up to."

"I should've thought of this before," Kurt said softly. Nadya didn't answer, allowing his mind to wander again in the ensuing silence. He stared at the floating purple Europa indicator, pointed at it, and spread his fingers. The ship's interface dutifully magnified his view. He repeated his motion twice more until he found himself gazing at the cracked, icy crust of the distant Jovian moon. A winding array of white and gray ridges worked their way down the frozen globe, pushing up against a haphazard sea of frozen ice floes. He recalled undersea images from a recent Europa mission showing a dark, deep but lifeless ocean that lay beneath the crust. It had all of the ingredients for life – water, dissolved minerals, and geothermal warmth – but just too much salt and ammonia to allow organics to survive. Pointing at the distant world, he moved his finger slowly to the left; Europa's disk slid aside as if his ship itself was pivoting to see another region of space. A distant field of stars filled his view. There were no hints of the Jovian system in which he was hiding – just uncountable numbers of stars.

Kurt spread his fingers again, and the stars rushed apart as if he were traveling through interstellar space at some impossible speed. Though he knew his view was only being magnified, the shift gave him a sense of vertigo. The starfield didn't look that different from the one before. New, dimmer stars took the place of ones that had shifted out of view. He magnified the image again. This time, a distant, spiral galaxy showed itself among the collection of stars. He focused on it, but its form was slightly fuzzy. It wasn't the galaxy, however, that had grabbed his attention. "Computer," he said. "What is the resolution limit of the imaging systems?"

"Zero-point-five nanoradians," the machine answered.

As if she were reading his mind, Nadya asked, "Do you think it's enough?"

"I'm not sure," he answered. Running the numbers through his head, he continued, "We're talking about distances on the order of a couple million kilometers between the Galilean moons. If their ships are about twenty meters long, it'd be above the diffraction limit, so technically, we could see them. The real question is: can this ship's systems first spot something that small, then track it, and finally recognize it as one of their ships."

"Then maybe," Nadya said thoughtfully.

"Yes, but it may take too long. Keep in mind that under that magnification, our field of view is tiny. If we're talking about maybe ten or twenty milliseconds between each exposure – including guidance maneuvers – we're still looking at maybe three or four hours to do the whole thing once. Whatever we'd spot would be long gone by the time we realized it."

"Remember," Nadya said, "It's Alpha's tech. It should be able to take images faster." Before Kurt could respond, Nadya called out, "Computer, how much time would be necessary to do a full, four-pi scan at this magnification?"

"Ten minutes."

"Impressive, but probably too slow," Kurt said. "Still, worth a try."

"Computer," Nadya called out again, "Begin scan. But lock on to the first non-natural trajectory you identify."

"Determining trajectories will require three images per region," the automated voice said. "Full scan time will be thirty minutes."

"Crap!" Kurt exclaimed.

"Computer, do it anyway," Nadya said. "Do the trajectory tracking in sequential images, not sequential full scans. It'll help us catch something quicker…if we get lucky."

"Commencing scan," the system replied.

"Now, I guess we're back to waiting," Kurt said softly.

Nadya didn't answer. Kurt stared at the collection of stars for a moment before suddenly saying, "Computer, remove magnification." The molten sulfur sea, with its sporadic bursts of white vapor returned. He didn't dwell on the view, however, and looked up at Jupiter's crescent and the surrounding stars. "Computer, cancel the full four-pi scan. Limit the scan to just the visible sections of the Io plasma torus…plus five degrees above and below."

"Understood," was the response.

"Display area to be scanned."

A belt comprised of small interconnected, iridescent blue boxes appeared to cut across the sky. Each box, he assumed, was the region contained in each image. The chain of squares started from below the horizon to his left, and looked as if it were rising out of the glowing yellow liquid. From there, the band continued diagonally across his field of view; it was maybe twice as wide as his fist held at arm's length and made it look as though he were viewing Jupiter through a mosaic of tiny, blue-bordered panes of glass. His eye followed the tiled belt beyond the edge of Jupiter's disk. It climbed high among the stars to his right until it arced back toward the giant planet – he knew it was simply following the path of the plasma torus. It accomplished what he wanted, though; it cut down their target area to a small fraction of the full sky. Kurt took a deep breath before asking, "How long to complete a scan of this target region, including tracking potential trajectories?"

"Four minutes," was the answer.

"Not a bad idea," Nadya said.

Kurt smiled in response but then added a quick, "Thanks," on realizing she wouldn't see his expression. He took a moment to admire the patterns created by the boxes overlaying Jupiter's cloud bands. There was no physical meaning to them. His eye, however, was simply accustomed to looking for patterns and reflexively sought out areas where some of the tiny eddies were entirely contained in a box. He caught himself staring at a minuscule red and gray swirl when a faint, thin, white streak shot across the sky. He tried to track the sudden motion, but it was already gone. Before he could formulate a question, the computer said, "Potential non-natural trajectory detected."

"Explain," Nadya said quickly.

"There isn't enough data to project a full trajectory," the machine answered. "Its speed and color, however, are completely atypical of natural material in this area."

"How fast was it going?" she asked.

"Zero-point-six-five c."

"So, we got one," Kurt said. "Do we break radio silence and tell Jack?"

"I'm not sure," Nadya answered. "It's got some pretty serious tech to be moving that fast here. I don't know if we want to expose ourselves with a broadcast."

"I wonder if they saw it too?" Kurt said aloud. Then before any answer could be made, he continued, "Computer, how far was the object from us?"

"At closest approach, between seventy-five thousand and one hundred kilometers."

"It might have been too far for them," Nadya said. "Jack's with the Europa drone…that's about seven hundred thousand kilometers out."

Kurt's eyes wandered about the molten landscape again, fixating on the silvery globe that lay ahead of them. It appeared to be slowly shrinking. Focusing on it a moment longer finally told him that it was actually slowly moving away while keeping a constant altitude above the Sulfur sea. Before Kurt could question the computer, it announced, "There is an inbound object moving at high velocity."

"Is it one of their ships?" Kurt asked.

Rather than answer his question, the system said, "A second object appears to be flying in formation with it. It is trailing the leading vessel by a hundred kilometers. The velocity of both ships is zero-point-four c and decelerating."

Kurt looked up toward the stars in a vain attempt to spot the inbound ships. "What's their distance?" he asked.

"One hundred ten thousand kilometers. Velocity has reduced to zero-point-one c."

Looking back at the horizon and the now rapidly receding metal sphere, Kurt asked, "What's their target location?"

"They appear to be heading toward the drone," the system answered.

"Distance between us and the drone?" Nadya asked.

"One kilometer and increasing."

"How long until intercept?" she added.

"The ships have decelerated to zero-point-zero-one c. Estimating constant deceleration rate, intercept will be in seven seconds."

"Are they both the same type of ship?" Nadya asked quickly.

"Unknown," was the answer.

Kurt stared at the now distant metal sphere a moment longer before allowing his eyes to look above it, anticipating where the enemy attack might originate. He immediately caught sight of a faint, but growing dot to his right. Within seconds, it morphed into a bright dart-like form. There wasn't time to formulate any thoughts before the enemy ship swept in. It skimmed above the molten surface, heading directly for the drone. Glancing to his right for a split second, he looked for its companion – but saw nothing. The enemy fighter slowed with unnatural speed until it hovered barely a hundred meters from the drone. The sharp point of the silvery vessel stayed aimed at the drone. Kurt wondered for a moment if it might have caught sight of his own cloaked ship. But before he could react, a second reflective sphere – identical in appearance to their own drone – approached swiftly from behind the enemy ship. The fighter spun around to challenge the inbound vessel but froze as a web of thin, blue-white lightning bolts embedded in a wave of fog leapt from the sphere and swept across it. The ship dipped as Io's weak gravity suddenly took hold of it. Almost instantly, their drone shot toward the enemy vessel and took position beneath it, catching it before it fell into the molten sea. The newer sphere circled the arrow-like fighter until it finally made contact on top of the vessel.

The comm came to life as Jack's voice said, "Kurt, Jack here."

"Yes, Jack," he answered. "What the hell just happened?"

"I think we caught one!"

"I thought we were trying to lure one in with our drone and watch it. When did you decide to do this?"

"We watched it do flybys of our drone around Ganymede and Don's at Europa. Its approach to yours was different. Alpha's analysis suggested it was going to engage either you or your drone, so we directed Don's drone to your position as a preventative measure."

"And capture it?" Nadya pressed.

"That was an opportunity that happened to present itself. When it held position near your drone, we figured it was worth a shot."

"Ok, but do we have a way to protect ourselves…I mean protect our minds from them this time?" Nadya asked.

"Alpha analyzed the implants from the one D-four killed. Despite the damage they took, he's determined how to suppress the technology it used on us. But, we shouldn't even have to use that; the plan is not even to revive any we capture. He wants to preserve them in some sort of coma-like state and directly extract their memories. Plus, we'll be able to get a good look at whatever tech's on board its ship."

Kurt shook his head, despite knowing no one would see it. All he managed was a weak, "I don't know."

Jack didn't say anything immediately – Kurt knew it was Jack's way of letting him voice any other concerns. When he decided to stay quiet, Jack continued, "We're going to tow it back to Alpha's main ship. Your ship will automatically follow it in."

PART 6: PURSUIT

Chapter 21

Jack walked slowly around the silvery, dart-shaped craft. Its sleek, narrow-body perfectly reflected the plain white walls and metallic gray floor of the landing bay. As he ran his fingers along the sharp, leading edge of the craft's stubby winglets, all he could see was a distorted reflection of himself looking back. Though this ship was somewhat larger than the first one they encountered, its thirty-meter length still appeared as if it were cut from a single piece of metal. There were no windows, doors, seams, or details – save for one unusual feature near the rear: the slightly uneven outline of a hatch. It was sealed tight and had no external controls or handles. It didn't show any signs of damage and only caught Jack's attention because he would have expected it to be a perfect circle, oval, or some other symmetrical shape.

"I am still unable to get a clear reading of the ship's interior," Alpha said from across the bay.

"I don't understand," Don said. "I thought your tech could penetrate anything."

"Some laws of nature hold firm, no matter how advanced your technology," Alpha answered. "This ship has a superconductive layer on top of its skin. It prevents any EM radiation from getting through. Plus, its hull is extremely rigid, so ultrasound can't penetrate it either."

"It's a damned Faraday cage," Sarah said as she surveyed the vehicle. Looking up, she met Martina's puzzled look, which prompted her to continue, "If you encase something completely in a conductor – or in this case a superconductor – then any EM radiation you throw at it will simply generate currents across the surface, but not interact with or see anything inside. We usually use them to shield sensitive equipment from electrical interference, but…"

As Sarah's voice drifted off, Jack stepped cautiously back from the ship and continued the thought, "It may have shielded whatever's inside from the EMP."

"Wait…are you saying there's a chance that whatever's in there is awake?" Don quickly asked.

"How sure are you that you can disable its…the device it used to affect our minds?" Martina asked nervously.

Alpha turned to Don and Martina as he answered calmly, "First, a Faraday cage – as you call it – works both ways. If it's shielding the outside from seeing in, it's also keeping whatever's inside from sending EM fields out. So, we are safe at this point."

"And if it's awake and we take it out?" Martina pressed.

"Your brains use periodic electrochemical impulses. The creature's implant was able to have an impact on us by emitting a varying magnetic field closely tuned to each of our neural systems. However, to do this, it needed to read your brainwaves first. The suppression system I've created is very simple. It's just an emitter that's tuned to each of your natural neural frequencies. When they try to read your emissions, my emitters will send a signal that will overlay your signals and overload their receivers. This will prevent their implants from working."

"But, right now, we can't see them, and they can't do anything to us, right?" Martina asked.

"That is correct," Alpha answered patiently.

"It's something of a standoff," Sarah added.

"More like a turtle," Kurt offered. "You know, it pulled everything inside of its shell and is trying to wait us out."

Nadya glared at Kurt as Jack said, "Something like that." He turned his attention back to the ship and said, "Alpha, what do you think about cutting through its hull and injecting an EM pulse of some sort? It'd have to happen fast – before they could react."

"It could work," Alpha said thoughtfully. "But, I don't know the interior layout of their ship. Depending on the materials they use and its geometry, there could be areas that would be shielded from the pulse's effects."

"So, if you don't get them in one shot, then they'll have an opening to retaliate," Nadya said. "It might be too risky."

"What if we play it safe and do this outside of our ship?" Sarah asked. When they turned to look at her, she continued, "If Alpha's robots can handle the vacuum, move the ship outside. Then have them pierce the hull, fire the pulse, and then put a sensor or something inside…to see if anything's still awake or alive. It'll keep us safe."

"Won't creating the opening kill them?" Kurt asked.

"Maybe," Sarah answered with obvious indifference. "But, I'm hoping

Alpha's tech can either revive them or get what we need from their brains. If we close the hole fast enough, they may even survive."

"It's possible," Alpha answered. "I have the…the equipment for lack of a better word, that we need."

Jack looked around the now-quiet room. Only Sarah and Kurt met his gaze; the others stared suspiciously at the ship. "Let's play it safe," he finally said. "Alpha…"

"I'm already working on it, Captain," the alien said. As he finished speaking, two silver orbs – each about two meters across – floated into the room. They attached themselves to either side of the enemy craft. Almost instantly, a small door in the bay wall opened next to Jack. Having become familiar with Alpha's less-advanced looking technology, he wasn't surprised at all when a silver, spider-like robot emerged. It walked over to the alien craft, gracefully hopped on top of the ship, and slowly walked along its length. On nearing the rear of the ship, it stopped and crouched down to the point where its body was in contact with the hull.

"I'll need all of you to step further back from it," Alpha said. "Move to within a meter of the wall."

A thick, clear, gelatinous fluid emerged from the floor as they took their positions. It flowed upward, piling on top of itself, forming a transparent wall. It solidified once it reached the ceiling resulting in a smooth, clear, glass-like partition between them and the enemy ship. At that moment, a thin, black horizontal seam appeared in the white wall on the far side of the bay. It widened smoothly and quickly, making it impossible to tell if upper and lower doors were simply sliding out of the way or if the walls themselves were dissolving. All that mattered, though, was that an exit for the enemy ship was now open. Alpha's attachments gently lifted it off the floor, pivoted the angular craft, and guided it smoothly into the darkness that lay outside. The silver spider held its position, apparently unfazed by the lack of atmosphere.

"How far are you taking it?" Jack asked.

"Five hundred meters should be adequate," Alpha answered. "Between the distance and my ship's shielding, we'll be safe."

As soon as the craft was clear of the bay, the opening vanished – replaced by the uninterrupted white wall of the room's rear. The glass partition melted as quickly as it formed, with the residue draining into a newly formed gap in the floor. Jack took a step into the now empty bay when a large, square section of the far wall turned pitch black. A view of the receding enemy ship appeared as Alpha said, "Once it's in position, we'll breach its hull and initiate the pulse. Several small probes will enter the vessel and provide us with a view and instrument readings."

"How long until we're ready?" Sarah asked.

"Just fifteen more seconds," Alpha answered.

Jack gazed at the sleek fighter's image and felt a tinge of hope run through him. They desperately needed some firm information – anything to help them know what they were up against.

"Preparing to breach the hull," Alpha announced.

Straining his eyes, Jack could just make out the slight movements the spider was making. It now stood over the oddly-shaped hatch. Though he couldn't see it, he imagined the drill must be piercing the skin. In a few seconds, it would emit the pulse and insert its probes. A blazing flash of white suddenly flooded the room. As Jack raised his arms to shield his eyes, the ship pitched sharply to the right, throwing him into the wall. He struggled to keep his balance, but something knocked his legs out from under him, and he hit the floor hard. Rolling onto his hands and knees, he came face-to-face with a disoriented Kurt. Jack didn't say anything, though, and jumped to his feet. Instinct drew his eyes to the far wall, but their view of the enemy ship was gone – only the plain white surface remained. "What the hell just happened?" He finally demanded.

"The enemy ship detonated," Alpha answered. "It is unclear what triggered the explosion – the unit I had on it had not yet started drilling into the hull."

Jack looked around the empty bay. No one seemed injured, but they all had similar, disoriented expressions.

"Did our ship take any damage?" Jack asked.

"It does not appear so," Alpha replied.

"What do we do now?" Martina asked.

Before Jack could answer, the lights went out. He found himself in an absolute, pitch blackness, unlike anything he'd ever experienced. There was no emergency lighting, glow from instruments or other minor sources of illumination. It was a smothering darkness that felt as if it were a blanket sitting only inches from his face.

"Jack?" Kurt's voice called out.

"Here," he said. Before Kurt could speak again, Jack called out, "Alpha, can you hear me?"

There was no response. He waited a moment longer – but the silence continued and unnerved him. He pushed any thoughts of fear from his mind as he called out, "Alpha," again and withdrew the flashlight he kept in his pocket. When there was no answer, Jack shined it in Alpha's direction. The weak beam illuminated their alien companion. He was sitting in his silver cart; however, rather than floating a few centimeters above the floor, the cart was firmly on the ground. A second light came on from behind him; he glanced back to see that it was Sarah.

"Alpha?" She said calmly. "Can you hear us?"

The alien turned his head to look straight at her but remained silent.

"I think his communications tech is down," Sarah said.

"Maybe he uses his ship's main computer system," Don added as he stepped into the glow of Jack's flashlight. "If the ship's power's completely out, then the computer's probably out too."

"That's not completely the case," Alpha suddenly answered. "I was linked to my ship's systems but have severed my connection from it. It just took a moment to complete."

"So, what the hell's going on?" Don asked, not even trying the hide the fear in his voice.

"I do not know," Alpha answered. "Nothing like this has ever happened before."

"Are you able to at least get the lights back on?" Martina asked impatiently.

"No," was Alpha's terse answer.

Jack slowly shined his light around the room. Nadya, Kurt and the others were now huddled close behind him. The flashlight's beam sent their long shadows across the empty landing bay's floor, where they blended into the darkness. Alpha's cart was floating again and was only a couple of meters in front of him. There were, however, still no other sources of light. He started methodically running the beam along the room's perimeter. When it reached a corridor to his right, his flashlight was only bright enough to show the hallway's entrance – otherwise, it was no more than a pitch-black tunnel. He pivoted slowly, allowing his eyes to carefully follow the white oval of his beam to the second of three entrances to the bay. Again, the corridor showed itself to be little more than another inky tunnel. Jack's beam continued its march around the bay, heading back toward them along the curved wall to their left. On reaching the third entrance to the room, Jack paused. The blackness seemed different, prompting him to angle the beam deeper into the corridor. Jack's eyes focused on the shadows just beyond the hallway's entrance. He was certain a shape was there – just barely beyond his perception.

Seeing him pause, Sarah turned her light to the same location. The additional beam, however, did little to pierce the blackness. Jack focused his eyes on the area; his mind tried to piece together what he was seeing. There seemed to be an oval of some sort within the darkness, though he wasn't a hundred percent sure his mind wasn't just playing games with him. The slightest hint of a reflection from their lights drew him in further. Suddenly, there was movement. He no longer needed to guess. A black helmet turned to look directly at him from the shadows. He stared at the reflection of their beams in its visor for a split second before the form dove deep into the shadowed corridor.

"Shit, it's loose!" Sarah nearly shouted with an urgency that was laced with fear.

"How the hell did it get on the…," Martina started but was cut off as Jack yelled, "Quiet!" Then in a level but firm voice, he added, "Not another word or sound." The room went silent. Jack stood still, staring at the corridor, listening for the slightest hint of movement. The room, however, remained perfectly quiet. Jack's instinct was to chase after it, but he had no weapons or idea of its capabilities. Instead, he listened to the silence a moment longer. When he was sure they weren't in immediate danger, he finally asked, "Alpha, is there any way to track it?"

"Unfortunately, my ship's systems are still down. The equipment I have with me right here doesn't give me much more range than what you can see. All, I can say is that there is nothing else in the room with us nor within a few meters of any of the entrances to the landing bay."

"What about that thing's neural abilities?" Sarah asked. "Can it do something to us again?"

"Not from that far away," Alpha said. "My analysis of the implants we recovered from the other one's corpse indicated that their ability to project neural signals onto your brains is limited. It needs to be within three or four meters of you for it to work. Plus, even if it was that close to us, the equipment I have in my chair includes an EM emitter. It will generate a signal that will overload the creature's receiver."

"What's the point of their implants being so limited?" Sarah asked with disbelief.

"Anything with greater range would require a significant amount of power – too much to run within a living being. My best guess is that they may use it at close range as an interrogation tool.

"There's one more thing you need to take into account," Alpha said. "My emitter is only effective if you're in relatively close proximity to my chair. The more powerful equipment I was going to use is integrated into the ship's systems – which are currently offline."

The room went silent again. Jack stared through the darkness at the corridor entrance – he couldn't let the enemy soldier roam the ship unchecked. However, they were defenseless. "Alpha," Jack said, "is there anything it can do to your ship or its system?"

"I am unsure. With power down, it won't be able to interface with the computer or access any data. But that doesn't mean it can't damage the hardware."

"How do we get power back online?" Jack asked.

"I'll need to get to the main control center," Alpha answered. "It's down that corridor," he added while pointing to the dark hallway through which the creature had escaped.

Jack stared back at the pitch-black entrance without saying a word.

"Do you have any weapons?" Sarah asked.

Alpha just looked back as if she had asked a stupid question. He kept his tone calm, though, as he answered, "No."

"What about your emitter?" Sarah pressed.

"I don't understand," Alpha replied.

"Maybe we can use it as a weapon."

"Explain," Jack said.

"Alpha talked about overloading its receiver when it tries to analyze our neural frequencies," Sarah said. "But, why wait for it to try and scan us. Its implant has to operate across the same frequency range as our brains."

"Yes," Alpha answered. "Its receiver will be tuned to that part of the spectrum."

"Then," Sarah continued, "all we've got to do is track it down and hit it with a high-intensity burst centered in that range. At the very least, we'll destroy its capability to directly interface with us. Best case, we actually knock the thing out or something."

"Make sure the burst uses constant power across the full frequency range that thing will be searching," Martina offered. Jack turned to look at her, prompting her to elaborate, "When searching for a channel – and it sounds like that's all each of our individual neural patterns really are – you scan across all possible channels until you find one with a signal. Since we won't know where it is in its scan, we'd have to have enough power in the burst to cover all possible channels. This way, it'll overload whichever one its receiver happens to be tuned to at that moment in time."

Jack nodded as he turned to Alpha and asked, "Can you do that?"

"Yes."

"Are you even able to make a portable emitter for us?" Sarah asked hesitantly. "I mean, we've got no power."

"There's no need to make one – the emitter's not integrated into my systems here. I can give it to you in a moment. I just need to adjust its settings." Barely ten seconds passed before a small drawer opened on the side of his cart. "You can take it from here," Alpha said.

Jack reached in carefully and withdrew what looked like a small silver pellet that was barely three centimeters long. His light revealed that aside from its smooth, oval shape, it was completely featureless. Jack looked up at Alpha, who said, "I've set it up to emit its pulse when you touch both ends simultaneously with your fingers."

"What's its range?" he asked.

"About five or six meters."

"So, a little further than their ability to get us," Sarah added.

Jack nodded as he looked at Sarah and said, "Ok, you and I will track this thing down. The rest of you stay here with Alpha."

"Do you have more of those?" Martina asked.

"No. I can fabricate more once we have the main power back online. For now, that's the only one I have."

"Damn it," Jack said softly.

Knowing what he was thinking, Kurt said, "There's no choice Jack, just take it and go after that thing. We'll be fine."

"You'll be ex…"

"Just go," Kurt said firmly, cutting him off. "And make sure you get that thing."

Jack looked back at them for a moment before saying to Sarah, "Let's do this quickly." He stepped to the entrance of the dark corridor before turning to Sarah and handing her the emitter.

"What're you doing?" she asked, though she knew the answer.

"I'm going to be the bait. Follow me, but stay out of its range…about five meters back."

"Jack, I should…"

"No arguments," he said preemptively. "Keep your light off and just follow the glow of mine – let's try not to let it know there're two of us."

"How am I going to know when I'm in range to activate this?"

"I'm going to keep talking while we're going – as if I'm on a comm-unit letting everyone know what I'm seeing. Once it gets a hold of my mind – you'll know. I'll either stop talking or…or you'll hear a difference in what I'm talking about. Either way, take another two or three steps tops, and activate the burst."

"It'll hear you coming," Sarah said.

"That's the idea," Jack answered. "You need whatever you're hunting to go after the bait."

"Godammit, you're insane," Sarah said, staring at him.

"You heard me, right?" Jack said, ignoring her statement. "Take two or three steps and activate the emitter." He kept his eyes fixed on her to make sure she understood what she needed to do. Sarah nodded and finally said, "Try to keep your voice deliberately monotone."

"What?" he asked as if the request were irrelevant.

"It'll force you to concentrate on the exact words you're saying and suppress your feelings. It'll make it easier for me to hear any changes that might suggest something's getting into your mind."

"Got it," Jack answered as he turned back to face the hallway. Before stepping in, he added, "I am going to have to stop talking every few seconds to listen for any sounds of it. I can't walk into it completely blind."

"Understood," Sarah replied. "Just make sure your pauses don't last more than, say, five seconds. I need to have a pattern to work with to know if something's going wrong."

Jack nodded and looked down the hallway. His light only managed to illuminate the nearest few meters of the plain white corridor. As he stepped into it, he dutifully started talking, "I'm entering the corridor now. There are no signs of damage of any sort. No debris either. I'm taking a deliberately slow pace so I don't miss anything. If I remember correctly, this one goes about fifteen meters before opening into…" Jack froze in his tracks as the sound of something rustling ahead of him caught him by surprise. The noise quickly ebbed as if its source was moving away from him.

"I think I heard some movement ahead," he said softly, continuing his narration. "But, there wasn't enough time to tell what it is." He scanned the featureless white walls of the hallway near him and continued, "Still no signs of damage or anything in the corridor. One might think that it would be searching for doors or other openings…maybe trying to pry something open. I'm about ten meters in now. In a moment, I should reach a junction. The corridor to main control will be to my right."

Jack stopped talking as he approached the dark intersection. His light cast arc-like shadows around the edges of the openings to either side and quickly died off to blackness as the central corridor continued into the distance. He stopped just short of the intersection and listened for any sounds before saying, "I'm at the intersection now. There are no more sounds or other signs of movement. I'm going to take the right-side path." He peered carefully around the corner and allowed his light beam to show that the hallway was empty. "This corridor seems completely empty and undamaged." He shined his light up to the ceiling and said, "Still no indications that it stopped here or anything. I'll continue down this corridor a bit further before…" Jack stopped as he kicked something and felt a slippery substance on the floor. He pointed his light downward and reflexively said, "Oh shit." In front of him were three of Alpha's creatures, sprawled and crushed along the floor. "It definitely came down this way," he said, making a deliberate effort to keep a level tone. "Two of the spider robots were stepped on or stomped on here. They're completely wrecked." He looked for a second longer and forced himself to keep describing what he saw, "It also killed D-four. It looks like it was stabbed and crushed. Its blood is all over the floor." He reached down and carefully touched its fur – it was matted with blood. "It looks like they were bunched up against the wall here. I think all three were hiding from it…or trying to get away from it."

Feelings of anger and fear welled up inside Jack. There was no need for them to be killed. "It could have ignored them," he said out loud. "They're just animals or…I don't understand; why would it kill them?" He shined his light ahead and saws more blood covering the floor. "What the hell is going on here?" he said loudly. The puddles were large. His eyes followed smears of blood up the sides of the walls. A large gray body was lying in the distance – blood oozing from its back. Its shape and size said it was another of Alpha's people. "Alpha, you said you were alone. Your shipmate…he's dead." Jack called out. "What did you have down here? They're all dead. What is this thing doing?" he shouted. Jack wanted to simultaneously run forward and get out of the area, as his anger fought against a primal fear. Loud footsteps approached from both in front and behind him. There was a sudden flash of light from both directions.

In an instant, the images of blood and bodies vanished. The hallway was perfectly white again. The sounds remained, though, as a tall, lanky form, clad in black armor and a helmet ran toward him. From behind him, someone shouted, "Jack, get down!" Without thinking, Jack ducked. A glowing white ball of plasma leapt from the form in front of him, grazing his shoulder. The burning sensation was easily pushed aside, though, as someone jumped over him from behind, meeting the armored soldier in mid-air. Sarah wrapped her hands around the creature's gun as they crashed into the wall. The corridor was tight enough that Jack had to roll aside to avoid getting tangled in the chaotic struggle. Pivoting quickly to a crouched position, he watched the alien stick out its leg to gain a better footing against Sarah. As it pushed itself up to its full two-and-a-quarter meter height, Jack gave a sharp kick with his heel into the side of its knee. It shattered easily, eliciting a howl of shock and pain. The creature spun up against the wall, using it to maintain its balance. Turning its attention toward Jack, the soldier swung at him with its free hand. That, however, was the opening Sarah needed. Maintaining a tight grip on its other hand and gun handle, she twisted sharply to her right. The creature's intended blow to Jack never landed. Its other wrist snapped with the sound of wet wood. The weapon slipped weakly out of its grasp as the alien slumped back against the corridor wall. Sarah moved quickly, though, grabbing the gun before it reached the floor and flipping it into position so that its muzzle was pressed against the soldier's helmet.

"We need it alive," Jack said calmly.

Sarah didn't budge and held the gun in place, prompting Jack to say, "We need to interrogate it."

She finally nodded and took a step back from the creature. It, in turn, slid the rest of the way down to the floor and cradled its broken arm. Jack watched as Sarah didn't say a word but instead stared at the pistol-like weapon in her hand a moment longer. She loosened her grasp of its handle and analyzed its silver, streamlined form. Raising it again, she aimed it down the hallway. Her index finger probed the junction between its handle and body for a couple seconds before a bolt of plasma leapt from its muzzle, striking a wall several meters away. Finally, she turned her eyes toward Jack and said, "I figured I should know where the trigger is if I'm going threaten that thing with it."

Jack allowed himself a half-smile before turning his attention back to their prisoner. The creature simply sat on the floor, its head tilted up toward them. Jack reached out, touched the base of its helmet, and made an upward gesture. The alien understood and, with its good hand, awkwardly unclipped and removed the helmet. As far as Jack could tell, it looked identical to the one they had encountered before. Its dark orange eyes and oval pupils stared straight at him. Its smooth blue-gray skin and tightly closed mouth gave no hint of any feelings it might be having. The creature simply sat still and watched them. "Keep your gun on it," he said, "I want to get the others."

Before turning to go, he looked directly at the alien, brought a raised finger to his lips, and softly said, "Shh." Turning to Sarah, he said, "Make sure it stays quiet." Jack didn't wait for a response and started back through the dark corridor. As he turned left at the junction, he caught sight of a flashlight beam glancing off the opening to the landing bay a few meters ahead. He paused and stared at the beam; it didn't wavier at all. Turning his own flashlight off, Jack crept up to the edge of the opening. Getting down to floor level, peeked around the corner. Kurt was standing upright, looking straight ahead but not focused on anything. Directly behind him was the unmistakable armored form of another alien soldier – it held Kurt's arm firmly behind his back, keeping Kurt rigidly in place. The others were slumped on the ground, though some subtle movements of their limbs told him they were alive.

Jack crawled back into the hallway, but Kurt's stressed voice started talking. "I know you're there. If you value your companions' lives, you will surrender now."

The fact that it was even making demands meant it was willing to negotiate. What he needed was time. Choosing not to answer, Jack retreated quietly back through the corridor to Sarah. As soon as she caught sight of him, she read his body language and asked, "What's wrong?"

"There's another one of them. It's got Kurt and the others. It seems to have somehow…interfaced with Kurt. It threatened their lives if I didn't surrender."

"So, it sees value in keeping us alive," Sarah said thoughtfully.

"Yes. But I don't think it knows about you. We can use that." Jack stared at Sarah and their prisoner for a moment before asking, "Do you have a utility knife or anything on you?"

She quickly patted two of her pockets before answering, "Yes."

"Good., give it to me. You keep the pistol."

"What've you got in mind?"

"We'll set things up for a prisoner trade," Jack said softly.

"You're going to let this one go?" Sarah asked incredulously.

"No. I'm just going to make the other one think we are. It'll be a distraction, so you can dive in and take a shot at it."

Sarah handed the knife to Jack, who immediately made an upward gesture with it while looking straight at the alien soldier. It understood and forced itself to its feet, using the wall for support. Looking back to Sarah, he said, "When we get to the landing bay entrance, stay out of sight. Wait until I have its complete attention, then get in and take your shot."

Jack immediately took position directly behind the soldier while putting his knife against its neck. He paused for a moment before applying gentle pressure and drawing it a centimeter across the creature's smooth, clammy skin. The soldier squirmed, at which point Jack stopped his hand but kept the pressure constant. A small trickle of blood ran onto his fingers. However, the soldier stayed completely still. "You get the idea now," Jack whispered.

Keeping his knife against its neck, he pushed it forward. The creature hobbled slowly but didn't resist. The light from Jack's flashlight was mostly blocked by the creature's body, causing their long shifting shadows to mix with the pitch darkness ahead. It gave them just enough illumination to see where they were going. As they turned the corner to head toward the landing bay, Jack pulled back on its uniform, causing it to stop. He surveyed the corridor, but it remained unchanged; as before, a light from within the landing bay showed on the edge of its entrance.

Jack gave the alien a push again, and it returned to its slow, hobbled pace. On reaching the entrance, Jack chose not to pause but gave it another nudge. The creature continued forward, and Jack only pulled back on its uniform once they had fully crossed into the landing bay. They stood still as Jack surveyed the room; it, too was unchanged. Kurt was still standing rigidly in front of the armor-clad alien. Jack chose not to speak first and waited silently.

The enemy soldier took its time analyzing the situation. After nearly a minute, it finally repeated its demand through Kurt, "If you care about your companions, you will surrender now."

Jack stared back at it and again took his time answering. Silence, he knew, was itself a weapon. Holding his position, he made a point of staring the alien straight in the eye before saying, "The way I see it, we each have something the other wants. We should discuss how to resolve this situation."

"There is no situation," it answered immediately through Kurt. "You don't have any leverage. You can kill your…your hostage if you want. He is aware of his duties. It doesn't matter to either of us."

Jack didn't break his gaze as he answered, "You're marooned in an alien star system. You only have a couple of ships and a handful of people. You're either lying or incompetent if you're telling me you don't need every asset you have."

Jack gave his prisoner a slight shove, guiding it toward the right side of the bay while keeping its body between him and the other soldier. He made a deliberate show of shining his flashlight on each of his unconscious companions' faces. The soldier pivoted, keeping Kurt in position between itself and Jack. It raised its weapon as if it were taking careful aim at Jack's head. Jack responded by pressing the knife harder against his prisoner's neck. The prisoner flinched, causing the other one to lower its weapon slightly.

"So, how do we resolve this?" Jack asked as he made his hostage take another couple of steps further to the right. The soldier again didn't break eye contact with him, but this time took a step forward, trying to close ground with Jack. As Jack pulled his prisoner back to maintain his distance, he caught a blur of motion out of the corner of his eye. Sarah dove into the room and rolled, moving too quickly for the soldier to pivot and track with its weapon. She fired twice. The first missed its mark; the second caught the creature in the shoulder. It spun around, ignoring the wound, and leveled its weapon at Sarah.

Jack kept his eyes on Sarah but felt a sudden shot of pain across his left thigh. His hostage had a short dagger in its hand, withdrew it from his leg, and moved to plunge it in again. Without hesitation, Jack forced his knife into the creature's neck and pulled the blade horizontally. There was a gush of warm blood flowing across his arm. The creature stiffened for a split second, then flailed its arms as it vainly reached for Jack. A second later it went limp. Jack, however, kept his eyes on the other soldier as it took two shots at a running Sarah. Its back was now to him. Jack immediately shoved the body of his prisoner to the ground and tried to run at the creature, forgetting for the moment that he had a deep stab wound in his leg. It heard him by his second step and turned. Jack knew he couldn't cross the last three meters between them fast enough but lunged toward his opponent anyway. The enemy brought his weapon around, trying to guide its muzzle toward Jack, but a brilliant ball of white buzzed by it, grazing its shoulder. The creature made a loud noise – Jack was sure it wasn't a groan of pain, but more likely some alien obscenity reflecting its anger with Sarah's shot.

It turned its head briefly back toward Sarah. Jack saw it as an opening and dove for the creature, but the alien's movement was a feint. Before Jack was within a meter of his target, it pulled its leg back and extended it violently, landing a kick to his midsection. The air rushed painfully out of his lungs, leaving him to fall to the floor with his chest convulsing. The pain spread across his lungs like a web, as they wanted to expand and take a breath of air. The tightened muscles prevented them from expanding, leaving Jack to gasp on the floor. He clenched his fists tight and pushed instinct from his mind. Instead, he used all of his strength to force his body to try to exhale what little air was in his lungs. The convulsions ceased, though the pain remained. Maintaining his concentration, he allowed his lungs a half-breath of air. It took all of his strength to keep focus and prevent them from taking in more – that would only start the convulsions again.

Jack rose to his feet as he strained his eyes in the darkness to see Sarah run laterally across the back of the landing bay. The creature tracked her with its gun, though, and fired several times. The shots barely missed but chased her into the corridor across from them. The creature turned around quickly, saw Jack standing, and leveled its gun not at him but at his crewmates. The first sounds of Jack's shout hadn't left his mouth before the creature fired. Two shots struck somewhere in the huddled mass of unconscious forms before another round of shots came inbound from across the bay. Sarah's volley missed the soldier but stopped the attempted massacre. It uttered the same growl, didn't bother taking cover and returned fire. Sarah ducked back into the corridor. This time, the creature didn't hesitate, and took off after her at a dead run. Within a second of leaving the room, Jack heard Alpha's voice – they were finally out of range of the alien's implants.

"Captain, the food production garden is at the end of that corridor. There's nowhere they can go from there."

Jack turned to shine his light on Alpha. Then directed it toward the others. Kurt and Nadya sat up, looking at him with expressions of sheer terror on their faces. Don and Martina, however, didn't move. Disbelief swept over Jack first before reason took hold. He kept his light on the two motionless forms until he could finally accept what he saw. Don had a singed wound in the center of his chest. His eyes were fixed and open, staring off to nowhere. The side of Martina's head was covered in charred skin and blood. Her hair covered the point of impact, keeping Jack from seeing how bad the injury might really be. She too, however, had a frozen, limp expression on her face.

Kurt's hoarse voice saying, "God No!" brought Jack back. He quickly directed his light again toward the far side corridor and took two steps toward it. However, his injured leg gave out, causing him to stumble to his knees.

"Jack," Nadya said. He looked back as she stared at Don and Martina. "We've got to do something for them. Alpha," she continued, "you can help them, right? They can't be dead."

"If we can get power restored quickly, I may be able to do something," Alpha answered calmly.

"How much time do we have?" Nadya asked with a wavering voice.

"We have to move quickly," Alpha repeated.

Jack didn't say anything but got back to his feet and just stared back at the darkened corridor down which Sarah and the soldier had just run.

"Jack," Nadya said again. "We've got to do something for Don and Martina."

He heard her, but his mind was fully focused on Sarah.

"Captain," Alpha said. "If you want me to do something for Don and maybe Martina, we have to act now. The other two are trapped down that way. There's nowhere they can go."

"Jack!" Nadya repeated loudly.

He looked down at his blood-covered hands and the small utility knife in his palm, and loathed the logic that told him he couldn't pursue them like that. He was of no use to anyone if he simply ran down the hall and got shot. Finally, turning back to Alpha and Nadya, he said. "Let's get power back up and get to work on them."

Nadya looked back and just nodded.

"But," Jack said as he directed his light back toward Alpha, "I'm still going to need something that can function as a weapon."

Chapter 22

Jack stood over the narrow table and looked down at the sheet-covered form. Smudges of blood shown through the thin white cloth, though it gave no other hints about the body that lay beneath.

"I am sorry, Captain," Alpha said. "I wish there was something more that I could have done for her."

Jack allowed himself a moment more of silence before saying, "It's not right. She wasn't even supposed to be here."

"Was there any choice?" Alpha offered. Jack wasn't accustomed to his alien companion showing empathy and simply answered, "I know. It's just not…fair."

"Forgive my bluntness," Alpha continued, "but remember, there is no such thing as fair. You did what you were certain was right when you took her when rescuing Kurt and Nadya. With what you knew at the time, you would never have considered doing anything different. So, there is no reason for self-doubt or remorse."

The words struck a nerve within Jack, but not for the reason Alpha had intended. They reminded him that there was simply no time to waste. Reflecting on his choices would have to wait until later. He turned to Alpha and, in a level tone, asked, "You said you had something that I could use as a weapon."

"Yes," Alpha answered. The alien reached out from his cart and handed Jack what looked to be a simple, palm-sized, silver box. "We know their implants are susceptible to EMPs. The best that I can do is give you this – it'll generate a focused pulse."

Taking it into his hand, Jack asked, "What's its range?"

"About fifteen meters," Alpha replied.

Jack held it firmly, extended his arm, and tried to get a feel for how to aim the device.

Anticipating his thoughts, Alpha said, "The pulse has a divergence of fifteen degrees, so your aim does not have to be that accurate. Keep in mind; it will only affect its electronics, so it won't do any physical damage to the soldier's body."

"Were you able to get all of your ship's sensors back online?"

"No. Power is still down in the garden area."

"Then, we've still got no idea about Sarah's situation."

"That's correct."

Jack looked at the table next to Martina's and stared at Don's unconscious form. Answering the unspoken question, Alpha said, "He will recover completely, and should regain consciousness within the hour."

Jack only nodded as his eyes continued to the last table in the row. There lay the partly covered form of their alien prisoner. A bright white collar covered the deep slash Jack had made in its neck. "Its condition has stabilized," Alpha said. "I will begin extracting information from its mind shortly. After that, I recommend that we dispose of it."

The coldness of Alpha's last statement was almost comforting – as if Alpha was validating Jack's feelings of hatred toward them. "Do you have anything that I can use for recon?" Jack asked.

Alpha stared back for a moment as if he were considering different options. He then looked to his left as a small, silver spider climbed out of the side of his cart. It paused for a moment, looked at straight at Jack, then jumped smoothly to the floor. Its animal-like behavior made it tough at times to think of the synthetic lifeform as a robot. "I've interfaced it with your implant," Alpha said. "This will allow you to communicate with it, and even see what it sees. Use basic commands when talking to it, it should understand."

Jack turned to Kurt and Nadya; they stood side-by-side, watching over Don. He felt a need to say something, but words weren't necessary. Nadya simply looked up and said, "Do what you have to. Just be careful."

Jack nodded as he took a step toward the corridor. He stopped briefly and glanced down at his robotic companion, unsure as to how to command it.

As if he anticipated Jack's thoughts, Alpha said, "Address it using its designation: S-three. I've told it to take you to the garden unit. You can adjust its speed by telling it to slow down and speed up."

Understanding Alpha's statement, S-three led the way down the bright, plain white corridor. Jack kept his eyes fixed on a junction a few meters ahead and, as they approached the turn that would lead them to the garden, said, "Stay ten meters ahead."

The knee-high unit picked up its pace, quickly pulling ahead. Without hesitation, it made the turn before slowing slightly to keep a nearly exact ten-meter lead on Jack.

The far end of the corridor was cloaked in blackness. Jack reached into his pocket for his flashlight before recognizing it would be more of a benefit to the enemy soldier than an aide to him – he'd simply be a well-illuminated target. "S-three," Jack said, "return here." The silver spider quickly scampered back to his feet. "Provide me with a thermal-IR view." His view of the shadowy end of the corridor was replaced with a clear, black-and-white, knee-level image of the path ahead. Jack took a step forward but quickly realized that S-three's ground-level perspective was too awkward to use for his own navigation. He looked down at the motionless robot and said, "What the hell," as the thoughts formed in his head. The creature looked up at him, not understanding if Jack's statement was a command. Jack then said more clearly, "S-three, can you…can you take up position on my shoulder?"

The robot leaped gracefully into the air, landing easily on his upper arm. The sensation was surprisingly similar to having a large bird, like a parrot, land on him. Jack looked to his left, but his IR view ended in a wall of blackness – he had reached the edge of S-three's field of view.

"S-three, can you track my head movements?"

The robot turned its head toward Jack, giving him an infrared view of himself. "Damn, you don't understand…" Jack looked straight ahead again and said, "Look where I am looking." It followed suit, giving Jack a view of the hallway. "Yes, that's it," Jack said with some encouragement. "Show me whatever is in the direction my head is facing."

Jack turned his head left; this time, the creature mirrored his action. Though there was a slight lag, it gave him an adequate view of what lay ahead in the darkness. He advanced cautiously and paused as he reached the entrance to the garden unit. Immediately in front were rows of plants – though he couldn't identify the type. Their stalks were not unlike corn, but they had distinctly broader leaves. In IR, they looked truly alien – their foliage having a gray-white hue. The urgency of the situation made it easy to suppress any fascination he might have with alien biology and focus purely on the strategic hurdles that lay ahead. Carefully surveying the room from left to right, he estimated it to be thirty meters across. The plants, unfortunately, provided a near-perfect screen, keeping him from seeing more than a few meters ahead. Their two-plus meter height meant that there was no way to see over them, even though the ceiling hung a full meter above the plant tops. Based on his limited knowledge of the ship, the garden might be forty or fifty meters deep. Deciding that caution was more than warranted, Jack chose to walk quietly along the perimeter, listening carefully for any sign of movement.

On reaching the far-left side, he slowed his pace and made his way deeper into the garden. The ghostly, black-and-white rows of plants continued without interruption. Perfect silence surrounded him. Growing concerned about an ambush, Jack paused every few steps and deliberately turned his head to the left and then to the right; S-three obediently followed suit. The resulting views told him nothing.

Jack continued slowly, closing in on the compartment's rear wall, but there was still no sign of either Sarah or the soldier. On reaching the last row of plants, he crouched down and whispered, "S-three, get down and show me what's around the corner."

The robot stepped off his shoulder and silently moved forward. Jack held his position and had the urge to glance around him but couldn't; S-three was still generating his view. He needed to see what the robot saw, but sitting blind like this was unacceptable. "S-three," he finally said, "I need to see using my own eyes too. Can you reduce the size of your image?"

Nothing changed. The robot simply stopped moving. "Damn," Jack muttered. "You can't really control my implant, can you?"

There was, of course, no response. "S-three," Jack said softly. "Disengage your view from my implant for one second, then re-engage."

Jack's world went black. There were still no signs of light from anything or anyone else. Before he could formulate another thought, the robot's IR view returned. "Continue around the corner," Jack whispered. "But, slowly."

Seeming to understand the situation, the vantage point of Jack's view suddenly lowered as S-three crouched down. Peering around the corner, Jack saw the IR-glow of a body. It was standing and appeared to be aiming a weapon in S-three's direction. A few meters beyond it was another form, its back was to the first one, and it too held a weapon. The two seemed to have taken up a defensive position together. Jack studied the scene closely, and it became clear that the form in front of S-three was human. Though it was difficult the recognize a person in infrared, her shoulder-length hair told Jack it was Sarah. The creature behind her was dimmer; its armor and helmet partially masked its infrared signature, confirming for Jack that it was the other soldier.

Jack's first instinct was to call out to Sarah – to warn her, but he held his tongue. He just watched as the soldier turned, looked in Sarah's direction, then turned back. Neither knew he was there. Sarah's form took two steps toward S-three; she slowly panned her weapon across her field of view but didn't stop at S-three – she was just as blind as he in the darkness. S-three, however, stayed perfectly motionless, allowing Jack to stare at Sarah's IR-rendered face. He strained his mind, trying to read any expressions that she might have – or any other hint as to why she wasn't opposing the soldier. But his efforts were for naught. In IR light, her face was simply a map of heat emissions – these told him nothing of her thoughts. He knew analyzing what Sarah might be thinking was irrelevant; it was obvious the creature had somehow taken hold of her mind. Whether it was giving her direct instructions or she was simply pointing her gun at some hallucination didn't matter either. Jack simply knew that he needed to avoid her. His true target was their common enemy, and it was several meters beyond the range of his small metal emitter.

The soldier spoke. Its voice must have been synthesized by a computer system as it sounded nearly identical to his own. It simply said, "It's out there somewhere. Fall back a few steps." The simulated voice reinforced whatever hallucination the creature had triggered, as Sarah obeyed and kept her gun aimed roughly in S-three's direction.

Jack whispered, "S-three, return."

His spoken words were too loud, though. The soldier spun around and fired three times. The bolts were aimed at torso height and tore through the rows of plants before passing only a few centimeters above Jack's crouched body. The burned stalks glowed with brilliant white light in his infrared view. Jack quickly flattened himself against the floor as Sarah fired wildly in his direction; her shots seemed almost random and didn't come close.

S-three quietly returned, backing up against his sprawled upper body. Both Sarah and the soldier stood with their guns raised, looking roughly toward him. Their heads, though, were turned in slightly different directions; they didn't know where he was. Jack wanted to back up but suspected that any noise his movements made would definitively give away his position. His only other alternative was to have S-three create a diversion. However, he knew the idea was flawed; he'd have to speak to tell S-three what to do. They'd zero in on him instantly. He stayed perfectly still, breathing as quietly as possible, and watched them. Sarah remained motionless with her gun held at arm's length. The soldier, however, kept surveying the area. His head pivoted back and forth, looking or listening for even the slightest hint of movement. It stepped carefully through the first row of plants, closing ground on him. Jack raised the emitter, holding his thumb only a few millimeters above its lone button. The creature stopped; it was at least twenty meters away – just beyond his weapon's range.

Jack needed to draw it in. His mind spun through the possibilities until he latched onto the nature of Alpha's tech. Alpha never really heard him when he spoke; he received and understood a projection of his thoughts transmitted by his implant. If his communication with S-three was the same, he didn't need to physically say anything to command the small robot. He just needed to concentrate on the words as if he were talking.

"S-three," he mouthed without making a sound, "run to the right for a few meters. Make some noise by hitting the plants. Then, return silently."

The robot immediately followed the commands. As it ran, it struck several stalks, making an obvious rustling noise. The soldier turned quickly; its gun tracked the sounds for a second before it fired. Expecting a human target again, it again fired at torso height. The shots singed dozens of plants as they passed safely above the small, scampering robot. S-three kept going, moving outward in an attempt to draw the soldier deeper into the room and into Jack's weapon's range. The alien, however, stayed in place. Instead, Sarah started walking forward. She suddenly stopped. As S-three returned silently to Jack's side, a low rumbling noise cut through the air. The soldier turned and shined a light on the rear wall. Its posture said it wasn't surprised by the sound but rather, it was expecting it. Sarah, however, remained still and didn't even look at the wall.

Guessing that there was finally enough light to see with his own eyes, Jack mouthed, "S-three, disengage IR view." Instantly he found himself back in the relative darkness of Alpha's garden. The beam from the soldier's flashlight easily gave him enough light to see it through the black silhouettes of the nearby plants. The soldier was carefully watching a section of the wall when a glowing orange oval started taking form. Jack shifted his position to get a better view, but the alien heard him. It spun around again and fired without taking careful aim. A dozen shots tore through Alpha's crops, igniting the ones nearest him. The sound and smoke, however, gave him enough cover the crawl back and away from the creature's line of fire. The relative safety, though, was not what he wanted. He knew another ship was trying to rescue it. A chill shot down his spine as the soldier's simulation of his voice called out, "Sarah, fall back. They're trying to surround us."

She didn't answer but started backing up toward the glowing section of the wall. A final spray of sparks shot out as the metal segment fell to the floor. Jack tried to get up to rush toward them, but the alien opened fire again. The shots were close, with the final one tearing through his left arm. Adrenaline and shock masked the pain as Jack fell to the floor; his only thoughts were to keep his eyes on Sarah. She continued shuffling backward toward the new opening.

"Sarah, move it!" the voice called out. "Get through there. I'll hold them off."

Before Jack could get to his feet again, the soldier sprayed the area with another round of fire. The nearest bolts buzzed past his head; their heat felt as if flames were licking his scalp. Sarah turned to run through the smoking opening, causing Jack to jump to his feet without thinking. "Sarah, no!" he shouted. He ran toward them, frantically pressing the button on his emitter, but it had no effect – they were still out of range. He didn't see the soldier fire again but felt intense heat cut through his leg. The momentum of his next step carried him on to it, but it had no strength. He fell hard to the floor, skidding into the glowing embers of Alpha's crops. Still, he managed to keep his eyes on Sarah and the soldier. She must have heard him because she paused for a moment.

The simulation of Jack's voice barked out an order, "Get through the hatch now! I can't hold them off." It laid down a round of cover fire as she turned again to jump through the opening.

Jack desperately tried to move, but his injured leg and arm sapped his strength. In an instant, Sarah's form was gone, disappearing into the shadows of the rough-cut hole. The soldier held its position, looking for any move that Jack might make. Jack's mind spun desperately, and he called out in a hushed voice, "S-three, come here!"

The spider was instantly next to him. He pushed his emitter up against the creature's body. It reflexively knew what he meant and used two of its legs to hold it close. "Follow them into that ship. Get into range and activate it."

There was no hesitation. As the alien jumped into its waiting ship, S-three shot toward the opening at a dead run. "S-three," Jack shouted, "transmit your imagery."

Jack's view of the nearly pitch-black garden was replaced by an infrared view of a fast-approaching, rough-cut hole in the hull. Just beyond it was a silver door that was slowly closing. S-three moved fast, though, and leapt through the opening just as the door slammed shut. There was a quick view of the alien soldier sliding by; S-three must have been skidding along the floor. The soldier, however, saw the small robot. Time felt like it almost stopped. Jack watched as S-three stared up at the muzzle of the alien weapon. The robot seemed frozen with fear. The alien's fingers tensed as it started to pull the trigger, but there was a sudden blur of chaos. A brilliant flash of light nearly blinded him. The room spun – Jack could only imagine that S-three had been thrown aside by a blast. The robot, however, quickly regained its footing and shot behind a stack of equipment. It held its position, doing its best to hide.

"S-three," Jack said, "if you can hear me, activate the emitter now."

There was no response – Jack wasn't sure it was even capable of verbalizing one. It simply sat with its back against the equipment and looked up. A shadow approached, but then held still. A second later, the soldier reached over; its gun squarely pointed at S-three. There was a sudden flash from the left. A burst of smoke stuck the alien in the arm. It shouted something unintelligible but held its gun on the robot. S-three did nothing but stare back. Jack's remote view instantly disappeared. He was alone in the nearly-dark garden. His only light now came from the burning embers of incinerated plants lying nearby. The floor briefly shuddered as the closed silver door of the alien ship pulled away. There was the sharp howl of wind rushing toward open space for a split second. But it disappeared almost instantly as the gash in Alpha's hull sealed itself.

Exhaustion finally took hold of Jack. Dizziness and numbness swept across him. He couldn't concentrate – too much was happening. A momentary wave of panic pulled at him as a single thought dominated his mind: Sarah was gone, and he had no idea what to do. Kurt's distant voice cut through the haze. He heard his friend shouting, "Jack, where are you?" He didn't want to answer, he needed to somehow get to Sarah. Kurt's repeated shouts pulled him back from his momentary feeling of despair. He still didn't answer but felt relief when his friend pushed his way through the splintered plants.

"Are you OK?" Kurt asked as he knelt down beside him.

The answer was no, but Jack simply nodded and said, "Yes."

Chapter 23

Jack hobbled into the room with his arm over Kurt's shoulder. Though each step brought a searing shot of pain, he didn't try to suppress it. It reminded him that they didn't have any time to spare. Pain kept him from succumbing to exhaustion. It kept guilt from taking hold. He used it as a tool. Together with his anger, it gave him the strength to push himself to his limits – to push aside any thought that finding Sarah was a lost cause.

Jack finally broke away from his thoughts and took a careful look around the room. In front of him were two plain, white tables set next to each other. One held their alien prisoner. It was strapped down and covered with Alpha's synthetic creatures. D-four was firmly wrapped around its scalp. No fewer than a half dozen silver spiders were spread across its limbs and torso. Alpha's intense desire to extract every piece of information from their prisoner was apparent in the behavior of his creatures – blood trickled down from each point in which they had inserted probes or tubes. There were no longer any attempts to be gentle or humane. Though the brutality with which Alpha was working stunned him, Jack also knew that his alien companion's logic was simple and in Alpha's mind flawless: survival was all that mattered, and a single soldier's pain or death was completely irrelevant.

Alpha stared intently at the restrained soldier and made no attempt to recognize Jack's entry into the room. Having no interest in wasting time on formalities, Jack asked sharply, "Alpha what's our situation?"

"There were only three ships that survived the collapse of the AGC. One was destroyed, we have one, and the last one is out there with your companion."

"I want to know where it is," Jack pressed

"I don't know at the moment. But, I will find it," Alpha said with blunt certainty.

Frustration drove Jack as he demanded, "How?"

"This thing knows what they've been doing in your solar system," Alpha said looking back at the soldier. "It may know what their backup plans were."

As he stared at their prisoner again, Jack watched as one of the spiders repositioned itself near the creature's neck. It inserted a sharp probe just under its ear, causing a small stream of blood to run onto the table. "I want you to keep it alive."

Alpha ignored his statement and pointed at the empty table as he said, "Sit down over here. We need to address your wounds."

Kurt helped Jack up onto the edge of the table, and almost immediately a silver spider, identical to the ones working on the soldier, appeared and ran to his leg. It moved quickly as one of its metallic legs acted as a syringe and injected an anesthetic into his thigh; it then pivoted gracefully and worked on the wound. Another one surprised Jack as it climbed up his side from behind. Without hesitation, it clung to his shoulder and tended to his injured bicep. Jack pushed any thoughts about them from his mind, though, and turned his attention back to the soldier. "I want you to keep it alive," he repeated.

"Why?" was Alpha's quick, emotionless response.

"We may need it later."

"I find it doubtful."

"I still want it kept alive," Jack pressed.

"You shouldn't consider it alive in the first place," Alpha said with a hint of irritation.

"What the hell are you talking about?" Jack asked sharply.

"I now understand what these are. The work that went into creating them is more than simply engineering individuals to be better soldiers.

These were programmed genetically and enhanced with cybernetics. From my analysis, they are only loosely based on the original beings that evolved on their homeworld."

"What difference does that make?" Jack challenged.

"It means that this one is nothing more than a tool – a hybrid biological machine," Alpha shot back. "Its entire decision-making process is pre-programmed, and its analog to instincts are just base commands on how to fight and survive. The only sophistication I can find in it is that it easily adapts to new combat situations – nothing else. I don't think it is capable of original thought or any other higher-level feelings."

Jack just stared at the soldier. The spider working on the base of its skull pushed its probe in deeper; the soldier's body tensed in response. Before Jack could continue the argument, Alpha said, "I've accessed more of its memories. This one's homeworld is located in star system K2-9 in your catalog. Its distance is two hundred seventy light-years."

"Is their ship already heading there?" Jack quickly asked.

"Give me a moment," Alpha answered. The soldier's body convulsed as the spider adjusted its probe. "I have access to its communication functions. It was linked to a central computer on its ship until they flew out of range." Alpha paused for a moment before continuing, "It appears that they shared a single, combined mind…it's as if each one of them is no more than a separate part of a single body. There wasn't communication between them in the standard sense…they were semi-independent components being directed by a central consciousness."

"Then you have to keep it alive when you're done," Jack said firmly. "We could use it as an interface. But tell me…did the other ship already leave?"

"Most likely…I am still searching for it."

"Damn it! We don't have time for…"

"I've got it," Alpha said.

"Where?"

"It is accelerating outbound toward K2-9."

"Can we catch it?" Jack demanded.

"It's complicated."

"What the hell do you mean, it's complicated? It's a yes or no question!" Jack practically shouted. "Sarah's on that thing!"

"The short answer is yes. But, they're accelerating to hyper-relativistic speeds. We will catch them, but time dilation will become a serious factor."

"Explain," Jack demanded.

"We'll get very close to the speed of light – within a small fraction of one percent of it. But, that means time in our reference frame will slow dramatically. It will be unlike anything you experienced onboard the Magellan."

This time Don asked the question that weighed on all of them, "How much time are we going to lose?"

"It depends on how fast their ship goes," Alpha answered calmly.

"Are we talking about months or even years?" Don asked, trying to hide the fear that lay behind his voice.

"Onboard my ship, we'll only experience an hour or two of time passing. However, several years – maybe as many as ten – will pass in the Earth's frame of reference."

"The year's 2132 right now, so we're talking about the early forties when we catch them?" Don asked with a slight tremble in his voice.

"In terms of the effect on you, it will be worse than that," Alpha said. We may be as much ten light-years out from Earth at that point. You'll lose just as much time returning."

"Twenty years total?" Kurt said softly.

"You won't be returning to the same planet you left," Alpha answered.

All eyes turned to Jack. The decision was easy for him, yet he found it impossible to say anything. Simply asking them to decide would be pressuring them to give up their lives on Earth for someone the rest of them didn't really know.

"So, it's either we do this or lose Sarah," Nadya finally said.

Jack refused to answer but didn't look away either. He watched as Kurt and Nadya gave each other a knowing glance. Kurt turned to Jack and said, "Seeing as they had already thrown me into an interrogation room before the destruction of Copernicus base, I don't see us having anything to go back to."

Nadya turned to Don. Meeting her gaze, he said, "None of this is fair."

"I know," she responded.

"If I say I want to go back, then I'm killing her."

"No," Jack answered. "You're not. No one person is more important than anyone else. I can't simply ask you to give up everything you have back home."

"I've got nothing left back home!" Don answered harshly. "It's gone. My position, my colleagues…they're not going to let me go back to them. Hell, it'd be a miracle if I don't get arrested on sight."

"I'm sorry," Jack said as he leaned forward toward him.

"Don't be! This isn't your goddamned fault!"

The room stayed silent. Don looked at each of them before turning

to Alpha and saying, "We've got to go after her. We've got no choice."
Alpha nodded and said, "I'm beginning the pursuit course now."

Chapter 24

Jack picked up the pistol-like weapon Alpha had fabricated. It was light but well balanced and fit comfortably in his hand. At its core was a pulsed UV laser, capable of piercing any armor the enemy might be wearing. Its power, however, was kept low enough so as not to risk breaching their ship's hull. Jack ran his thumb up to a button near the top of the weapon – it would trigger a carefully tuned EMP, capable of disabling the soldier's implants and, most importantly, cutting off its communications with the centralized consciousness. Standing next to him were two more of Alpha's synthetic creatures – generically designated as S-four and S-five. The silver spiders would conduct reconnaissance for him. Realizing that total immersion in their imagery left him vulnerable, their data was now integrated into a pair of augmented reality goggles. They had the look of un-tinted sunglasses but would project images from the spiders onto only a portion of Jack's field of view.

"We're approaching the vessel," Alpha announced. "This one is roughly the same size as the one we captured – thirty meters in length. There appears to be a hatch in the rear – I'll get you onboard there."

"I'm ready," Jack answered as he rubbed the bandage on his leg; there was no residual pain. He looked to his right, where Kurt stood admiring a nearly identical weapon. "Remember," Jack said, "you're staying here. Just make sure nothing gets aboard."

"Got it," Kurt answered without hesitation.

"Nadya, Don," Jack called into his comm-unit. "You're with Alpha, right?"

"Yes," Nadya's voice replied.

"I thought about it some more…I want you two to review a continuous feed from the spiders. Let Alpha worry about sending me intel from his sensors."

"You sure?" Nadya answered.

"Yes. I want you to take direct control of one. Direct it as you see fit throughout the ship, and tell me what you see. I'll have the other one stay close to me. Keep an eye on its video feed too. I won't be able to concentrate on both its data and what's going on around me."

"Got it," Don answered.

"Fifteen seconds until contact," Alpha said with some urgency.

Jack stared at an oval outline on the featureless white wall before him. It was a far cry from the steel-reinforced hatches he was accustomed to, but he'd learned not to doubt Alpha's tech. Jack took a step to the side, making sure he wasn't potentially in the line of fire of anything that might be waiting for him. "Take cover back there," he said to Kurt, pointing to a corner in the hallway.

Kurt moved into position as the ship suddenly shuddered – they had made contact. There was a sharp loud hiss, followed by the echo of metal being forced open. Jack kept his eyes on the oval. Its border became thicker and deeper. Another hiss cut through the air; the oval pushed a few centimeters out from the wall and slid aside. Jack found himself staring at a small, cylindrical airlock; it was large enough to hold maybe two people. Stepping carefully toward it, he saw that its inner door had already been forced open.

Suddenly one of his two spiders dashed through the airlock into the alien vessel. A second later, Nadya called in over the comm-unit, "The hallway is clear."

"Got it," Jack said as he stepped through. Holding his weapon in at chest height, he peered down the ship's plain, metal-lined corridor. The walls were lined with textured aluminum plates and small access panels with recessed handles. Bright white lights were spaced evenly along the ceiling and ran the length of the short, ten-meter corridor. It ended at a junction with paths that led to his right and left. Jack paused halfway down, listening to the soft flow of air through a ventilation system and the hum of distant equipment. The hallway was perfectly clean, with the exception of two blackened marks on the far wall of the junction. "S-four," he said softly, "give me a look up ahead."

The small robot dashed silently around the corner – its view was embedded in Jack's glasses. To the left was another short corridor; this one ended at a closed hatch. The spider spun around, showing Jack that the path to the right was identical – except that its hatch was partially open. Jack walked calmly ahead and examined the damaged wall – the blackened marks were the result of weapons fire. It gave him hope.

"Nadya," he said softly into his comm-unit, "Where's S-five?"

"I've got it moving slowly a few meters ahead of you. It's already through the open hatch. So far, we haven't seen anything."

"Don't let it get too far ahead of me. If they see you coming, it'll give them too much time to prepare."

"Got it," Nadya answered, "I'll hold position here."

Jack walked up to the open door and took a moment to examine it. The material was thinner than anything he might find on a human ship and perfectly smooth. On tapping it with his knuckles, he found it to be solid – as if it were carved from something as dense as stone. His eyes ran along the door frame, spotting a streak of red. It was blood, though there was too little to tell if it were human or alien. "Alpha," Jack said, can you show me my position?"

A glowing blue outline of the enemy ship appeared, hovering within arm's reach in the middle of the hallway. It was simply a signal transmitted onto his glasses, but it was effective. Embedded within it was a partial map of the corridors he and the spiders had traversed. Thin, iridescent red tubes identified the path from his entry point up to his current position. He was in a central hallway that seemed to run the vessel's length.

"Nadya," Jack said, "send S-five ahead."

There was no verbal response; the small robot just took off down the corridor.

"Alpha," Jack said into the comm. "I assume they know we're here. Have they taken evasive action, or are they trying to somehow break away from your ship?"

"Nothing so far," Alpha answered.

"That doesn't seem right," Jack said mostly to himself.

"Agreed," Alpha answered.

"We need to know what's going on. Are you able to get into their computer system?" Jack asked.

"Not at the moment," Alpha answered. "They're using open-path EM comms with entangled state encryption. It's going to take some work to find a way in."

"What about…" Jack started but stopped as Nadya cut in, "Jack, you need to see this."

"Go ahead," he answered quickly. The map of the alien ship disappeared and was replaced by S-five's view of a closed-door embedded in the metal paneled wall. Along its edge was the unmistakable form of a bloody, human handprint. "Sarah," was all he got out before S-five's view shifted. Something was running at it fast. The robot turned on its own and sprinted back down the hall. "S-five," he practically shouted, "take cover behind me."

Jack quickly dove to the floor and carefully held the pistol out in front of him. Though he didn't hear anything, he saw the small silver spider running toward him. Its pursuer was barely keeping up and was still partially hidden behind S-five's rapidly approaching body. The spider leapt while still a couple few meters away, giving Jack a clear view of the attacker. It was metallic and about the size of a large dog. As S-five glided over him, Jack focused his attention on the attacker's body. It had no discernable head or other features – just a thick body and fast-moving legs. Jack held his fire as it closed ground, looking for a weak spot. It was barely five meters away when he adjusted his aim and zeroed in on its shoulder joint. It showed no intention of slowing as Jack shifted his weapon slightly and pressed the trigger. A bright white targeting spot shined on a bundle of wires running under the joint. In an instant, sparks and smoke flew from the mechanism. The leg gave way, and the robot toppled to the ground, skidding toward him. Keeping his finger on the trigger, Jack swept his aim up and across the sliding creature's metal body, splitting it in half. He barely had enough time to jump up as the robot skidded beneath him, finally coming to a stop. It lay motionless; small streams of smoke leaked from the points where he struck it. When he was satisfied it was no longer a threat, Jack turned to see S-four and S-five standing still behind him, as if they were waiting for a command. A twinge of remorse entered his mind as he uttered the obvious one. "S-five," he said, "head back down the corridor and see if there are more of them."

The creature didn't hesitate as it ran down the hallway as ordered; Jack followed its progress through the image overlaid on his glasses. It stopped at the door and looked up again at the bloody handprint. "S-five, continue five more meters, and keep watch."

The spider again did as ordered. Jack then walked slowly toward the door. On reaching it, he stared at it for a moment, looking for a button or some other sort of actuator, but there was none. He waved his hand by it, hoping to trigger a motion sensor, but it remained sealed. "Alpha," he called into the comm-unit. "Have you hacked their system yet? I need to get in here."

"I'm still working on it," was the response.

Jack resisted the urge to demand that Alpha solve the problem – he knew it would be nothing more than a pointless display of frustration. But, his frustration was real. He raised his gun, aimed it at the edge where the door met its frame and fired. The white targeting spot showed that he was striking the intended area, but nothing happened. After holding the trigger for the better part of a minute, he finally released it. Reaching out to touch the spot, he felt the heat radiating from the metal. Though it was undamaged, the laser had heated it to some high temperature.

Jack stepped back and stared at the handprint. He needed to get in. He raised his gun again but stopped as Nadya shouted over the comm, "Jack, left!"

He spun to see another of the enemy robots tear down the hall. S-five caught sight of it and tried to run, but its legs struggled to gain traction on the smooth floor. As it finally got moving, the enemy closed to within a couple of meters. It jumped at S-five, narrowly missing the agile spider, and skidded toward a wall. Rather than slow it, though, the robot simply allowed its body to slide sideways, and when all four legs made contact with the wall, it jumped again. This time, one of its front legs was close enough, and it swept S-five's legs out from under it. The small spider rolled over, trying to quickly right itself, but it wasn't fast enough. The enemy robot pounced on it, smashing the spider with its torso.

Jack stared down the corridor at the new threat. The enemy robot got to its feet and held position as if staring back. Jack raised his gun, but before he could take aim, the metal creature dove into an alcove and out of the line of fire. He kept his eye on the alcove for a few seconds before turning back to the sealed door. Jack ran his forefinger along the side of the weapon until he reached the EMP trigger. "It might work," he said to himself as he pressed it. There was no noise as it generated the pulse, nor was there any other sign that it was doing anything. However, a small wisp of smoke leaked from the edge of the door. A second later, it slid aside. "It looks like I've overloaded the control mechanism," he said into his comm unit, "it's open."

He didn't wait for a response as he looked down at the waiting S-four and said, "Go in. Show me if there are any hazards."

The spider jumped through the door. Jack's glasses automatically activated a window showing him the robot's view. It was a large supply room containing neatly stacked rows of metal cases, with a meter-wide path between each. S-four worked its way deeper into the room, turning to give Jack a view down each row – there was nothing there. Impatient to make progress, Jack stepped in and quickly moved along its perimeter. Being barely ten meters wide, he reached the far left side in a matter of seconds. He moved fast toward the room's rear but stopped as his foot hit something. Glancing down, he saw an extended leg. His eyes worked their way up the motionless body of an alien soldier. It was lying face down; a pool of blood was by its head. A smile crept across his face as he called "Sarah" in a hushed voice. There was no response.

Jack surveyed the area more closely and spotted a damaged weapon near the soldier's hand. A few meters ahead were two blast marks on one of the stacks of boxes, along with a smear of blood on the wall. It could well have been Sarah's. His best guess was that they traded shots and she escaped – possibly not realizing she'd killed her opponent.

Jack called out Sarah's name again as he walked deeper into the room.

There was still no response. On reaching the rear of the room, he came face-to-face with S-four.

"Don, Nadya," Jack called into his comm. "Have you been tracking S-four's video?"

"Yes," Nadya replied. "There's been nothing of interest."

"I've come across some of Sarah's handiwork," he said. "She killed one of them here. It looks like a clean shot to the head."

"That means she's still alive," Nadya said with a voice laced with hope.

"I want to believe that, but she may have been injured. We need to find her," Jack said softly. "Alpha, what's your status? Are you in their system yet?"

"No," he answered without elaborating.

Jack looked down at S-four; the spider stood perfectly still, looking up at him. He opened his mouth, ready to give it an order, but stopped. Instead, he simply said, "She could be trapped or hiding."

"Come again?" Nadya replied.

"Sarah can handle herself; we've seen that," Jack said. "What if whoever's on this ship decided capturing her was too dangerous – at least for now. Isolating her would be the next best thing."

"Are you saying she's still loose but cornered or something?" Nadya asked.

"Maybe that thing that attacked S-five is the key," Don added.

"Go on," Jack said.

"I'm just thinking it's either there to keep you from getting to her or keep her from escaping wherever she's holed up. Either way, it means you're close to her position."

Jack stared at S-four again and finally said, "S-four, work your way down the corridor, but do it quietly. I'll be a few meters behind you. If something comes at you, do everything you can to get behind me."

The spider moved at a walking pace to the room's exit. As it turned down the hallway, it looked back, making sure Jack was following. Jack waved it ahead and surveyed the utilitarian corridor once more. No attempt had been made to hide or integrate the various pipes and conduits into the ceiling or walls. The corridor's lights were simple boxes spaced every few meters and connected by a plain metal tube carrying its power. The only thing that struck him was the complete lack of markings – there were no signs or labels in some alien language. He suddenly stopped midstride and said, "S-four, hold position."

The spider did as ordered. Jack stared at the row of conduits and thought again about the robot that had attacked before. Pointing at the tubing, he said, "S-four, can you climb along those instead of using the floor?"

The spider leapt up and caught hold of the lighting conduit with two of its legs. It gracefully swung its body around so that it was inverted and able to easily crawl along the metal tube. Jack just smiled and said, "Continue down the hall. Feed your view to me."

An upside-down image of the corridor appeared in the corner of his glasses. Without thinking, Jack said, "Can you invert your imagery?"

S-four paused and looked back at him, but the image didn't change.

"I guess there's a limit to…"

"Give me a second," Alpha said over the comm-unit. "I can take care of that."

S-four's image of the corridor suddenly righted itself. "Thanks," Jack said. Then looking at S-four, he said, "Continue down the corridor."

The spider returned to its silent, fast-paced shimmying along the ceiling. Jack stayed back, though, carefully keeping an eye on the video feed. On reaching the next junction, S-four froze. Two short corridors led left and right; S-four's attention was firmly fixated on the right-side path. Two of the enemy robots were standing just around the corner, waiting for him to approach. Jack, however, marveled at the sloppiness in their design; they should have seen S-four or at least sensed its presence using a motion detector, lidar, or some other non-visual technology. Instead, they stood still, staring at the junction in the hallway, waiting for something to come to them at floor level.

"S-four," Jack said in a hushed voice, "look around, give me a full, three-sixty view of what's there."

The video feed slowly panned around, showing three closed doors – one at the end of each short side-hallway and a third that lay a few meters ahead, where the central corridor ended. The door at the end of the main hallway had a reinforced frame and appeared to lead to the front of the ship – perhaps the cockpit. The other two looked identical to the one he had opened a couple of minutes earlier. The walls, however, showed signs of a firefight. There were blast marks on either side of the cockpit door, as well as on the door to the right. "Are you getting this?" Jack whispered into the comm-unit.

Nadya answered, "We see it."

"Safe bet, Sarah's behind the one to the right," Don said.

"That's what I'm going with," Jack said. He stared at S-four's video feed a moment longer before taking two steps forward. The video showed the two robots suddenly move closer to the junction's edge. Jack froze in place. He thought about moving some more and drawing them out – he already knew his gun was capable of disabling them. But he also remembered the old adage: never assume your opponent made a mistake. They likely had integrated weapons he hadn't yet seen – anything else would have been a mistake.

"S-four," Jack whispered, "I want you to jump down to the floor behind them on my command. I want them the hear you."

Though it couldn't respond, Jack was confident it would follow his instructions. Keeping a careful eye on the video feed, he took another couple of steps forward. In response to the sound of his approach, the two robots leaned forward but kept out of Jack's direct line of sight.

He was barely five meters away from the junction now, but that was still too far – S-four wouldn't have a chance. He inched closer, putting his back against the right-side wall. The two metallic creatures held their position, waiting for Jack to show himself. When he was within three meters, Jack crouched down and said, "S-four, now!"

The silver spider dropped from the ceiling, landing hard. As the two robots started to react, Jack launched himself forward. They spun to face S-four as Jack crossed into the junction. On seeing him, S-four launched itself back toward the ceiling. Fixated on their original target, they ignored Jack and tracked S-four as it latched onto a conduit and headed toward the far wall. Jack trained his weapon on the one to the left, but before he could press the trigger, they opened fire on S-four. A line of high-speed pellets cut across the metal ceiling, ricocheting in all directions. The spider leapt across the small corridor, deliberately bouncing off the far wall and dropping to the floor. Simultaneously, Jack pressed the trigger, but two sharp stabs across his arm caused him to flinch and miss his target. Blood seeped from wounds created by two ricocheting projectiles.

Jack kept his eyes on his targets and S-four. The spider had successfully dodged the first round of fire. The robots, however, regrouped. The one to the right spun around to face him. Jack, however, had the advantage – all he needed to do was make a simple, quick adjustment to his aim. There was no sound as his weapon fired. The result, however, was definitive. A bright, glowing line appeared across the machine's midsection as Jack sliced it in half. Jack turned his attention to the other one as it opened fire again on S-four. The spider instantly jumped, aiming for the lighting conduit in the ceiling. The enemy robot, however, anticipated the move. Its stream of projectiles cut across S-four's path, intercepting it in midair. The spider's body shattered into uncountable numbers of small fragments. Rage guided Jack's motions as he held the trigger firmly and swept his weapon's targeting spot across the robot's body in multiple directions. It never had the time to recognize that it had destroyed S-four, as its body burst into flames and fell into several pieces.

Jack stood up and surveyed the short corridor. Smoldering pieces of alien machinery lined the floor. What was in front of him, though, was vastly more important. The sealed door showed small smears of human blood on its frame. Jack looked around to be sure that there were no nearby threats. But, without his small robotic companions, he could only guess that he was safe for the moment. As before, the door had no obvious controls. Jack chose not to waste time searching for hidden buttons and simply pointed his weapon at the door. He ran his finger up to the EMP trigger again and pressed it, generating a silent but effective pulse. There was a burst of smoke as the door's control mechanism failed, and it opened slightly. Grabbing the door's edge with both hands, he pulled hard, creating a large opening for him. As he started to lean into the room, two bursts of weapons fire shot just past his right temple. He dove inside, rolled left, and took cover behind a metal column. His immediate instinct was to return fire. Instead, he held his fire, kept his weapon at the ready, and called out, "Sarah! Hold your fire."

There was no immediate response. Jack called out, "Sarah, it's Jack. Are you ok?"

This time, a voice answered, "How am I supposed to know if it's really Jack Harrison? You've simulated his voice before. So, don't take a single step forward, or I will fire."

"Sarah, I'm going to step out into the open, so you can see me. You can decide then what you need to do."

Jack took a breath and said, "I'm stepping out now." As he walked out from behind the column, he raised his hands and held his position. He stood in silence for the better part of a minute before saying, "Sarah, are you there?"

A silhouette appeared against the lights in the rear of the room. It held its position for a few seconds before uttering the words, "Jack, thank God!" Jack started walking toward her; she met him halfway and embraced him. "I didn't think it was possible for you to get here."

For a moment, all that mattered to him was that he'd found her. He didn't comprehend the level of anxiety that had gripped him until this moment when it evaporated. There were no words for the relief that swept across him. His reflex, though, was to push emotion aside. They were still on an enemy ship. "There was no way we would leave you behind," was all that he managed to say.

Sarah just looked at him and smiled as she released him from her embrace.

"I saw the one you killed back there," Jack said. "Are there any others on board?"

"I think just the pilot," she answered as she looked past him and out the door. "I'm not sure what really happened. It had me in some sort of hallucination. I thought it was you…we were retreating into this ship…but at that moment, it was Alpha's ship. Almost immediately after the hatch closed, the hallucination fell apart. Suddenly we were standing there with guns in our hands, facing each other. We both fired. It nicked me on the arm. I must have winged it too, because it took off down the hall. I chased it into some room. I just hid there until it screwed up and exposed itself as it looked for me. It was an easy shot. But then another one showed up. It didn't expect a fight and took off down the hall when I raised my weapon. We exchanged a couple of shots when we got to this door. I know I hit it, but it had these other things…robots that it deployed. They chased me into here. That's the last I saw of it."

Jack just looked back at her. Before he could say anything, the comm-unit came to life. "Jack, what's your status?" Nadya said. "We lost the feed from S-four. Are you ok?"

"I've got Sarah with me – she's ok. But there's one of them alive on the ship. We're going after it."

Jack stepped back into the corridor and stared at the cockpit door. As Sarah joined him, she looked at her gun and said, "I tried blasting it open with this thing. It didn't work. But then again, I only got one shot off before I was attacked." She looked at the wreckage on the floor and kicked a smoldering piece of robot torso before saying, "You certainly made quick work of them."

Jack only smiled in response. As he raised his gun toward the door, Alpha's voice came in over the comm. "Captain. I need their computer system in one piece. Whatever you do, don't destroy it."

"Are you saying you've finally hacked your way into their systems?"

"No," Alpha answered. "But if you do kill or disable the pilot, I'll be able to directly access the systems from their ship."

"What difference will that make?" Jack asked. "We'll have already won the battle."

"I need to see what's on their systems," Alpha answered. "I'll show you once this is over."

"Got it," was Jack's reply. He moved to the side of the door and said, "Don't stand in front of it. I don't want you getting hit if whoever's behind it starts shooting." Sarah stepped to the left as Jack aimed his gun about chest-high near the door's edge and pressed the EMP trigger. As before, a small stream of smoke leaked from the door's edge. This time, however, it remained sealed.

"Shit," Jack muttered as he stared at it.

"What were you trying to do?" Sarah asked.

"This thing generates an EMP. It fries the circuitry, which releases the internal locking mechanism…at least that's what it did to the other doors."

"Maybe it worked, but this one's just too heavy to move on its own," Sarah offered.

Jack nodded and looked along the door's reinforced structure for a handhold…something he could grab and pull on. Its design was simple. It was perfectly smooth with the exception of two ten-centimeter wide support beams that crossed near the door's center at an angle. They made an 'X' that was raised a couple of centimeters above the surface – just high enough to offer a handhold. Jack dug his fingertips in, put one foot up on the door frame for leverage, and pulled hard. His fingertips burned from the pressure. The door budged slightly. He only needed to get it open a few centimeters – enough so that they could grab the edge of the door itself. He pulled hard again; it slid slowly with a heavy metallic scraping sound. It had moved just far enough.

"Grab it hear," he said to Sarah, gesturing to the door's lower half. "I'll take the upper part. Pull on my mark."

"Got it," she replied.

"Three, two, one, pull!"

With their combined force, it slid more easily this time. They made enough progress that Jack actually had to take a step to maintain his leverage. "We're almost there," he said.

Sarah didn't answer but didn't let up pulling either. Jack glanced at the opening. It was nearly half a meter wide – enough to squeeze through. "That's good. We can…" Jack started, but his words were cut off by a sharp crack followed by a searing pain across his forearm. He tried to jump directly away but collided with Sarah, who seemed to be flying back from the opening. He kept his eyes on her as he banged into the wall. She fell directly backward, hitting the floor hard. A small stream of smoke emanated from her abdomen.

Jack stayed low as he crawled to her. Two sharp cracks echoed through the hallway as more weapons fire came from within the cockpit door. He leaned over her for a split second but heard something running toward him. Instinct drove him to roll onto his side and then hold perfectly still. He grasped the gun with both hands, aiming directly at the opening; his right forefinger hovered over the trigger. It felt as if minutes were passing as he waited for his inbound target. A four-legged, metallic creature leapt through the door; it didn't even reach the apex of its jump before the laser from Jack's weapon cut it down. Two of its severed legs fell separately from the rest of the machine. It hit the floor hard but made no movements of its own.

The charging robot, however, was a decoy. Jack still had his weapon held up in the air as two more shots came from the cockpit. One squarely struck his left hand, searing it with plasma and throwing the gun halfway across the corridor. Reflex drove Jack to roll back toward Sarah. His eyes were fixed on the half-open door, but he caught sight of Sarah's gun with his peripheral vision. There was no time to think. He lunged for the weapon as an armor-clad form stepped into the corridor. Its eyes found Sarah first, and it brought its gun to bear on her. Jack was sprawled across the floor; her gun was just at the edge of his fingertips as he shouted at the soldier, "I'm over hear your goddamned piece of shit!"

Jack's tone was all that was needed to convey his message. The soldier looked toward him as Jack turned his back on it. His body blocked the creature's view of Sarah's nearby gun. Jack shouted, "What the hell do you want?" as he got up on his hands and knees and made it look like he was trying to crawl away. The soldier said something in a calm voice. Jack couldn't see what it was doing, though. As he crawled haltingly away from it, he grabbed hold of Sarah's gun. The creature barked out an order of some sort. Still unable to see if it was preparing to fire, Jack played up his injuries and deliberately stumbled and fell to the floor. He curled up into a fetal position and cried out in his best imitation of excruciating pain. The soldier shouted the same command. Jack stayed on the ground, waived his injured left arm in the air, and yelled, "I give up!" He knew the creature couldn't understand him, but his body language would tell it he was no longer a threat.

Jack stayed in place as the soldier shouted the order for a third time. There was the sound of approaching footsteps. Then a brief pause, followed by the sharp pain of it kicking him solidly in the shoulders. The alien shouted again as Jack once more got up onto his hands and knees. Keeping his back to it, he tensed his body and waited for the next kick. It finally came, landing squarely on his hip. Jack rolled to his side in mock pain but exposed his gun-wielding hand. The soldier barely had time to begin raising its weapon before Jack got the shot off. The first blast caught it squarely in the chest. Jack squeezed the trigger twice more, hitting once more in the torso and finally in the head. Jack's eyes, though, darted to Sarah's motionless form before the creature hit the ground. He crawled to her quickly and put his ear over her mouth. She was breathing.

"Alpha!" Jack shouted. "I need help in here now!"

Chapter 25

Jack stared at Sarah. She was lying on Alpha's version of a med-bay table and had just opened her eyes. She looked around the room, making eye contact with Kurt, Nadya, and finally Don. Then looking back at Jack, asked, "Did we get them?"

"Yes," he said with a smile. "They're all dead, except for one prisoner we have here. Nothing's left for Earth to worry about."

Sarah answered with a smile that showed pure relief. Then, after taking a breath, she asked, "How long was I out?"

"Just a day," Jack answered. "You took quite a beating, but you'll be fine."

Sarah made it obvious that she was looking at his still-bandaged hand and said, "It looks like you took a bit of a beating too."

Before he could reply, Alpha glided into the room and said, "I'm glad to see that you're awake. You're going to make a full recovery."

Sarah raised her head from the table and answered simply, "Thank you for what you did."

Alpha nodded in response.

Jack looked at their alien companion, but Alpha deliberately avoided making eye contact. If it was an attempt to evade discussing some uncomfortable topic, it was poorly done. Jack intended on letting him off the hook, at least for now, but Kurt appeared to have noticed too and asked, "Alpha, what is it?"

Alpha looked at each of them before saying, "I was able to access their systems and communication logs."

This time, curiosity got the better of Don as he asked, "So, what did you find?"

"We know that one of them hacked my ship's systems and downloaded data. The problem is that I've identified exactly what they took and what they did with it."

When Alpha stopped speaking, Jack asked the obvious question, "How serious is this?"

"They downloaded technical data. If used correctly, it's equivalent to a few thousand years of progress. Worse yet, this ship managed to transmit the files in the direction of their star system."

"What does this mean?" Kurt asked.

"They're already dangerous," Alpha answered, "This could make them a much bigger threat."

"Is there anything you can do about this?" Don asked. "I mean, you threatened to delete the knowledge we downloaded from the archive. Can't you just do something like that to them?"

"This isn't the same," Alpha said. "In your case, I gave you an archive that fed the data at a specific rate and tagged it so that it could be tracked. None of that's in place here. They have already accessed the information. They sent it. It's effectively in their possession."

"You mean to tell me that they just got tech that'll make them as powerful as you?" Don said with disbelief.

"Not as powerful, but significantly more dangerous than they are now."

"Don't split hairs with me," Don pressed. "There has to be some way you can stop this."

Alpha just stared back at Don without saying anything.

"Answer me," Don demanded.

"It's already been done," Alpha replied. "They stole and sent the data. It can't be undone."

"What about going after them?" Sarah asked softly.

All eyes turned to her. Sarah looked back and said, "Why can't we follow the transmission and see what we can do to stop them from using the data."

"I don't think you fully appreciate the sacrifice you would need to make," Alpha said.

Jack tried his best to hide the feeling of dread that was now sitting in his gut. He knew exactly what it would entail. As he looked around the room, his friends' expressions told him they knew – at least to some degree – what would be involved.

When no one spoke, Alpha continued, "It's a simple matter of physics. We can't intercept the transmission; it's moving at the speed of light. Their homeworld will receive it in about two hundred seventy years. If we follow it, as you suggest, and push this ship to its limit, we will arrive in their system about two months after they receive it. There's no doubt in my mind that the data would no longer be localized. That is, it would be spread out in various storage systems and thus impossible to isolate and delete."

"So, you're saying it won't be easy," Kurt replied.

For the first time, Jack was sure he could read Alpha's alien facial expression – it was akin to rolling one's eyes in disbelief. "No," Alpha replied, "Take it as fact; we won't be able to delete the data. I have no idea what we would even be able to do."

The room went silent. Jack didn't believe in giving up; there had to be options. "More importantly for you," Alpha continued, "relativistic travel at these distances will have a devastating effect on your lives. To put it bluntly, you will lose over two hundred seventy years going there. You will be two hundred seventy light-years from Earth. The return trip – if we even are able to head back – will take just as long. That means it would be sometime in the late twenty-seventh century before you returned to Earth."

Kurt tried masking his trepidation with another flippant remark, "As far as everyone back home is concerned, we've already been missing for ten years, and I'm sure presumed dead. So, this won't change anything for them. That's done and over."

"But," Alpha said, "can you live with the fact that if we do this, you will never be able to see any of those people again? They will all be dead when you return – dead for over half a millennium. All of your connections on Earth will have been long forgotten. The world you go back to may be more different to you than your current Earth is to someone from the European renaissance. There will be no going back. And, keep in mind, I don't think there is anything we could do even if we go to their star system. Can you live with that?"

As the room went silent, Alpha added, "You also need to consider that none of what just happened will ever affect your lives. If you go back to Earth now, you, any children you may choose to have, and over twenty more generations of your decedents will live without being affected by any of this. These creatures will only pose a threat to an Earth in a future that is far, far removed from your lives. Are you willing to give up your lives for this?"

Jack looked around the room at each of them again. Their expressions told him that their decision had already been made.

ABOUT THE AUTHOR

Andreas Karpf is an experimental physicist with a life-long interest in the space program. He enjoys a good space adventure, but lives for the hard sci-fi novel set in a plausible future that doesn't get weighed down by too much technology – a story that takes him for a ride and lets him dream about what may lie ahead for humanity.

As an undergraduate, he earned a degree in Physics and Astronomy and minored in English. This led him to begin his career as the assistant editor for a physics magazine. He moved into software development, designing business applications. His love of science though drew him back into Physics where he earned his doctorate and has pursued a research career. Andreas' work focuses on designing new spectroscopic techniques to detect trace gases in the atmosphere. His interests are varied and include art and Taekwondo (where he's a 4th-degree black belt). Through his different positions, his love of writing has persisted, leading to his debut novel, "Prelude to Extinction" and now its sequel, "Latent Flaw." Here he's combined his scientific background with his deep belief in keeping his audience both engaged and entertained. It is his desire to keep his readers thinking and involved in the adventure that drives his writing.

Made in United States
Orlando, FL
07 December 2022

25734601R00114